Praise for *Summer, in Between*:

'Smart, funny and oh-so real. I wish I could've read this book when I was 17!'
— *Gabrielle Tozer, award-winning author of The Unexpected Mess of it All, Remind Me How This Ends, Can't Say It Went To Plan, and The Intern*

'A beachside summer that captures the thrill and heartbreak of first love with pitch-perfect authenticity and whip-smart laugh-out-loud moments. It's a portal into your own experience of first love, except the love interest, the protagonist's family, and the setting are better than yours were. Cat knows her own mind but needs to get out of her own way – and yet, she never compromises her dreams for love. This book will make you wonder why you don't read more YA.'
— *Anne Freeman, multi award winning author*

'I hugely enjoyed Cat as a character – I loved how authentic she was as an Australian teenager with Australian teenage problems that she would blow out of proportion. I loved that she was moody and flawed and stressed out, and how well Paul's calming energy balanced her out. Their relationship hit the sweet spot.'
— *Bek Diskett, reviewer*

'Heartfelt, humorous, deeply relatable. Pulses with emotional clarity, vivid storytelling, and wit. A standout novel. I couldn't put it down!'
— *January Gilchrist, author of The Last Chapter*

'A brilliantly told, soulful, unputdownable novel for the young and young at heart. It is captivating from the first sentence, laugh out loud hilarious, relatable, and at times, heartbreaking. A truly touching story with depth. Absolutely wonderful.'
— *Lorena Otes, author*

Praise for *Summer, in Between*:

'Holly Cardamone perfectly captures the tender moments, while deftly exploring deeper themes of identity, cultural heritage, and anticipation for the future. A sweet romance brought to life with writing so evocative you can feel the heat of the sun on your shoulders, the grit of sand between your toes, and the salt encrusted on your eyelashes.'
— *Camille Booker, award-winning author*

'This book is a delight! A coming-of-age tale full of romance and humour. Firecracker Cat and her noisy Italian family will win your heart, while the charming and often misunderstood Paul finds his way into Cat's.' — *Sarah Todman, author of Forgotten*

'An absolute joy, brimming with voice, humour, romance, and a huge amount of heart. I devoured this gem!' — *Miranda Luby, author*

'Cat is kind-hearted and passionate, working hard to carve space in her life for Year 12, and the ache and pull of a summer romance. Her life is coloured with the richness of her Italian-Australian family, delivering laughs, plenty of trouble, and just the right amount of hand pressed to heart moments. *Summer, in Between* feels like it will deliver *this* generation a fresh bitey take on life that *Looking for Alibrandi* gifted us in the nineties.' — *Jenna Lo Bianco, author*

'Perfect for a mental holiday, the kind of book you'll finish in a week.'
— *Gabrielle Davis, author*

'Funny, hot, relatable. An absolute page turner that I'm proud to have signed, particularly because *Summer, in Between* proves that booklovers are not the shy nerdy stereotype. I am absolutely and totally in love with Cat. What a summer!'
— *Carolyn Martinez, Director, Hawkeye*

Summer, in Between

HOLLY CARDAMONE

HAWKEYE
PUBLISHING

First published in Australia in 2025 by Hawkeye Publishing

Cover Design by Isabelle Uy

A catalogue record of this book is available from the National Library of Australia.

Hawkeye Publishing recognises the Traditional Custodians of the lands where we live and work. We pay our respects to Elders past and present and extend that respect to all Aboriginal and Torres Strait Islander peoples. We celebrate more than 60,000 years of storytelling, art, and culture that continue to shape and enrich our world.

ISBN 9781923105591

Proudly printed in Australia.

www.hawkeyebooks.com.au

For Gabriella and Alessia,
my beach babies.

1

HOW much can one singular New Year's Day sucketh? Let me count the ways.

First up, I couldn't be more of a loser loner if I tried. I have no friends for the whole entire summer. Here I am, stuck in this tiny little town on the edge of nowhere with no one to hang out with.

Number two? Let's not forget the beach, *my* beach, my happy place will be filled with grandmas, Neanderthal surfers and kids with noses dripping like sandy snot candles.

And for the biggest suckage scenario of all? I've planned to get a head start on the most important year of my life. Year Twelve. The big one. It's taken forever to get here, but now it's finally happening. It's *the* year, hurtling towards me like all those shrieking little kids out of control on their Christmas boogie boards. Year Twelve. It's massive, yeah? So, imagine my *absolute* delight when my beloved parents tell me on day one of the shiny new year, that instead of peace and quiet, or as much as you can have with two brothers, Dad's renovating our house, to make – wait for it – a home within our home for Nonna. My grandmother will be moving in. Here. Where I live. All while I'm trying to get my act together to smash Year Twelve. I explain these three points as if I'm in a debating competition, but my parents just keep shuffling paper around on the dining table.

'You heard what the principal said,' I say. 'I get one shot. If I work hard and focus, the whole wide world will open for me. If I don't, I'll be stuck in this crappy little town for the rest of my crappy little life.' Well, okay, she didn't say that last part, but I can read between the lines.

What if I stare at my books long enough? They'll materialise into the best university, the best career and then the best life? Yeah, right. Talk about feeling doomed.

I slump in my seat, sighing, not that my parents even pretend to notice. There's six weeks until school starts and I'm already behind. We're supposed to read all the textbooks over summer, and the English novels until they're reprinted into our brains. Well, that'll be hard when the delivery only had half my books, and the bookstore is closed for two freakin' weeks! How ironic. I wasn't happy that I'd be a loner all summer without my friends. I'd accepted it with the consolation of getting stuck into my textbooks, yet half of them didn't land because of some kind of delivery debacle, and they wouldn't send another delivery driver to a place that barely shows on a map until after the silly season. I have almost nothing to distract me from Em being on the other side of the world and Sal up North with her girlfriend. My best friend JB is working, so there's no chance of seeing him until school goes back either. And now add to that a soundtrack of a power saw and a nail gun.

'What the actual, Dad? Do you really not get how big this is?'

Dad barely looks up from the plans strewn across the table.

'Calm down, cowgirl,' he says. 'You'll be all right, you'll hardly notice.'

'Calm down? Are you for real? You're turning our house into a construction site. I need to work out what to put down for uni selections. Do you even know how many decisions I have to make?'

'Here, I'll make one for you.' Mum hands me her credit card. 'Go get me a roll of foil. Get Matty from the beach while you're at it, please.'

'Happy New Year to me,' I mutter. 'So nice that you don't even care that I'm having a mini-freakout.' I grab an apple from the bench.

'The walk will help. Off you go.'

'Can't Tommy go?' I say, biting into my apple. 'It's so hot.'

'You can go to Sadie's, or you can help Dad gut fish. You choose,' says Mum, as if that's even an answer.

'Fine,' I say, 'but just so you're aware, I'm not happy.'

'Noted,' says Mum.

2

2

LITTLE kids crouch by the roadside using sticks to prod the tar, soft and pliable from the heat. The sun has started its slow submerge into the ocean, but the air's still, as if the sun's heat is trapped within the atmosphere. The day's sluggishness refuses to give way to twilight cool. I cut through a vacant block; its boundary defiantly marked by the sweet citrus smell from the gums standing guard by each corner. I close my eyes and inhale the eucalyptus scent, so fresh, so clean, like the land's counterpart to the ocean.

Batter's Cove is full of empty blocks, most of which are unkempt, overgrown illegal rubbish dumps and fire hazards, the perfect hangout for tiger snakes. Nonna forbids us to go near any of them in bare feet or bare legs, which we ignore as soon as the temperature rises, and the lure of a shortcut is stronger than the fear of venom-induced paralysis and possible death.

Poor Nonna. She's convinced that Mum and Dad moving us out here was equivalent to their signing our death warrants. If we don't lose extremities from snakes, sharks will tear off our limbs and we'll drown in a sea of our own blood. Her words, not mine. She has conniptions if we walk on the rocks because of blue ring octopuses, not that I've ever seen one. She's no fan of spiders, either.

I don't think Nonna is much of a friend to any creature. Even her chickens, which she frets over and refuses to leave the house for more than a night because of their regimented feeding schedule, but the minute they stop laying, she goes all Mary Queen of Scots on them.

Only a month ago, I was in her living room, staring at whatever crap Matty had on the TV, trying to muster up the motivation to read my exam notes for the gazillionth time when Nonna appeared in the doorway holding a limp chicken by the claws. A long strip of something gross petered out from where its head should have been.

I screamed.

Nonna laughed and shook it, then took it outside. Two minutes later, we heard her singing. I looked out the window and there's Nonna, sitting on a deck chair under her fig tree, yanking out feathers with her bare hands. Beside her, amid scattered white and brown feathers, was the tree stump used for the dual purposes of chopping wood and beheading chickens. Leaning against it was the axe, blade shiny in the late afternoon sun, as polished as a samurai sword. Tommy was poking the chicken's head with a stick. Its head lolled, horrible beady eyes staring into nothingness.

On Batter's Cove Road, the citrus of the lemon-scented gums is replaced by the smoky, palpable smell of hot barbecues blasting the cells of helpless sausages and steaks, turning fragile meat into carcinogenic charcoal. Music blares from balconies and I walk close to the shoulder of the road as cars drive past flicking melted tar.

Sadie's, our local and only general store slash fish and chips shop slash hang out place, is the final of a strip of three shops. I catch my reflection in the shop window. My face is a glorious shade of scarlet and I can feel a moustache of sweat on my upper lip. Sexy, and perfectly timed. The Neanderthals are sprawled across the picnic tables out the front, some bikini-clad girls in their midst. The remnants of what was a parcel of hot chips rests in the middle of the table, the corners of the wrapping held down by drink bottles. A Neanderthal balances a skateboard on two wheels, flicking it up into the air and catching it. *Ugh. Awesome.*

I don't know these guys very well and they don't know me. I mean they'd have a vague idea of who I am — you can't live in a small town and not know people, especially when your dad's a tradie and the likely career path for these guys is some kind of trade. And while I've never spoken to any of them, I've been observing them like an assignment for years. They're quite the sociological phenomena, this subset of the human male species. They travel in a pack, and if you do see one alone in the wild, they must let out a dog whistle, because within minutes, there will be the rest of them, draped en masse on the bonnet of a car, or perched at a lookout assessing the waves, or like now, taking over all available surface area outside Sadie's.

When I was younger, I thought those guys were like gods, King Neptune's offspring come to life. Even the ugly ones have a certain something. In basic terms, they're a group of good-looking guys, perennially salt-encrusted with abs that come from hours of paddling a surfboard which you could… well, there's a few things you could do. Picture tanned faces, white teeth, some in a better state than others, salt-dotted eyelashes which probably make them look longer than is fair and hair bleached by sea and sunshine.

Bottom line: they look like they've just walked straight out of a cheesy music video. I'll never forget Sal's reaction the first time she saw them. She'd come to stay for the weekend so we could work on our biology assessment task. They were in the beach car park, gathered around the older guys' cars, music blaring. They'd just finished surfing, and the king of the Neanderthals, the hottest of the hot of them, stood under the beach shower peeling off his wetsuit.

'Oh my freakin' God,' said Sal. 'He looks like Adonis come to life. Is he even real?'

'Are you okay?' I mimicked wiping my mouth. 'You're not going to drown in all that drool?'

'Who in the name of all that is holy is he?'

'Paul Lightwood,' I said. 'He's a chippy, like Dad. Although unlike Dad, he's obscenely gorgeous.'

'You know him?' Sal asked. 'How have you kept his existence such a secret?'

'I don't know him, he's just a local. We've barely even exchanged eye contact.'

'Cat, you need to exchange bodily fluids with that guy. It would be a crime against humanity if you didn't. He's almost enough for me to see a guy as doable.'

I walk towards their table, head down, ostrich-style. If I can't see them, they can't see me, until I hear a freakin' skateboard coming straight at me. I'm no skater, but by some miracle of the sea gods, I manage to stop the skateboard from smashing me straight in the shins by blocking it with my foot. I put my weight on one end to flick it up and I grab it. Maybe I should be a skater.

'Is this yours, Einstein?' I glare at the kid standing before me, a wild-haired teenager that is definitely not one of the hot ones. He smirks, lip curled.

'Cheers.' He reaches for his skateboard.

'What, no apology?'

He snatches it from my hand and skates to the table.

One of the older guys sits facing me, leaning back, elbows resting on the table behind him, his legs outstretched. He yanks them out of the way of the skateboard as it careens towards him, partially dislodging the girl sitting on his lap.

'Mate, seriously?' He pulls the girl back against him.

She giggles, and as she flicks her hair, we lock eyes.

'Oh, look, it's Kitty Cat,' Isabel Dillon drawls. 'Didn't see ya last night at the Pav. Where were you? With your rich loser friends?' She's with some random girl from town with a high-pitched giggle like a drill in my ear. They're flicking their hair so hard it's a miracle they stay upright. In the late afternoon I find myself standing in their shadow. If they were anyone else, I might see that as symbolic.

Isabel is like that feeling of sand in your sneakers. No matter how much you shake it, there are always annoying grains rubbing against your skin. We were friends once. We met when we were 13, both of us with a mouth full of metal. For that first summer we were inseparable, hanging out every day, both of us trying to hide our crushes on the Neanderthals. But then her braces came off, and she stopped being intimidated by them to the point where she was happier hanging out with them than me. Scrap that: she wasn't just happier hanging out with them. She became actively nasty, vicious and vile towards me. Two can play that game.

I lift my sunglasses and make a show of looking at Isabel's neck, a mosaic of purple welts speckled with red.

'Classy. Which three were the unlucky guys?' Stuff the sisterhood and the very concept of female empowerment and girls supporting girls – for her, anyway.

'You're just jealous,' she snarls, smirk completely gone. 'We were at the best party on the biggest night of the year and where were you? At midnight Mass? Were you praying for a personality?'

'Maybe she was praying you'd grow some tits,' a Neanderthal mutters.

I can't help but laugh and Isabel gives me the middle finger salute.

'Ooh, catfight!' The skateboarding ignoramus circles me. 'You know what that'll turn into. Come on girls, give us a show.' He wriggles and thrusts as he skates, his hips jutting like razors from the top of his board shorts. He wraps his arms around himself and his potato face goes side to side as he smooches the air.

'Yeah right, Steve,' says Isabel. 'As if. Don't you know SUBs don't catfight?' Leaning against a Neanderthal's legs she takes his hands and tugs until his arms encircle her bare waist.

She, like everyone else in town, calls me a Stuck-Up Bitch, SUB for short, just because of the school I go to. It's not just me. SUB is the collective noun for the girls at our school. It's very important and significant to note that this is only given to the girls and not the boys. There's the patriarchy hard at work. Given this is decreed by the type of girls who wear their uniform so short you can almost see their belly ring, it's not hard to see Stuck-Up Bitch as a source of pride. And look, there's me, also a slave to the patriarchy *and* a snob.

I am miffed, though. It's nice to have your presence noticed, even if it is by one's eternal nemesis. I *was* at The Pav last night. There would have been a good two or three thousand people packed into the space that's smaller than a football oval, but still, I'm not invisible, surely? Although I didn't hang around long. It was too depressing, me there all alone, completely sober with every second testosterone-filled and alcohol-fuelled dipshit between the ages of 12 and 42 shouting *Happy*

New Year in my face, trying to follow up with a tongue down my throat. No, thank you.

Last year, I had such a great night with my friends, but this year? Surrounded by people, I couldn't have felt more alone. I would have killed to have my friends with me to see in the new year at The Pav. It was two hours to midnight when I saw someone give my 14-year-old brother a beer. He wouldn't have been the only barely adolescent puking his guts out on New Year's Eve, but still. I made my way over to him and the crowd surged as two men began fighting and wrestled each other to the ground. The people around them took the brawl as an invite to throw punches so I grabbed my brother and we pushed through the crowd to the edge of The Pav.

We took a path to the beach and laid on the sand for a while. Eventually he stopped his drunken jabbering and we watched the kaleidoscope of stars. That's one of the best things about this place. At night on the beach, away from the streetlights, the sky forms a perfect arc filled with stars. It would have been bliss, if not for the sound of people having the best New Year's ever. Ugh.

Every year, I promise myself I won't let Isabel Dillon get to me, and here's that resolution broken already. Steve keeps circling across the footpath. Skirting him, I push open Sadie's door. I pause to let a family exit and see Isabel reflected in the tinted window, laughing with her friend who has just started a sentence with, 'I'm not racist, but…' Steve is wheeling, swearing at the top of his lungs, and a woman holding hands with a little girl shoots him daggers before crossing the street. I step into Sadie's and crash smack bang into the chest of Paul Lightwood, aka Sal's Adonis come to life, the hottest of the hot, the king of the Neanderthals, a beautiful, walking surfer god.

3

'YOU okay?' He reaches above me and grabs the door, holding it open.

I step back, looking up past his (perfect) pecs into his (perfect) face. I'm gaping at him like I've never seen a walking god speak.

'Yeah, good thanks, you?' I have a visceral urge to kick myself, hard. The cringe factor is next level.

'Yeah, good, a bit dusty. It's Cat, yeah? I'm Paul.'

As I step through the door, he lets it close and holds out a hand. I shake it awkwardly, acutely aware that he's gripping my clammy palm. His wrists are twice the size of mine.

'Cat,' I say and release his hand to wave at Sadie at the counter, her rheumy eyes watching some young teenagers lurking around the lollypops. I walk across the store, past the ice-cream freezers and the dine-in tables straight to the drinks fridge and stare into it as if the contents are the most intriguing sight I've ever seen.

'Can I buy you a drink?' says Paul.

I turn away from the fridge to look at him. He's standing with his thumbs tucked into the waistband at the back of his deep blue board shorts, right behind his hipbones.

'Can you buy me a drink?' I repeat, rolling my eyes. 'That's one I haven't heard in Sadie's before. Thanks, but no. I'm all good.'

'Really? You look hot,' he says.

'Seriously?'

'I just meant it's hot,' says Paul. 'Not that you're not hot, of course you're hot, but it's hot, you know? You want a drink?' He's blushing, which is almost as startling as him apparently flirting with me.

'No thanks, I've got to get my brother.' I open the door. The bell jangles, reminding me of why I'm even at Sadie's in the first place.

'Forgot the foil,' I say to no one, and I wind my way around the two aisles scanning the shelves.

Paul is leaning against the counter, two glass bottles of water in his hand. I pay Sadie for the foil, my breath hammering around in my chest like I've been dumped by a wave at the very thought that Paul Lightwood, the most ridiculously good-looking member of the male species in the entire history of the male species, knows my name. I know he's nothing more than a massive flirt, yet I'm one more 'can I buy you a drink?' from collapsing into a Jane Austen-style swoon. I drop my change into the charity tin beside the register and Sally smiles at me in gratitude, patting the back of my hand with hers, age spotted and crepey.

'Here you go.' He hands me one of his bottles. 'Tell your old man I'll catch up with him tomorrow, yeah?'

'My dad?'

'Yeah, Mick. Your dad. I was happy to kick off today, but he said New Year's and all that.'

'Kick off? What are you talking about?' Now I really am on the brink of hyperventilating.

'Your reno?'

'You're going to work with my dad? At my house? But how? What?'

'You probably know more than me,' he says. 'Your old man spoke to my boss about needing another set of hands for a build and look at this.' He flips his hands, palms up. Callouses dot the base of each finger and the deep lines would be a palm reader's dream. 'How's these for hands?'

'I have to go.'

The bell jangles again as he holds the door open for me.

'I'll be seeing you, Cat.'

'Ooh, Paulie and the SUB,' I overhear as a car does a burn out, music blaring, tires screeching and smoking. I zip around the corner out of sight as the Neanderthals whoop and I half run to the beach, the foil tucked under one arm. Condensation from the glass bottle pools in my hand.

<h1 style="text-align:center">4</h1>

THERE'S a lookout high above the beach, barricaded on three sides by a timber fence to stop people from accidentally plummeting over the cliff edge. A teenage boy walks the top rail like a tightrope, nothing but air beside him. He's barefoot, tall and skinny. I see the ripples of his rib cage. He's concentrating hard, and I grab his hand, yanking him down to the safety of the grass at my feet.

'Cat! You scared the crap out of me!' Matty yells.

'Yeah, well you scared the crap out of me,' I say. 'I've told you before: don't freakin' do that! It's dangerous! Now, grab your stuff, let's go.'

'I think you pulled my shoulder out of its socket,' he says.

'Yeah, right.' I sneak a look. He's holding it funny, letting it hang awkwardly away from his body.

When our younger brother Tommy was a toddler, we were walking on the beach with Mum and Dad, and he was holding Dad's hand when he stumbled, Tommy, not Dad, and we all heard this loud pop. Tommy screamed, his elbow dislocated. Mum still gets emotional when we bring it up. I think she imagined him maimed for life. Instead, the doctor at the local hospital nonchalantly popped the joint back into place, gave Tommy a lollypop and told us it was the third most common injury in kids under two. The most dramatic part of the whole thing wasn't the fifteen-minute drive to hospital that they did in five. It was the tantrum Matty threw about not getting a lollypop too. Now, twelve years later, he's swinging his beach towel over his head like a lasso as he walks beside me, talking at a million words per minute. I'm pretty sure his shoulder is fine.

'Jeez, Cat, the beach is packed, isn't it? Gonna be a long summer, hey? Jeez, it's hot, isn't it? Did you swim? It's flat, isn't it? Did you see any waves? No waves, hey? Should we go for a snorkel later, what do you think?'

He doesn't pause for breath – he rarely does. If I weren't 17, if he weren't 14, if I didn't think it would gross him out completely, I'd scoop him up and snuggle him like I did when he was little. I settle with an arm around his shoulder and squish him. He's all hard angles and between the elbow to my ribs and the pure evil adolescent smell radiating from his pits I sincerely regret it.

'And here's me thinking you're a good kid.' I rub my ribs and scrunch my nose. 'Even though you're basically just walking, stinky sweat.'

Matty tosses his towel at me and swings himself over the metal access gate that separates the carpark from the path to the beach.

'Let's go the back way,' I say. I'm not in the mood for another Neanderthal run in, so we cut through the streets towards home. There's only a couple of hundred people who live in Batter's Cove, but over summer that number explodes as all the holiday houses fill with people determined to squeeze every bit of summer out of their vacation. Towels hang over balconies, garages are open exposing the bowels of beach houses filled with bikes, ping pong tables, boogie boards and boxes. The drone of lawn mowers is pervasive as people make up for months of neglect while their holidays houses were empty over winter.

As we move further from the beach and higher up the hill towards home, the tarred roads turn to gravel. Matty's barefoot and I can tell by the way he minces along that his feet are still fleshy, soft and tender from months upon months in school shoes. By the end of summer, he'll be able to walk on glass. Mum will tell him off about not wearing shoes and if Nonna's there she'll really give it to him for walking around like *poverati*, poor people, as only my politically incorrect grandmother could put it. We approach our house. From the street, it's three levels of glass balconies and windows reflecting the sky and the trees, and there's Mum on the side balcony with her back to the street, Nonna sitting beside her, white hair shining.

'What do you think about the whole reno thing?' I ask Matty, but he's scooping up a rock from the road and tossing it up into the canopy of the gums. There's a raucous flurry as a cloud of red lorikeets take to the sky in objection.

Nonna and Mum turn to see us walking up the driveway, Matty's feet filthy with red gravel dust and the dirty grey soil from the nature strips. We're going to cop it.

5

MATTY dumps his towel in front of the garage and flies straight up the stairs to the balcony. Directly above my head, Nonna's delight at my brother's appearance is as obvious as it is unbridled. It's OTT, even for her standards. He's *my cherished boy* this, *my darling boy* that, all in a rapid Italian staccato. After following Matty up the stairs I toss the foil to Mum, sitting at the outdoor table with Nonna, a bottle of bubbles between them.

'Thank you, darling,' she says.

'How dare you let your brother walk through the streets like that?' Nonna says.

'Happy New Year to you too, Nonna.' I pretend to take a sip from her glass of bubbles.

'Don't you dare.' She snatches it back, the liquid protesting its rough handling with a flurry of disturbed bubbles. 'Your mother and I are toasting in the new year.'

'I love that colour on you, Nonna.' I nod at her new scarf, a Christmas gift from Mum that I helped pick out. She runs her plump fingers over it and smiles.

'Anything to eat?' Matty interjects.

Well, if that isn't the most ridiculous question. Here comes Exhibit A, Mum with a giant platter in her hands. She places it on the table and Matty and I pounce. On one side, there's cold chicken, avocado, cheese, lettuce and tomato, on the other, sliced watermelon and pineapple.

'Wait, I'll grab the rolls.' Mum disappears inside.

'Forget about it, Angela,' says Nonna. 'They're like a pair of animals. Anyone would think you haven't eaten for weeks.'

'Where's Dad?' I bite into some watermelon, then spit the pip over the edge of the balcony.

'Caterina!' my mother and Nonna say in unison.

'What?' I ask. 'It's for the garden. Anyway, where's Dad? We need to have words.'

'He's downstairs,' says Mum. 'Words about what?' Last night's eyeliner sits smudged well below her eyelids and her hair rivals mine in the dishevelment stakes, twisted into a bun at the base of her neck.

Mum and Dad had friends over last night to watch the Batter's Cove fireworks from the balcony. When Matty and I got home the party was in full swing. We managed to get Dad's attention from the shadows and kissed him goodnight before we skedaddled to our beds to avoid being dragged into a room full of dancing fossils. Around one in the morning, Tommy climbed into bed with me, crying from over-tiredness. I drew on his back until he fell asleep, texting my friends and trying not to wake him by laughing. It was such a bad sleep, being woken every now and then by the sound of clinking bottles, a shriek or laugh, and then the farewell shouts as people left. I have no idea how any of them managed to make it down the stairs. Soon after, Dad's snoring echoed through the house. I'd just drifted off when the sound of the vacuum started, and then ten minutes later I could hear my brothers fighting over the television remote control. Happy freakin' New Year!

'Words about the fact that I just had the king of the Neanderthals inform me that he now works for Dad.'

'It's a big job, Cat,' Mum says. 'You think Dad can do it on his own?'

'You know they call me a SUB, right?' I glance at Nonna who is rearranging the gaps in the platter left by Matty. I lower my voice. 'That's Stuck-Up Bitch, you know.'

'That's not going to happen, Cat,' Mum says. 'From what I hear, he's a good kid.'

'He's a Neanderthal and he'll be here, at my house.' I spit a watermelon pip into my hand.

'How is you calling him a Neanderthal any different from this *stuck-up* rubbish? You don't think that's a bit unfair and hypocritical?'

'Fine, you've got me. I'm an unfair hypocrite.' I take a big slug from the water bottle Paul gave me, swallowing the last of the dregs. 'Hey, Tommy, can you bring out the water?' I yell over my shoulder.

'How many times must I tell you? It's Tommaso,' says Nonna. She's the only person who doesn't contract our names. None of this Anglo Cat, Matty or Tommy for our Nonna. Dad might call us the Dirty Three, but to her, we are Caterina, Matteo and Tomasso, whether we like it or not. Mostly, we lean towards not, but with all things Nonna, we're fighting a battle we'll never win. My name is the perfect example. In her house I am Caterina, complete with full rolling of the 'rina'. I'm named after Nonna's mother who by all accounts was a complete and utter witch, and not the good kind. My mother doesn't have a single nice thing to say about her, yet there's her name on my birth certificate.

'I think I know my brother's name, Nonna, thank you.'

'Cat…' Mum shoots me a pleading look. It's a familiar one that says that she knows Nonna gives me a hard time, but can I please just suck it up for her sake?

'And do you have to sit like that?' Nonna leans down and pushes my knees together.

We lived with Nonna while Dad built our house. That was fun. So much fun! Dinner at five, soapies all night long. There's a high probability she loves the soapie characters more than she loves her actual family. The only good thing about them is you can say anything you want when Nonna's watching; she doesn't hear a thing. We lived there for almost a year, and when we left, moving a whole fifteen minutes away, both Mum and Nonna cried as if our house were interstate.

I think Dad probably missed Nonna most of all because she fussed over him and my brothers like they were crown princes. She sent him off to work with lunches that could have fed a factory, and

Dad still gets a packed lunch courtesy of his mother-in-law every single day.

I didn't shed a single tear. I was too excited about my new room. A new room, and the fact that we'd be seeing her every day after school anyway. Every. Single. Day.

Our school bus drops us off in town after school and we walk the few blocks to Nonna's, where either Mum or Dad pick us up. Dad works everywhere, wherever he's building, and Mum's office is at home, but she spends a lot of time back and forth to the city depending on what she's working on. When we arrive at Nonna's we fling our school bags through the kitchen door and yell, 'we're here!' Matty races straight into the kitchen to find what treats Nonna has left out for us, Tommy's focus is the TV, and I head to the percolator and jam it full of espresso. My conversation with Nonna is a daily ritual performed as she watches me make coffee.

'Caterina, you need sugar! Put some sugar in.'

'Nonna, no, I don't like it.'

'Just one teaspoon, it takes the bitterness out of the coffee.'

'No, it's fine, it's not bitter.'

'Here, I'll do it for you.'

'Nonna, no, I don't like sugar.'

'I don't know how you drink it like that.'

Rinse and repeat that conversation five times a week, fifty-two weeks a year. Still, I have a horrible suspicion that I'm going to miss sitting at the table with my Nonna. When I was a child, I thought Nonna's espresso cups were the most gorgeous things ever. Picture pastel cups a quarter the size of normal ones, all the colours of gelato. We've drunk hardcore espresso out of Nonna's tiny cups since we were toddlers. Okay, maybe not toddlers, but I honestly can't remember a time when I didn't sip from a cup. It's amazing that all three of us don't have Type 2 Diabetes. One of my earliest memories is Nonna feeding me spoons of sugar stained with coffee. That's what she'd do; she'd make us our own espressos, in the beautiful, magical cups of course, and then to weaken the caffeine she'd add sugar, at least three teaspoons. In a tiny espresso cup. Yes, caffeine might make a child hyper, so let's add sugar. Now I can't stand the slightest sweetness in a hot drink. I still adore the cups and at least once a week I remind Nonna that when she dies, they're to go to me. I know that sounds macabre, calling dibs on a living person's belongings, but it's one of Nonna's expressions: 'You like it? You can have it when I'm dead.'

It's not only a miracle we're diabetes free; by all measures we should be morbidly obese. Most kids get home from school, maybe have some fruit, perhaps some crackers or biscuits. Nothing too heavy to spoil their dinner, right? Not us. We come home to a feast. A bowl of pasta. Some eggplant that's been crumbed and fried in olive oil. A frittata. Cake. Pastries. Biscuits. A giant bowl of jelly. One time even scones that she'd made from a packet mix, God knows why. The boys love it. They easily put away a bowl of spaghetti, reach for the pastries sitting on the table, then work their way through the salad she's picked that was originally destined for at least two neighbours. So basically, after school we get to my Nonna's house, leave our shit everywhere, eat all her food, the boys go play with the local kids in the street, I get started on my homework, Mum or Dad walk in after an hour or so, tell us to clean up our shit, Nonna waves us out her door, we leave, and she cleans up after us.

When we were younger, I used to play with the other kids in the street too. I was the only girl in a group of about seven and the moment I turned eleven, without a hint of approaching body changes, my grandmother began standing at the front gate watching us play. Or more specifically, watching me, her eyes like red target lasers circling me, following my every move. No amount of ducking or weaving could make her lose track. Even with my back turned I felt her eyes drilled into me. That was bad enough, but then, just to ramp up the mortification, she began calling me from the gate. If I waved her away, or yelled, 'five more minutes,' she'd hit me with her most powerful weapon in her arsenal.

'Caterina! Come away from the boys!'

As if Italian wasn't her native tongue, her shrill voice would ring across the street, her English flawless. Heads would turn, equating the panic of an elderly woman's voice with a situation of grave danger: a wolf pack, an out-of-control car, the local creepy old man. Nope, it was just my Nonna's warnings about the dangers of a young girl hanging around the terrifying prepubescent boys of the neighbourhood. Never mind the fact that most of them were my brothers' ages, and that both she and I had known them all their lives. No. According to my Nonna, at eleven I was on the cusp of the terrifying descent into womanhood, and as such I was a magnet for debauchery and depravity. The boys wouldn't be able to fight my subconscious bewitching siren calls nor their own willpower to hook up with me in the street. According to Nonna, I'm in constant danger of being ravished. As if reading my mind, she starts up again.

'You're a woman now, Caterina,' she hisses at me. Her eyes narrow as she takes in my posture, sprawled in a deck chair, my feet resting against the balcony glass balustrade. 'Sit like a lady. The whole town can see your underwear.'

'It's okay, Nonna,' I say. 'I'm not wearing any underwear.'

Nonna pins me with a glare as unforgiving and merciless as the stony mountain ranges of her ancestors. She opens her mouth to strike but Mum steps in.

'Mama, enough. She's just teasing you,' she says. 'At least, I hope she is.' She reaches for the edge of my skirt, and I push her hand away. I sit up and wriggle my skirt back down over my hips.

'There, Nonna, all sorted. Virtue intact.'

'You go on and laugh. One day you'll see that I'm right and you won't be laughing then.'

'Right about what, Nonna?'

'Right about being proper. I never had the opportunities you have. I never had the opportunities your mother had. Don't waste them by hanging around boys, being reckless.'

Mum and I exchange glances. Mum has told me many times that the only reason she was able to go to university was because her father suddenly died when she was in her final year of school, relinquishing any say in the matter. According to Mum, he was a lovely man and she adored him, but he didn't believe in educating girls, and he *really* didn't believe in women being architects. His early demise was Mum's long-term good fortune in a bizarre, mournful way.

'Don't you two go pulling those faces,' Nonna continues. Man, she could tell me off underwater. 'Be smart. If you're careless just once, *just once,* Caterina, that's it. Your whole future ruined. Forget about boys. Concentrate on your books.'

'Nonna, I don't even have a boyfriend. If I even had the hint of a boy around here, you'd scare him off.' I stand and hug Nonna, her face bright red, a mix of the heat, the champagne and her pure outrage.

As I turn to go inside, she slaps me lightly on my butt.

'She's a smart mouth. You watch that one.'

'I don't need to watch her, Mama,' says Mum. 'You're here.'

I give up on waiting for Tommy to bring out the water. I slam the fridge door. 'Seriously, Mum?' I wave the empty water jug. 'There's no cold water. What is wrong with people?'

Mum comes inside. 'Is it that big a deal, Cat?' She reaches behind me to the freezer, shaking some ice into a glass. 'Problem solved.'

'It's not even about the water, Mum,' I say. 'It's everything. Freakin' hell, is this my summer? Arguing with Nonna about my non-existent love life? Trying to study with no books and a house full of Neanderthals?'

'It's one kid, Cat.' She puts her arm around me in one of her perfect mum hugs. 'And you might want to pull your head in. It's the first day of the year. If I were superstitious, I'd be worried that this tone you're throwing around is what you'll be stuck with for the whole year. Come on, darling girl, this isn't you! What's wrong?'

Damn it, I feel my eyes burning. How does she always know how to get to me?

'It's just… everything.' I tuck myself into her arms. 'That one kid? It's the whole Neanderthal world entering mine and I don't want them here. Not now. It's too much, what with school and Nonna and everything.'

'It's a lot, I know,' she says. 'But believe me, we'll all be okay. I promise.'

6

I'M sipping a coffee on the balcony with my English notes and the newspaper, blue highlighter in hand, when I hear the heavy tread of work boots on the stairs behind me.

'Global warming or drowning children?' I say over my shoulder.

'Well, they're both pretty messed up, aren't they?'

I spin so fast I probably have whiplash. There, right on my balcony, is Paul GD Lightwood, looking like he's just stepped off the pages of a surfing magazine. It hurts to look at him, and not just because of the glare. His board shorts are green camouflage and he's wearing a black t-shirt with a surf logo right in the middle of his chest. He's passing a pair of sunglasses between his hands.

'Hey, Cat.' He smiles, just quickly, flashing teeth that look as expensive as mine, then looks down at his hands.

As I squint against the sun, I'm painfully aware that he wouldn't be mistaking me for a surf model, not by a long shot. While I've spent the last half an hour multitasking while circling articles and mentally debating the merit of global issues, I've also been squeezing the hell out of a crop of pimples on my chin, including its centrepiece, a flaming, throbbing volcano. It's so big that even though I know it's not physically possible I swear I can practically see it in my peripheral vision. My pyjama pants are covered with fluffy kittens and sit below my hips, not from any sense of style, but because they're hung with age. Last year, when they were rising up my shins, I cut them into shorts, and have since picked at the loose threads, so an uneven, unravelled hemline sits across my upper thighs. I've paired them with a singlet top that was Dad's and has long since lost its shape after spending many an hour stretched over my knees. To top off this ensemble, my hair is a big, tangled knot on top of my head with my pen stuck through the bun. The ultimate horror of horrors? My bra is a world away, abandoned on my bedroom floor.

Paul takes the chair to my left, sitting at the table as if he's been here a million times. He leans back, surveying the view which, thank the sea gods, isn't me.

'I've always wondered about what you could see from up here,' he says. 'This is such an incredible house. Any chance of one of those?' He nods at my chest.

The captain of the Senior Debating Team finds herself speechless.

'Or a water, whatever's easier.'

'What? Yes, coffee's not a problem.' Thank you sweet baby cheesus. I've remembered how to speak.

I rise from my seat and pause, a clammy hand on the kitchen door. 'Um, how do you take it?'

'Stock standard,' he says. I look at him with a blank stare. 'White with one.'

'Ah, okay,' I say. 'Be right back.'

I fire up the coffee machine and bolt upstairs into my bedroom. I should get dressed. But would that look like I'm trying too hard? I wriggle into my bra and pull on some denim shorts and a singlet that has never belonged to my father. I run my finger over my teeth and rub the sleep out of my eyes. Using my fingertips I go over my eyebrows, smoothing them down. In the kitchen, I hover over the coffee machine.

My stomach reminds me with a deep growl that I haven't had breakfast. I open the fridge and find a bowl of mashed avocado. My mother is the actual best.

I slice up some ciabatta and take it outside with two plates and the avocado. The second I put it on the table it feels completely over-elaborate, but Paul starts loading up a plate, piling bread with avocado.

'This is awesome,' he says. 'I haven't had breakfast.'

The coffee machine beeps and I go back inside. When I return with two coffees, he's put two pieces of avocado bread on my plate. I place a mug before him.

'Thanks, babe.' His eyes widen. 'Sorry, I mean, Cat, I mean thank you.'

'You're welcome, *babe*.' The word on my tongue makes me shrivel with cringe. 'Dad isn't here, he's gone for a walk with my mum, but I don't think he'll be long.' I peer into my coffee cup like I'm reading a fortune, and the steam fogs my glasses.

'It's all good,' Paul says. 'I don't mind waiting, not when you're feeding me like this.'

'Don't get used to it. I'm not your waitress while you're working here.'

'We'll see,' he flashes me that grin again. 'What's all this then?' He nods his head at my scribbles and takes another bite.

'It's for school.'

'Aren't you on holidays?'

'I'm going into Year Twelve next year. Well, this year, now. I can't believe that in ten months I'll be all done.' I look into his sunglasses to where his eyes should be. It's unnerving that I can't see where he's looking.

'Ten months? Is that all?'

'Yep. Look, I have a countdown.' I hold up my phone, the lockscreen showing the months, weeks, days and hours until the last official day of school.

'You're on a countdown?' he says. 'And you have homework, now? Don't you need some down time?'

'You sound like my mum,' I say. 'I'll worry about work life balance next year when it's all behind me.'

'That's a first.'

'What?'

'Sounding like a mother. What subjects are you doing?'

I tell him, and he whistles.

'My highest level of achievement was veggie maths,' he says. 'Do they still call it that?'

'Not at my school,' I say, 'we're a little more evolved.'

'What?'

'Doesn't matter,' I say. 'But you can't talk. Aren't you about to work the entire summer? Where's your work life balance?'

'I need a new car,' he shrugs. 'I have a good excuse.'

'You don't think smashing Year Twelve is a good excuse?'

'I didn't say it wasn't.'

I take a piece of ciabatta. At least if my mouth is full, I can't speak.

'What were you saying when I got here? Global warming or kids who can't swim?'

I swallow. 'Asylum seekers. Kids and their families drowning for the chance of a better life. It's for English,' I shrug. 'It's a yearlong assessment, following an issue of our choice. I'm thinking that or global warming, the melting of the polar caps and all that.'

'Why don't you do plastic in the ocean?' he asks. 'Something that means something.'

'People fleeing persecution doesn't mean anything to you?'

'That's not what I meant.' He runs his hand across his hair, cut short against his scalp. 'You really like making me look like a deadshit, don't you? I'm just trying to chat with you.'

'I'm not making you do anything.' My face is hot, mind racing. Have I lost the ability to have a conversation without being snarky? The gum leaves shimmer, their silver undersides flashing. The silence stretches. I take a slug of water, more to occupy my hands than to quench any thirst.

'Stop! It's mine!' The sound of squabbling kids reaches the balcony. Grateful for the distraction, I peer down to the street. Through the gap in the trees, I see children playing in the street in front of a holiday house. Mum and Dad are at the foot of our driveway, talking to some temporary neighbours. Dad looks up and sees me, or sees us, more specifically. He nudges Mum who stares, eyes wide. She waves distractedly at the neighbours and yanks Dad by the hand up the stairs behind her.

Paul takes off his glasses and stands as my parents approach. He introduces himself, shaking both of their hands. Mum's eyes dart between me and the walking surfer god on our balcony. Wow, Mum. Smooth.

'Another coffee, Paul?' Mum says, composing herself into the ever-accommodating Italian host.

'We've just had one,' I say.

'Is your name Paul?' Dad says to me, his head tilted. 'Paul, would you like a coffee? Some water?'

'I'm actually okay, but thank you,' says Paul.

'I need one desperately,' says Mum. 'Lovely to meet you, Paul. We've got a lot to talk about. Cat, would you make us a coffee and get some water too, please, darling. Mick? Grab the plans.' She shoots her *do not challenge me* face in my direction. I leave the door open so I can listen.

'So, the two of you are going to spend your holidays from working as builders to work as builders,' says Mum, taking a seat. She gestures for Paul to sit down. 'Are you sure you're happy to start this soon, Paul? You don't want another week or so?'

'No, it's all good, Mrs Kelty.' He sits and shifts forward in his seat. 'I'm actually stoked. I've always wanted to work on a place like this.'

'It's Angela,' she says. 'We're really happy to have you on board. It's a big job and Mick can't do it on his own.'

'Man, I love this house, so I hope I do you proud! So, what are we looking at?' Paul nods at the plans Dad's spread across the table. I wouldn't mind a look too, so I hand Mum her coffee and put a water glass in front of Paul. He thanks me, smiling, before returning his gaze to the plans.

'It's the subterranean level. We always knew that we'd use this space down the track, and so these plans, this reno, is what Angela intended all along,' says Dad.

It's the first I've heard of it, this plan to renovate our house.

Dad explains to Paul that they'll turn the space under the house, between our garage and the hill behind it, into a bedroom, living room and bathroom for Nonna, basically a built-in granny flat. He's also including a cellar in the project and we're all under strict instructions to call the reno exactly that, so Nonna doesn't get wind of Mum and Dad's plan to 'future proof' her life.

'What? So Nonna doesn't even know about this?' I say. 'Why the rush? Does it really have to happen now?'

'Cat, you can see Nonna's going to need us more and more. We need everything set up in case she can't stay at home anymore,' says Mum. 'Unless you want her to share your bedroom if she needs to?'

'Nonna will outlive the zombie apocalypse,' I say, and Paul laughs. 'I just don't see why it has to happen this summer when there's already so much going on.'

'You're a smart girl, Cat. You'll handle it,' Dad says. 'So, Paul, you in?'

'Absolutely.' Paul nods, as enthusiastic as a golden retriever going for walkies. 'Bring it!'

'Shall we do a quick tour?' Mum clasps her hands and a grin breaks across her face.

'Let's do it.' Paul stands and pushes his chair back in under the table.

'Let me just finish this,' Dad nods at his coffee. 'Cat, can you show Paul inside? I'll meet you downstairs.'

'Okay, so we're here, this is the top.' I take a deep breath and tell myself this is decidedly not weird, flinging my hands around like a tour guide as I show Paul my house. 'We're basically four levels because of the hill, right? This first one is the kitchen and dining room and laundry.' He follows me down into the living room. 'Those steps down there? That's the parentals' room, and if you turn to your right? That's me and my brothers.' I point to what Dad calls the nosebleed section, the corridor that runs the length of our living room with our three bedrooms and the bathroom we share which is the bane of my existence.

'Man, this is a nice house,' Paul whistles. He turns slowly. 'So, what, it's two, four, six stairs to each level?'

'And the twenty-two from the garage to the balcony,' I say. 'It's one thing we're not short of.' Between the stairs all over my house, the stairs up and down to the beach, the stairs at school and the stairs to get on the freakin' bus, all I do, all day, every day, is climb stairs. Some days I get to the car, ready for school and realise I've left something in my bedroom, so back up I go. How don't I have the knees of a geriatric? Funnily enough, the stairs are the only things Nonna doesn't whine about when she comes over. She'll spend an hour having a go at me about my hair, having a crack at Mum about working too hard, telling Dad off about not growing veggies, but she plows up and down the stairs without a murmur.

'I can't believe I get to work on this house.' Paul grins, looking around like he's casing the place.

'Hey, Paul,' Dad calls us from the balcony. 'Do you mind if we take a rain check? Angela has to go pick up her mother and I have to go get the boys.'

'Yeah, that's sweet,' Paul says. I follow him out to the balcony. 'I have a few things to do at home for the old man, but before you go, can Cat come to a party at the Gap with me tonight?'

'Well, you'll have to ask Cat,' says Dad. Three pairs of eyes turn to me, one set almost doing cartoon-style loops out of the owner's skull. No prizes for guessing who.

'I don't know.' I gesture vaguely at my notes on the table. 'I need to finish all this.'

'Cat, you have all summer.' Mum shakes her head. 'You can have a night off.'

'Come on, Cat, it'll be fun,' says Paul. 'A bit of work life balance for both of us, what do you think?'

'Um, yeah, sure.' I'm as articulate as ever.

'I'll pick you up around eight-thirty?'

'It's okay, I'll meet you there.'

'No, Cat, you won't be wandering along the beach alone in the dark,' says Dad.

I could punch him.

'So, I'll see you here at eight-thirty,' says Paul. 'What time do you need her home?'

'Midnight,' says Dad.

'One thirty,' Mum counters.

Paul laughs. 'Shall we meet in the middle and go for one?'

'One is fine,' says Mum, and now it's Dad's turn to receive her *do not challenge me* face.

'See you tonight, Cat, and thanks for breakfast. Nice to meet you, Mrs Kelty, I mean Angela.' He shakes their hands again, kisses me on the cheek – *kisses me* – and then he disappears down the stairs.

'You didn't tell me your new chippie is a model,' says Mum.

'Funny,' says Dad. 'He's not just a pretty face, so I hear. Good guy. Smart. Truckloads of initiative. Works for Jaz Smith.'

'Wow, what a looker,' says Mum. 'And Cat? A chippy, just like your old Dad.'

'Who's old?' says Dad. 'And here's me thinking I'd have to watch Cat with the hired help.' He pulls Mum down onto his lap. 'So, the ladies still love the tradies, hey?'

'We sure do, don't we, Cat?' She snuggles him.

I roll my eyes and leave them to it. Apparently, I have a party to go to tonight, and a demon in the form of a pimple to exorcise.

7

THE sun belts through my blinds. It's still ridiculously hot outside, and the heat of the day is fighting hard against my AC. I've slept for hours, my face heavy and bloated, my head thumping with a dehydration headache. My book is on the ground beside my bed, spine cracked. It's going to look a lot worse in a few more months once school is really humming with exams and assessments and all that — dog-eared, scribbled all over, assaulted with sticky notes, streaked with highlights. I pick it up and take it downstairs to the kitchen where I stick my head under the tap to guzzle water. I could drink the entire ocean. Although, given its salt content, I'd still be thirsty. And dead, but whatever. Mum is rustling in the pantry behind me, peering into the depths of its corners.

She turns and spots me. 'Seriously, Cat? You can't stretch your arm just a tiny bit to pick up a glass?'

'It's all good.' I wipe my mouth with the back of my hand, more to annoy her than anything.

'Lovely,' she says. By the look of her hair, she's had a nanna nap too.

Just to emphasise the point, Nonna lets rip with one of her famous snores from the living room below us, waking herself momentarily. She looks around, dazed and wild-eyed, then her eyes droop, and her chin drops back down onto her chest. Startled, Matty and Tommy look up from their video game and then crack up laughing.

'For such a tiny thing she has a shocker snore,' I tell Mum. 'When did she get here?'

'About an hour ago,' she answers. 'We could hear you snoring from outside.'

'Funny.' I reach behind her for one of Nonna's home-made lemon cookies. 'Man, how hot is it? Is the air con even on?' I lift my ponytail off the back of my neck. A little river of sweat channels down my spine. If I think about it, the metaphor would probably be a creek. Or do I mean analogy? I'm already sick of searching for metaphors.

I look down towards the beach. The ocean's like a millpond, and hello, there's another analogy. Ugh. Even from here I can see the tide's edge a long way out, without a hint of waves. Well, that explains why Paul was here, wanting to work. The Neanderthals always seem at a loss when there are no waves, unsettled, like the entire purpose of their being has been swept away with the tide.

'How weird are time zones?' I wave my phone at Mum, notifications empty. 'It's the middle of the night in London. Em will wake up to messages from me and when she answers I'll be asleep.'

'Hmph,' says Mum. 'Well, that's good timing with Paul, isn't it?'

'What "with Paul"? What are you implying, Mother?'

'Nothing, nothing, of course. It's good that you have someone to hang out with.'

'It's hardly hanging out.' I turn back to my book. 'He's working for you and Dad. It's not like we're friends. Until yesterday I'd never said two words to him.'

'Well, you are going on a date with him tonight, that's hanging out. You can get to know him more before he starts.'

'A date? Hardly! It's a party full of Neanderthals and deadshits, and I don't even know why I said yes. I have far too much to think about to be surrounded by shitheads. If he turns up, which I highly doubt, you can just tell him I'm not home.'

'I'll do no such thing, Cat. If you don't want to go you can give him the courtesy of telling him yourself. Anyway, why wouldn't you want to go? You love parties.'

It's true, especially school parties. My school is the only private school in a one-hundred-kilometre radius. So, when there's a party, we travel from all over to get there. The collective vibe of parents is that it's preferable for some poor sucker parent to host the kids. We party, we go back to someone's house in a big group to lie on their living room floor in sleeping bags. We chat for hours, sleep for maybe twenty minutes, then the host mum or dad cooks us up bacon and eggs before our parents pick us up.

'I love them when I have actual friends to hang with, not just some random here to make some cash with you guys.'

'I think you're being unfair, Cat. He seems like a nice guy, good manners, polite, and, well, there's no denying he's super cute. Speaking of which, what a meet-cute!'

'A what?'

'You know, when you meet someone and it's sweet and romantic. Very Hollywood. Meet cute. Or is it cute meet? If we're talking Paul, it's cute meat, m-e-a-t, let's get real, am I right?' She holds up a hand for me to high five, and mock groans when I leave her hanging.

'That's objectifying, Mother. I'm truly ashamed of you.'

'You're right, and while I might be your mother, I'm not blind, Cat. That boy is yummo.' She bites her knuckle and winks at me. I can't help but laugh.

'Anyway,' she says. 'It will do you good to get your head out of a book for a while. You're going to burn yourself out before you even begin.'

'Ugh, Mum, again? You've been on my back about not overdoing it since the Information Night. There's no chance of burning out when I don't even have half my books, is there?'

'Let's worry about your books next week when the bookstore opens. Tonight, forget about Year Twelve for a while. Have some fun.'

She's just getting warmed up, so I brace myself.

'All right, I'm ready. Give me your speech.'

'What speech? All I'm saying is, you've been invited to a party, you've said yes, your date's a nice guy, you're a beautiful, lovely girl, together you'll have a fun time.'

'Mum! Can you please stop calling him my date? It's just a beach party!'

'I used to love beach parties.' A look of nostalgia washes across Mum's face. 'But be smart. Walk on the beach, not the bush paths. And don't go off on your own, stay with your "date".'

She uses her fingers as quotation marks with the word 'date'.

'You know the keep safe rules. Don't have more than three drinks, make sure you open them yourself, if someone hands you an opened drink just say, "no, thank you". If you put your drink down, don't pick it up again. I had my drink spiked at uni. I woke up in your father's car with no memory of getting there. He could have had his wicked way with me but there's nothing wicked about him. Or nothing wicked that I can share with you, my darling daughter.'

'That's a beautiful story, Mum, thank you,' I hold her hands and stare into her eyes. 'I genuinely have no words to describe how much I'm enjoying this conversation. This closeness between us? Can it stop? Please?'

Mum holds my gaze. 'All I'm saying is don't do anything that you couldn't comfortably tell us. But if you do, make sure you use protection. I'm not talking about Paul, obviously, or tonight. Although, I hope you know you can tell me anything. Anything and everything, Cat.'

'Okay, Mum, I think we're done here.' I pick up my book.

'Cat, you're 17-years-old,' she says and walks to the kitchen. 'You know we trust you, and you know our expectations of you. You have a whole summer in front of you to get ready for Year Twelve. Stop overthinking everything.'

8

JUST before half past eight, right at the moment between dusk and night when the lingering light from sunset has dissipated, Paul knocks on the sliding door. Of course I'm ready. I'd been dressed for hours, and thanks to the miracle that is modern cosmetics, I'd been able to camouflage the red demon on my chin. With a 'see you later' over my shoulder, I shut the door behind me, pushing Paul back onto the balcony.

'What, I can't say hello to your parents?'

'Nope, let's go,' I say. Tommy's up against the glass making a kissing face. 'That is Exhibit A of why we're out of here.'

Paul's Hilux ute is immaculate – not a takeaway wrapper in sight and no empty drink bottles rolling around my feet, smacking into my ankle on every corner. I'm wearing my favourite skirt, ombre moving from green to blue with a white singlet knotted against my midriff. I sit gingerly in the front seat, expecting the grit of sand against my thighs, but there's only the smooth softness of nylon cloth.

'Is this the car you're so desperate to replace that you're willing to give up your entire summer?' I say. 'There's nothing wrong with it!'

'I need a bit more grunt.' He keeps his eyes focused on the road.

'I thought you're a tradie?'

'I am.'

'Have you told your car? It's nothing like my dad's. His is a cesspit.'

'So was this one a couple of hours ago.' He flashes me a grin.

Paul parks at the Surf Life Saving Club. When he pulls the handbrake up, I spring from the car, tugging my skirt down. As we pass the clubhouse, the dunes take turns concealing its light. The beach is dark, but I can tell that the tide has come back in as the waves fill my ears, the only indication of their presence in the blackness of the night. As my vision adjusts, the foam cuts the beach in half with a white smudge. I stop as the path reaches the beach line to take off my sandals, balancing on one foot at a time. Paul holds out a hand.

'I've got it.' The words are abrupt and loud, cutting through the darkness. He drops his hand and shrugs.

It's much cooler down on the beach, the air moist with sea mist, the night's warm, humid air high above the sand dunes. I shiver and wrap my arms around myself, my sandals digging into the soft skin of my waist.

We reach the Pee-Pit, the tannin-stained channel carved into the sand where the storm water runs from the cliff into the sea, dotted with ancient rocks that form perfectly placed steppingstones through the effluence. Although, as Dad says, it's not really effluence, just rainwater and whatever chemicals people have used to wash their cars. I don't care what Dad says: it looks like urine to me. Paul steps ahead, leaping onto the first rock, hand outstretched.

'I've been jumping these rocks my whole life.' I smirk as I leap, losing my balance momentarily as we share the same narrow footing. He grabs me by the waist to steady me, and together we leap off the final rock onto the sand. Stable and surefooted on the other side of the Pee-Pit, his hand rests on my waist and as we start walking it slips down and across my bum.

'I think we need to get something clear.' I stop, shifting away so his hand falls to his side. 'You don't need to pretend to have this sudden interest in me just because you're working for my dad. You've got the job. It's a done deal, without my involvement, and so nothing is going to happen. Nothing.'

'I don't know what you're talking about,' says Paul. There's a hint of offence in his tone, as if he's biting down on the words. He's standing with the sea behind him, his features hidden in the shadow of the cliff face.

'I know what you're like. You'd sleep with a stop sign if it looked at you the right way.'

'You don't know anything about me,' says Paul. 'Up until yesterday we'd never even spoken.'

'That's exactly my point,' I say. 'I've seen you around for years. You're part of Batter's Cove furniture. Up until yesterday, you have never acknowledged my existence.' I can hear myself, and worse, I can see myself, hands on hips, face thrust out. I sound exactly like Nonna. Maybe she's put one of her crazy Italian Nonna curses on me and is inhabiting my body, making me as untrustful as she is when it comes to the male species.

'You know what, let's just sit here for a bit,' Paul says. He sits on the sand, then leans forward to take off his hoodie. I glance at the golden tan of his abs that peek beneath his t-shirt as it lifts slightly with his arms. He holds it out.

'I'm fine, thank you,' I say, sitting beside him. 'Actually…' The sand is cold under my bare legs. I pull on his jumper before my stubbornness takes hold again and can smell… what? Shampoo, laundry powder, aftershave, a hint of salt. If clean and fresh had a smell, this is it. In fact, does this guy smell like sunshine? I roll away from him to pull his jumper down over my hips. The waves smash into the rocks, as relentless as a heartbeat. Fires glow up and down the beach and the thrum of a bass line pulses in the distance.

'You were saying?' Paul shifts beside me, stretching out a leg, leaning back on an elbow.

'What was I saying?'

'That I'd have a crack at a light pole, or something like that.'

'Actually, it was a stop sign, but my point stands. Listen carefully – I know you think that something's gonna happen between us, but anything you think is going to happen is never going to happen.' And to mortify myself more, I spell it out. 'N-E-V-E-R.'

'What exactly is it that you think *I* think is going to happen that's never going to happen, Cat?'

'You know.'

'I really don't. Enlighten me.'

'You know exactly what I'm talking about. It all goes back to the stop sign.'

'Yes, the stop sign,' he says. 'That's it. That's beautiful. Touching. Can't wait to tell my mum that's what I'm known for, she'll be so proud. And of course, I know who you are, Cat. It's a small town, and a girl like you? I'd be dead if I hadn't noticed you. It does go both ways, though. You've never even looked me in the eye. Would it have killed you to say hello to me? Even at Sadie's yesterday, I'm trying to talk to you, and you ignored me.'

'Number one: I didn't ignore you. Number two: you weren't trying to talk to me, you were... who knows what you were doing?'

'Number three: I was just saying hello. It's not that deep,' he says. 'I'll be at your house all summer, so it's weird that we don't talk, don't you think? I wanted you to come out tonight so we could talk, have some fun. Not *that* kind of fun, obviously. Which you already know, don't you, private school girl, so much smarter than an ignorant, dumbarse tradie like me.'

'Wow, that didn't take long,' I say. 'What's next? You going to call me a Stuck-Up Bitch too?'

'I'd never call you that,' he says. 'N-E-V-E-R. See, I can spell too.'

'Impressive.'

'Thank you. I've been reading the dictionary all arvo, hoping I'd get the chance to spell something out to you.'

The low boom of a firework echoes from a bonfire down the far end of the beach.

'Merv will be in all kinds of pain tomorrow,' I say. Like a horrible case of chicken pox, the Batter's Cove foreshore is dotted with signs prohibiting open fires. Apparently, the local authorities issue severe penalties to people caught building fires, which is patently unfair given the huge number of constituents that have barely evolved beyond the wheel. Every day of summer it's almost impossible to walk on any local beach without coming across the scattered remains of the previous nights' bonfires. I've never heard of anyone being fined for it. No one seems to police the no-fire decree. No one except Merv, a man employed to manage the camping grounds. He wears his quasi-officialdom well, like he's wearing an invisible sheriff badge. He flies around the back streets and camping ground trails in a tiny little car. He's always harried and busy, fuelled by self-importance, like one of those people who talk with their hands, waving them around to make it harder to see that if they stopped the incessant moving, you'd realise they weren't actually saying anything at all.

'Oh man, I can't stand that a-hole,' says Paul. 'Although, he gave me the best laugh of my life a couple of years ago, I'll give him that.'

'When he had the fight with the fire brigade?'

'Yes! Were you there?'

'The whole town was.'

And it was: Batter's Cove had come alive the night some brainiac set fire to a rubbish bin. We'd seen the lights of the fire engines from home, and we jumped in the car with Dad to bolt down to the foreshore to see two massive fire trucks, monoliths of red lit against the black of the night sky. Twelve big burly men in full firefighting get up were arguing to the point of a brawl with Merv, who had dialled it in as a major outbreak threatening people and property.

'How did I not see you?' says Paul.

'There were a lot of signs fighting for your attention.'

'Funny. Shall we go to the party now? Or would you like to talk more about me and my attraction to road signs?' He stands and holds out his hand. This time, I take it, and he pulls me to stand before him.

'Thanks,' I say and go to wipe the sand from my legs. 'Um, can I have my hand back now?'

'If you must,' he says but pulls it against his chest. I can feel the heat of him against the back of my hand. 'Cat, everything you think you know about me is crap, I just need you to know that.'

'Okay, whatever,' I say, keeping my eyes firmly on my hand still pressed against his firm chest.

'Whatever? That's not very convincing. Good thing the night is young, hey? Let's go, yeah?'

He turns, and my hand goes cold at the absence of his heat. He starts walking, and after picking up my sandals I trail him up the beach before remembering that this is not the twelfth century and that I, Cat Kelty, walk behind no man. I scurry to catch him, kicking up sand, and match his step. I mean I'm tall, but he's taller and has a good thirty kilos on me, so instead of walking casually I'm doing a little half skip-limp thing. Very glamourous. The music gets louder and as we follow a curve around the cliff, we enter the Gap, a small beach with a narrow bay formed by a split in two cliff faces eons ago. The Gap's lit with the orange glow of a huge bonfire. We've arrived.

Around a hundred people litter the Gap in groups. Surfers, campers and locals alike sit sharing eskies, drawn to the ocean in celebration of summer and beach and surf, having drifted down from the camping grounds, the general store or the pub. There are younger kids, Matty's age, right through to some of the fossil surfers. There's the obligatory group of surfer groupies who turn up at all these things with the sole purpose of hooking up with a surfer. Sitting to the side of the bonfire are the Neanderthals who hoot when they see Paul. Across the fire from them is Isabel Scuzzbucket Dillon, sitting on an esky, drinking ouzo straight from the bottle. We lock eyes, hers narrowing before she turns her back to talk to a shirtless guy next to her who is leaning back on an elbow, bare feet crossed at the ankles, a modern-day Jesus with his long shaggy hair and matching beard, if Jesus were in his twenties and used the f-word like punctuation.

Paul takes my hand and leads me towards his friends. I discreetly shake free, and it flops hard against my body, as if it were a limb belonging to a stranger. He sinks to the sand surrounding the fire and pats the space beside him. I sit as gracefully as my short skirt and Paul's giant hoodie allows me. I didn't think my outfit through at all. Looking across the beach, I see many other girls clearly thinking the same thing, flicking sand off bare legs, doing that telltale short skirt adjustment, trying for subtlety but if they're anything like me they're feeling painfully obvious. The heat from the bonfire is intense and so I unzip Paul's hoodie to my waist.

A Neanderthal stands before me, three bottles in hand. 'Hey, Paulie,' he says. He tilts the bottles at us. 'Beer?' he asks. They still wear their metal caps. Mum would approve, slightly.

'Thank you,' I say, feeling prim. He wrenches off the top before handing it to me.

'Paulie? Beer?' He tosses the caps into the fire.

'I'm Ant.' He sits on the sand in front of me. Though we've never spoken, I know him as Antonio Scamporelli. His nonni go to the same Italian club as my Nonna.

'Cat.' I tip my beer in greeting.

'You here for the summer, Cat?'

I look at him incredulously. 'No, I live here.'

'Really? You just move here?'

'Not really. I've lived here since I was a kid.'

'Hang on. Cat Kelty? Mick's daughter? Signora Maria's granddaughter?'

'The one and only,' I say, lifting my hands in a shrug.

Paul offers no comment, seemingly content to sip on his beer and listen to our awkward greeting. I glance at him, and he offers a quick smile.

Ant looks me up and down, his head tilted in confusion. 'Man, I can't believe I didn't recognise you! What have you been up to? How's JB? You catching up with him over the summer?'

'I wish,' I say. 'He's working with his dad all summer.'

'Bummer,' says Ant. 'His old man's a bit of a prick, isn't he?'

'Just a bit,' I say, 'but he pays well.'

'I haven't seen him since the season finished. How'd he go with everything?'

'Really good,' I say. 'He works his arse off – he's going for physio.'

'He's a smart one,' says Ant. 'Too smart for us dumbarses at the footy club, that's for sure. Say hi to him for me.'

'I will, but don't you have preseason coming up? You'll see him before I do.'

He takes a swig of beer, and his eyes do another sweep of me. He shakes his head. 'I can't get over how different you look.'

'Different how?'

'They're called tits, Scampo.' A Neanderthal flops on the sand in front of me, the little shitbag who nearly took out my shins with a skateboard at Sadie's. Steve. A wiry, short, towheaded, barely teenaged kid from an estate in town with the telltale black front tooth. He openly stares at my chest. I try not to squirm under his insulting gaze but wrap Paul's jumper tighter. Of course, the loud-mouthed tool somehow managed to time that insightful comment right in the break of music between songs. While the logical part of my brain knows that between the roaring of the ocean and the multitude of simultaneous conversations there's no possible way he was heard by anyone beyond the people in my immediate vicinity, it seems that every person at the party turns their head to chance a glance at my (admittedly spectacular) rack.

'They're great tits. Give us a proper look.' He reaches out and I slap his hand away.

'Touch me, and I'll break your nose,' I say.

'Come on, don't be a Stuck-Up Bitch all your life.' He goes for me again.

Before I even register what's happening, I punch him right in his face and he falls back against the sand holding his cheekbone. My knuckles throb but I keep the sharpness of the pain from showing on my face.

'You fucking bitch,' he yells. He gets to his knees and lunges, his fist clenched. Years ago, at a funeral, one of my cousins accidentally punched me in the eye and I've never forgotten the sound of her fist making contact, the pop, and that tear of pain. I brace.

Suddenly, I'm covered in sand as Paul leaps to his feet. He has Steve by the neck of his t-shirt, his feet lifted off the ground.

'Fuck off, mate,' he says, quietly.

'The Stuck-Up Bitch just fucking punched me!' Steve kicks in the air, trying to see past Paul. 'You're dead, bitch.'

'Shut the fuck up.' Paul shakes him by the shirt.

Ant moves across the sand, his back to me. There's a high-pitched squeal. Isabel's lying sprawled in the sand with another girl, laughing, kicking the sand with their heels, their underpants flashing.

'You better watch your back, bitch,' Steve yells at me over Paul's shoulder.

'Off you fuck, mate,' Paul says. 'You stay away from her, you hear me?' He shakes him again, then shoves him away. Steve stumbles from the release, looking around, almost pleadingly, but the party has continued as if nothing had happened. Someone across the Gap sings along out of tune to the music and a group of people join in, arms around each other.

'Don't make me tell you again.' Paul sits back beside me, brushing sand off my shoulder then wrapping his arm around me. 'Mate, don't even look at her. You see her, you walk the other way, you hear me?'

Steve turns and crosses the beach, climbing the stairs up the cliff face.

'You okay?' Paul whispers into my ear. 'You're shaking.'

'I'm fine.' I pull away and he drops his arm. 'Just embarrassed. My Italian temper. He caught me off guard.' A trickle of sweat moves down my spine and my teeth are chattering. I zip Paul's jumper up to my chin.

'Don't worry about that dickhead,' says Ant. 'He knows better than to cross Paulie.'

'What's "Paulie" got to do with it. He should know better than to cross me. *Non ti preoccupare.*' I try to smile to bring down the tension, but it comes out as a grimace, my face burning all the way through to my ears. What a goddamn scene! Although, I don't know how much of a scene it was. I nearly get bashed by a loser who would likely stab me with a dirty syringe and a group of girls danced right through the whole thing, completely oblivious to what was going on over at our side of the bonfire.

'*Esattamente.*' Ant gives me a wink.

'Don't worry about Steve,' says Paul. 'He won't go near you. Ant, grab us another drink, hey? Cat?'

'No, thanks.' I shrink a little into myself, grateful for the security of Paul's jumper.

'Hey, Paulie, how's your new board?' Paul turns to one of the Neanderthals. Thankfully Ant joins in, asking inane questions about rails and outlines and about travelling the world, surfing every break they came across. Across the circle, Isabel and her friend lean against each other, legs twisted, their faces lit by the fire. Their gazes lock onto me and Paul. Her friend cups her hand over her mouth, whispering into Isabel's ear. Ugly laughter fills the cove. Isabel totters to her feet, heels sinking into the sand, and lurches around the fire.

'You're here!' she yells and drops into Paul's lap, her back to me, her hair whipping me in the face.

'What the fuck?' He rears back, but she clings to him, her arms around his neck.

'We need to talk,' she slurs.

'Yeah, nah we don't,' he says, and stands, dislodging her into the sand in front of us.

The wind shifts, blowing smoke into my face. My eyes sting and fill with protective tears.

'I'm just going to go chat to those girls over there,' I say to Ant, coughing through the smoke.

'Cat, wait—' Paul puts his hand on my arm.

'It's all good,' I say and make my way to a group of people in the shadows of the cliff. Looking over my shoulder, Paul's standing side-on, talking to someone, so I move behind the randoms under the cliff, following its curve to the edge of the Gap. I'm not game to take on the bush path alone in the dark, especially if Steve is hanging around, so I walk back along the beach. The moon lights up the sand and the tide's retreating. The clouds have parted long enough for the waves and the sand to reflect off the moon, giving me light to see my way.

Between the top of the beach stairs and the clubhouse the path curves around a bend, enclosed on each side by the dense tea trees. I can barely see, and with the ocean roaring behind me I can't hear a thing. The path is a faint silver line. I sprint, only four or five seconds until I'm in the openness of the streets, but it feels so, so much longer.

It's weird, but sometimes the streets feel safer here in the dead of winter when there's no one around. It seems like every second house is having a party tonight. At one house I catch the attention of a group of losers who whistle and yell at me. 'Hey, babe, where you going? Come have a drink? Don't be shy, babe!' I keep walking, eyes straight ahead, my ears tuned to their laughter, waiting to hear footsteps behind me, ready to bolt. As I move into shadows past the streetlights, they give up on me as quickly as they'd noticed me.

Mum and Dad are sitting in the dark watching TV when I get home. It's just after eleven. Dad has an empty wine glass beside him, a faint tinge of pink around the rim. They startle as I open the sliding door, Mum spilling the water from the glass she's cradling.

'You're early,' she says. 'Where's Paul?'

'At the party.'

'He let you walk home on your own?' Even in the low television-cast light I can see that Dad's livid. 'That little prick…'

'No, Dad, it's fine. I'd had enough so I just left.'

'You didn't ask him to take you home?' asks Dad.

'Why didn't you call us?' Mum stands and puts her hands on my shoulders. 'Are you all right? We don't like you walking around on your own at night, especially in the holiday season. It's not safe, Cat. You know that.'

'There're people everywhere.' I kiss my parents good night and go upstairs to my bedroom.

I hear the clink of glass on the granite bench and Dad's footsteps moving through the house. 'I'm going to strangle that little prick with my bare hands.'

9

'BOOM!' Mum slams the newspaper on the dining table and my sticky notes scatter. 'Here's an issue for your assignment, Cat.'

'What?' I pull the paper closer and spread it flat.

'This is the world you're living in. We've been fighting this for years, and look, here we still are.'

'"She asked for it."' I read the headline aloud. 'Is this for real?'

'I wish it weren't. I honestly can't believe it.' Mum winds open a window to let in some fresh air and a trickle of water from the early morning rain moves down the glass.

I scan through the article of a young woman sexually assaulted by a group of men, footballers, at a party in a beach town just like Batter's Cove, but in New South Wales.

'So, sexual assault?' I writhe in my chair at the thought of months upon months of researching violence against women.

'It's not so much the act,' Mum says, 'but how it's being reported. That's your issue. "What was she wearing?" "Had she been drinking?" Next there will be character witnesses about the men, what good blokes they are, how they're the pillars of the community. Sadly, there'll be more than enough articles for you to analyse, and that's only the ones that make the papers.'

My stomach squirms. Last summer, Isabel in the manky toilet block, a deep red scratch down the length of her leg, the rumours that followed. I grab a sticky note and scribble a love heart and a smiley face before tearing it off.

'You're the actual best.' I slap it gently on Mum's forehead and laugh as she goes cross-eyed looking up at it.

Dad honks his car horn twice. Tommy leaps up from the living room floor where he's been playing. He and I kiss Mum on the cheek and bolt down the stairs.

'Don't run!' Mum yells but the command comes too late.

Tommy's feet hit the second last step and slip from under him and my stomach lurches as he skids down the stairs, the path slick with rain. His head slams into the last step with a loud thunk that rings in my ears. He blinks rapidly, his eyes focused on mine. Bile rises in my mouth.

'Muuummmm!' I scream and kneel beside him. Tommy lays on the ground blinking as a procession of misery moves its way across his features, his eyes becoming luminescent with tears, his brow furrowing, his mouth opening. He wails and in that moment I see him as baby Tommy, as toddler Tommy and preschooler Tommy. Mum appears at the top of the stairs, her face blanched.

'Just walk, sweety,' Dad says to Mum as he slams the car door behind him, 'or you'll be on your arse too.' He kneels over Tommy. 'You okay, mate? Don't try to move. What hurts?'

'My head,' Tommy sobs, then sits up, rubbing his crown. My legs are shaking; I feel almost swamped with relief. I thought for sure he'd be spending the next six months in a spinal unit and I'd be hand-feeding him jelly that he'd let dribble out of his mouth just to annoy me. I love him so much I'd let him.

'He's fine,' I say. Tommy's been skidding down these stairs at least once a week since we moved here.

'I'm not fine, dickhead.' He tries to kick me.

Mum's at the base of the stairs by now.

'Enough with that filthy language,' she says. 'If you can kick and talk like that then you're fine. Upstairs with me, you need an icepack for the back of your head.'

'No, I want to go with Dad and Cat,' he whines, but by the way he clutches his head his protest is completely by rote. As he stands, he rubs his sacrum. 'My arse is fucked too.'

'What did your mother just say?' says Dad. 'The language in this house is beyond a joke!'

'It doesn't help that you call your offspring the Dirty Three, Dad,' I say. 'It's like we have a genetic predisposition for profanity.'

'Bullshit,' says Dad, proving my point times infinity.

'Come on, Tommy.' Mum places an arm around him and guides him up the stairs. 'Don't be hours,' she calls over her shoulder.

'You're driving.' Dad moves to the passenger side of the car and throws the keys over the car roof to me.

I catch them, and clap my hands and jump on the spot, then curse myself for acting like a silly schoolgirl. Which I am, for the next ten months, anyway. I slide into the driver's seat and pull Dad's tattered seatbelt over my shoulder. I clip it in and it hangs limply across my torso, as ineffective as a strand of cooked spaghetti. I yank it tight and with my hand on the seat lever, I use my body weight to jerk forward so I can reach the pedals. This movement is just a flick of a button in Mum's, but Dad's battered work car has no such luxury. I adjust the mirror as Dad clicks in his seatbelt. We're off, puttering down the dirt road, the potholes making the car shake and shudder.

It's cold today; yesterday, it was over 40°C and it felt as though my lungs were about to spontaneously combust. The northerly wind felt like a blast in the face from a hairdryer. Today, I'm in my favourite yoga pants even though I'm no yogi, and I'm wearing last night's singlet under my puffy jacket.

'What do you think's worse? Extreme heat or cold?' I ask.

'I'd prefer heat. You can always find a way to cool down. But imagine being stuck in the snow with no way to warm up. That would be hell.'

'Hell is a car without seat warmers. You live like a savage, Dad.'

He laughs, and points to his right. 'Let's hit Boomers.'

We have the roads to ourselves, the storm keeping everyone contained inside their holiday homes, a win for my self-esteem. Dad insists that I drive not so much the speed of light but at the speed of custard, and not the runny kind – imagine custard that could hold a metal spoon upright. That speed.

One of Matty's favourite ways to give me hell is to give us a head start on one of my practise drives and then catch up on his bicycle, riding beside me with greatly exaggerated movements to pretend it's an accomplishment of massive physical exertion to keep up with the car. He takes the hilarity to new levels, that kid, especially when he dismounts and holds his bike above his head, walking backwards. Dad always says to ignore him, to ignore all distractions, then leans out the window to yell at Matty to stop distracting me, which, funnily enough, is highly distracting. Helpful, Dad. Thank you.

We roll to the end of the street, by gravity more than actual acceleration, and I look left, right and then left again, the indicator sounding like a drum beat. There's nothing. I change gears.

'Hang on,' says Dad, 'check again.'

'I did, there's nothing.'

He knocks the car out of gear, and I know we're not going anywhere. I sigh, then physically lift myself out of the seat, twisting my entire body to look in both directions.

'Okay,' he says.

'You sure?' I keep switching back and forth, right and left. 'Should I just keep looking?'

'You want to walk?'

'It would be faster.' I ease my foot off the clutch and rev the accelerator. Nothing happens. I rev harder and the car shudders beneath me. 'What the hell?'

It's not in gear.

'Very funny, Dad.' I bang it into gear and take off. A car blasts its horn and I slam on the brakes, throwing us forward. An old wreck of a station wagon passes by, veering sharply around our front end, missing us by centimetres. A hand protrudes from a window, middle finger saluting. I stare in shock, hands glued to the wheel and my heart thrumming, the staccato snare to the still ticking indicator drum.

'Head check!' Dad yells. 'Fuckwit, driving like that. Did you see his rego?'

I turn off the engine and burst into tears.

'You're fine,' says Dad. 'Get back on the horse, it's not your fault. That goose was driving a hundred miles an hour. But see what I'm talking about? Always, always, *always* check each way. How many times do I need to tell you?'

'Stop yelling at me!'

'Come on, Cat.' Dad pats my knee. 'We're fine. Do your head checks and let's go.'

'Are you sure?' I say, doing the shaky-voiced sniffly thing I do when I'm crying. I rub my sweaty hands on my pants and wipe the back of my arm across my face. There's a fine film of snot glistening off my sleeve. 'Okay.'

I'm still trembling when I turn the ignition and the car rumbles back to life. I take a deep breath and check each way, check again, and then check again. I grab hold of the gear stick, push it into first, then slowly take my foot off the clutch. The car hops along the gravel. Dad and I lurch, then I hit my stride. My nerves calm as the car settles into a smooth roll, the only shudders from the potholes and not my gear changes. We pass dozens of beach houses, holiday makers standing forlornly on balconies. The road takes us out of town, along Back Road, a boundary of sorts between the town and the nearby farms, little more than a goat track built to access Dad's fishing beach. We drive to a clearing smaller than a standard house block. We're the only car, thank goodness, so I pull up next to the log barrier that marks the walking track to the beach.

'You know what, Dad, I really don't like driving.' My knuckles are white as I grip the steering wheel in the perfect ten to two position. 'I don't think I'll worry too much about getting my license. Next year, I'll just take public transport in the city.' I turn off the ignition and toss the keys across to Dad. 'You're driving home. I'm done.'

'Spoken like someone who has never had to take public transport in their life,' says Dad.

'What? I take the bus to school every day!'

'That's not public transport, Cat. Not even close. Anyway, how do you plan to get home on weekends or your holidays? Are your mother and I supposed to drive you backwards and forwards?'

'Could you? That would be fantastic. Thanks Dad, you're the best!'

'Hang on, Cat,' he says as I take off my seatbelt. 'Before you get out, about last night…'

'Ugh, here we go.' I roll my eyes. 'I know, I know, I shouldn't have walked home alone, blah, blah, blah.'

'Don't be a smartarse. You have an incredible brain; we all know that. But you don't have a lot of street smarts, and walking home alone last night proved it.'

'Quick question, Dad. Would Matty have to sit through this or is the safety chat just for me because I'm a delicate, vulnerable girl who can't take care of herself?'

He holds my eyes as he continues, concern heavy in his face. 'Why'd you leave the party? Did something happen that I should know about?'

'I told you I was over it. Like, I won't be seeing the king of the Neanderthals enough?'

'Bella, you need to lose the attitude about Paul. Everyone's dealing with their own crap. Remember that and don't add to it. Yeah?' Dad only calls me Bella when he is in full protective father mode and the nickname cleaves through my stubborn annoyance.

'Yeah, all right, Dad. I get it. It was stupid, and I'm sorry, okay? Are we doing this?' I really don't want to think about Paul GD Lightwood and what's looking like my undeniably bad call sneaking off last night. He's occupied far too much of my brain space this morning as it is, the way my hand felt in his. Enough! I get out of the car and zip my puffy jacket right up to my chin. I pull the hood over my face so only my nose is poking out. Matty always says the jacket makes me look like a burnt marshmallow, but I love it. Even today, it's so cold that I can see Dad's breath as he takes his fishing rod from the car, yet I'm already covered in a fine sheen of sweat. It's like walking around in a doona.

I take Dad's tackle box and walk ahead of him down the path.

Once away from the carpark, the trees absorb the light, turning the morning into a strange twilight. A pile of poo, hopefully canine, is crawling with flies, the buzzing an assault, yet somehow thankfully assuaging the smell. The path twists and turns through the bush, then gently ascends. Eventually, sand wins over soil, the trees recede, and the path crosses a dune that leaves my calves burning as I reach the crest. The ocean is a calming sight, spread before me like a galaxy of blues and I am greeted by its salty kisses.

I yank the hood off my face and unzip my coat to my belly button, the cold air delicious on my skin. I wait for Dad at the top of the dune. When he emerges from the trees, he uses his rod to point right.

I run down the dune to Dad's fishing hole. It's a rocky outcrop just behind the shore break, an area of water the size of one of the tennis courts at school. The water barely ripples despite being surrounded by an ocean of supreme grumpiness.

Since we were kids, we've had it drilled into us that we are never to swim where the waves don't break. The smooth sea seems enticing when the waves are violent, and the shore break alone looks too big to navigate without being pummelled.

Every summer at one of the local surf beaches someone always gets swept out by the rip. There's rescue after rescue when it's hot. If people are lucky, they get caught when the surf is pumping, because they drift into the surfing lineup who begrudgingly drag them onto their boards and paddle them back to shore, abusing them relentlessly, calling them every name under the sun and accusing them of ruining the chance of catching the best wave of their life. By the time they get the poor, bedraggled, terrified person back to standing height, the surf lifesavers are barely up to their knees in the water.

No wonder the lifeys hate surfers, and vice versa. The surfers see themselves as martyrs giving up their fun time to do the lifeys' jobs for them while they parade up and down the beach with their wedgies. The lifeys see them as the interlopers who step in and get all the hugs and gratitude and glory for saving lives, while they get stuck rinsing sand out of kids' eyes and treating sunburn.

I place Dad's tackle box on a flat rock shelf high above the point of any rogue waves. There's a line of foam high on the beach and the tide is making its way out. Away from the dune's protection, the wind tears into me. I zip myself back into my coat, wave to Dad and start walking along the beach.

The sand is soft beneath my feet but too wet for the wind to flick into my face. I find a gorgeous piece of driftwood, thick, narrow and gnarled. Attach some straw to the end and it would be a perfect witch's broomstick. I use it as a walking stick, my footprints left with a deep, round indent beside them. When we were kids, Dad's favourite beach trick was for all of us to walk with stretched, exaggerated steps in the sand so the next people at the beach who came across our footprints would think they were following the trail of a family of giants.

A wall of white crashes and bounces off the rocks in a steady pounding. At the foot of the dunes is a carpet of seaweed, torn, twisted sheaths of rubber. If the tide doesn't reclaim it overnight, by this time tomorrow when the heat returns it'll be hard and cracked, its shine reduced to matte. Entwined and tangled in the seaweed is rubbish. *Ugh*. I grab a giant discarded crisp bag and step in the gaps between the seaweed to start collecting. I pluck tin cans, plastic bottle lids, fishing line, straws and beer bottle tops. There are the disgusting remnants of cigarette butts, so many cigarette butts. I barely walk half the beach, and the chip bag is full. Still, the air smells clean, the scent of salt and wind clings to my skin and hair.

I place my stick under a giant pile of seaweed, its stem as large as my torso. I flick hard and it flips over, revealing thousands of scrambling sand fleas. I leap over them, using my stick to clear a path of sorts towards the cliff face. I hate stepping on sand fleas, but not as much as on seaweed. I'm always waiting for something to reach up and grab me by the ankle.

It's sheltered at the point. I sit in the soft white sand, my back against the cliff face, cradled by rock. It's so quiet below the wind, the waves muted. All I can see is a trinity of sand, sea and sky. The horizon is clear. The light between sky and sea is opaque, as if someone has taken a white chalk and drawn a line to separate the two.

It's easy to imagine being the only person on the planet today, until far in the distance, the triangle of a boat moves across my vision. Closer in, shapes are moving just under the surface of the water, a strange shimmering. Seaweed, I think, until I see what's unmistakably the tip of a fin flick above the surface. The shape shifts, separates, rejoins and then two dolphins rise above the water, their white bellies blending into the waves' foam. They drop, and rise again, joined by another, and then another. One leaps high from the water, launching itself across the face of a wave, its landing sending a torrent of water splashing. I'm on my feet, wishing for them to return but their forms are replaced again by the waves. They've gone, and I'm both exhilarated and bereft. I grab the plastic bag of other peoples' crap and my stick and run back to Dad.

'Did you see the dolphins?' I yell from the beach. His face is beaming, and he points to the bay beside him. The pod is chasing each other up the beach. We watch them until they are indistinguishable from the white caps. It's cold, my puffer no match for the wind blowing off the ocean. Dad's had enough and so have I. We're putting away Dad's gear when another two cars of fishers arrive to fish the low tide.

'Good haul?' They note our elevated moods.

'Yep,' says Dad as he turns to leave. He hadn't caught a thing.

10

'DIE, die, die!' shrieks Matty at the screen.

I sit on the bottom of the steps and take off my shoes and socks, leaving a miniature sand dune in their wake.

Mum's in the kitchen, faffing around with the fruit basket, lining everything by colour. The fridge door is open and she's an island in a sea of shopping bags strewn haphazardly around the kitchen. Dad and I timed that well, not having to carry them up the stairs from the car. I help Mum unpack the groceries.

'It's okay, Cat, I've got it,' she says.

'Yeah, I wouldn't want Tommy or Matty to break a sweat,' I said. '"From every region, apes of idleness!"'

'You're the weirdest teenager, Cat. Lose the Shakespeare and go play with them.' She turns back to her fruit arranging.

I stand at the top of the living room watching my brothers wrestle their controllers. No thank you.

I'm lying on my bed flicking through my science textbook. It's big, overwhelmingly so. There's no way I'll be able to read it this summer. There's no way I'd be able to read it in six summers. Not even an hour ago I was mesmerised by science at its most magnificent; now I can't focus on a single page. I am not looking forward to spending the next ten months or so dragging this to and from school. My back will be twisted and gnarled like the witch's broomstick I found on the beach. I turn a page with more force than is needed and hear the sharp tear of paper over the banging from under the house — the *took, took, took* of Dad's nail gun belts out a tune against my temple. What will it be like with two of them under there, and one is the hottest of the hot?

I walk down to the living room where through the window I see dark, nebulous clouds shift and move through the sky high above the coastline, the ocean clear, the storm making its way out to sea.

'The campers will be happy when it stops raining.' Tommy stands beside me to look out the window.

'You're so right.' I'm almost bouncing off the walls from half a day of bad weather. I can only imagine how hideous it must be for the people trapped in caravans and tents and mouldy old holiday houses playing endless card games. When it's cold, wet and windy, the days feel so freakin' long and oh so boring, like the days after I finished school, but at least then I could go to the beach. I want some sunshine, pronto. I want this wind to blow its way back out to Antarctica so I can walk on the beach without feeling as though I'm pushing through quicksand. I'm sick of the books sitting on my desk, gloating, swollen with information I'm in the wrong headspace to access, let alone absorb, and I'm sick of worrying if the missing ones will arrive in time for me to read them before school starts. 'Hey, Tommy, if it clears up tonight, do you want to go watch the sunset from top of the Bay?'

It's something we've done together since he was little. Tommy loves to watch the colours shift through the sunset as much as I do. He grins up at me and I stick a finger into his rib, tickling him. He giggles and scoots back down to the living room.

Mum's playing karaoke with Matty. Oh, the horror of my mother playing air guitar, bellowing alongside my brother. Cats all over Batter's Cove could take up the chorus and still hold a better tune. I make Dad a coffee and escape downstairs.

The garage door's open, as it always is whenever anyone is home. It's empty. Mum's car is in the driveway and Dad's is parked on the street in front of the house. Tommy and Matty's bikes are in a jumble at its entrance. Dad's categorically told us not to use it while he's working on his Taj Mahal of cellars. It's a big garage, I suppose; it's basically the bottom level of our house and is the frame on which half the house sits. It fits two cars easily, and Dad's wide workbench extends along the back wall. Above the workbench Dad built shelving and hooks for his gazillion tools. A full length of cupboards lies along a side wall. The doors are closed, but I don't need to open them to know they are on the brink of exploding. Mum's a bit of a hoarder. She still has all our baby clothes and the toys we stopped playing with long before we even moved here.

'Dad?' I call out from the middle of the garage. I can hear him banging around behind the wall beside me. 'I've made you a coffee.'

He backs out from the manhole at the side of the garage, and I'm greeted by the lovely view of his tradie's cleavage. A small triangle peaks his chest, tanner than the rest of him from wearing an unbuttoned shirt all day.

'You're a good one, you are! I knew you'd come in handy eventually.' He takes the coffee from my hands. He's filthy with cobwebs and the strange, pale coloured dirt we have here at Batter's Cove.

'You'd be a good one too, if only you took advantage of modern life. There's this new invention, you might have heard of it, it's called a belt?'

'A belt's the least of my problems,' he says. 'I need to get this wall open so I don't have to crawl in and out. I'm too old for this.' I crouch down to look through the manhole. The space under the house is cavernous, easily the size of our kitchen and living room combined. It's such a big space, used up until now as an undercover junkyard to keep lengths of timber, flooring, bits and pieces of building who-knows-what, hidden out of sight. Dad likes his garage pristine. For all these years it's only ever been accessed by the small manhole, the height of my thigh, wider than it is tall. 'Go in, take a look,' Dad says.

I shuffle through the manhole, my hands above my head as a buffer against the thick beam of its opening. There are spotlights set up, lighting every angle.

'This is supremely cool, Dad,' I step carefully over the piles of timber. 'How's it all going to work?' He talks me through the plans, showing me where the new walls will go, the plumbing paraphernalia that's been here since we built which will become a bathroom and a kitchen. Begrudgingly, I can see why he needs help. There's more timber stacked against the far walls. They're stark in their newness and the space has a strange smell, a mixture of timber and earth and stale air. He's spray painted a giant W against a wall. It looks like Nonna's new living room is going to have a view directly into the garden. There's a narrow section marked out in the opposite far corner, where the house meets the hill. 'Is this "the cellar"?'

'Yep,' says Dad, 'and it is a cellar, so you don't need the air quotations, Miss Smarty-pants. But just so we're clear, this is a room you are prohibited from entering. Last year, you ate four hundred dollars' worth of salami by yourself.'

Each July at Nonna's house, we have a day, an annual festival if you will, to celebrate all that is freezing cold and nauseatingly gross in our culture. Salami Day is its official title, but I prefer to go with Annual Vegetarian Hell Day. Yes, it's a cliché, but we spend the day up to our elbows in pork flesh that we mince ourselves. We fill the intestines of an unfortunate, recently-wallowing-happily-in-mud pig with its own flesh.

We start before dawn, or Dad and Nonna do, when they go to a local farm to collect a newly indisposed pig, butchered to Nonna's precise instructions which must make the farmer want to take to his own intestines with a blunt and rusty boning knife. The worthy sacrifice is one that Nonna would have chosen the week before, selecting which among them to grace our grazing platters for the year ahead. The next eighteen hours are then spent freezing in Nonna's shed and arguing over salt and chilli ratios. We finish up late at night, the fruits of our labour hanging over laundry airing racks, and the smell of dead animal firmly wedged in our nostrils and in the very fibres of the clothes we wear. In fact, a change of clothes is mandatory packing before we leave home in the morning and Mum won't let us in her car until we shower and scrub the living bejesus out of our every pore and follicle in Nonna's tiny bathroom.

'No offence, but you can be a bit of a smartarse yourself, Dad,' I say. He's right though. I do love Nonna's salami, and I have no issue eating it three times a day; with eggs for breakfast, on crackers and cheese when we get home from school and in a frittata for dinner. My arteries are probably more clogged up with cholesterol than a sixty-year-old chain smoker.

'What's that around your leg?'

I look down, and there's fishing line wrapped around my leg in a tangle. I've dragged metres of it through the manhole and across Nonna's future home. I follow its trail to an old reel in the corner of the garage. Dad drinks his coffee, and I sit on his workbench, untangling the fishing line and rewinding it on the reel, swinging my legs. It's raining again; water runs down the driveway in tiny rivulets. We're laughing about the rock concert coming from the living room above our heads when a voice calls from the garage entrance.

'Hello?'

It's Paul.

11

WHAT is with this guy turning up when I'm looking my absolute most shitful? The annoying part of all of this is I'm usually not one of those people who gets in a flap about how I look. I mean, I know I'm no supermodel, but I was the first grandchild and remain the only granddaughter of my Nonna. You can't have seventeen years of being told in no uncertain terms that you're the most heavenly, beautiful creature on the planet in great danger of ravishment without a fraction of it sticking, causing just a smidge of vanity.

'You didn't say you're working today, Dad?' He hasn't changed position. He's still next to me leaning against his work bench, staring at Paul – not exactly hostile, but without his usual 'g'day, mate' vibe. I'm sitting on Dad's workbench like a child and so I launch myself with a little more vigour than necessary and land on my feet, graceless, but at least upright. 'Your jumper is upstairs, I'll go get it.'

'Keep it, Cat,' says Paul. 'I'm good, thanks for asking.' He turns to Dad. 'Mick, Mr Kelty, before we get going, I'd like to apologise to you and Mrs Kelty for not bringing Cat home last night. It's not the best way to start a job, losing the boss' daughter. She just disappeared.'

'She walked home alone last night.' Dad downs his coffee and then straightens. 'Alone.'

'I know, and I hate that.' Paul holds his gaze. 'As soon as I knew she'd left I came past, and I saw you guys upstairs through the windows.'

'You're not planning on asking her out again, are you? What if you took her to the city and let her hitchhike home?'

The air has become stuffy and heavy, and it's not from the dust

61

particles floating around under the house.

'I'm right here, Dad.'

'I haven't asked anyone anything,' says Paul, 'but I'm feeling like it might be a bad idea if I did anyway, and I don't blame either of you. Once bitten and all that, but again, Mr Kelty, I'd like to apologise, and Cat, I'm sorry you felt like walking home in the dark was a better alternative than hanging out with me.'

'Well, that's not completely accurate.' I dart a glance at him. I can feel the heat in my cheeks. 'I'd just had enough of the party. Not you. It's not that deep.'

Dad takes a moment to assess Paul's speech and I hold my breath in anticipation.

'We've got to get this formwork up,' says Dad. Paul holds out his hand and Dad shakes it in one firm thrust. 'I appreciate your apology.' He crouches and disappears through the manhole.

Paul squats on his haunches in the doorway, his hands gripping the door jamb above his head. His board shorts creep up his thighs and as he leans forward his t-shirt rises, exposing a patch of skin, startling white against his tanned lower back. I fight an urge to flatten my hands against it.

'What are we working on?'

I can't hear Dad's reply.

'So, all the formwork?' Paul moves into the space and all I can hear is faint builder-babble.

'I'm going upstairs,' I say to the hole in the wall. There's no answer. The rain hasn't let up, but I bolt up the stairs anyway.

A couple of minutes later, Paul runs through the rain to his car. Mum comes to stand with me at the window. 'Is that Paul here already?'

'He apologised to Dad about not taking me home last night.'

'Well, that's pretty sweet.'

'Sweet? You don't think it's chauvinistic? That he seems to think it's the 1950s? Who are you and what have you done with my cool, feminist mother who has spent the last seventeen years telling me to fight the patriarchy, burn my bras, and rise from the oppression of men?'

'Well, I don't know that I was ever that emphatic,' says Mum, 'and fun fact: did you know that the feminists never actually burnt bras? It's a misconception that's floated through time. Anyway, there's a big difference between being a chauvinistic pig and being someone with basic manners. I hope you can recognise the difference.'

'What freakin' manners?' I say. 'He left me to walk home alone in the dark. Anything could have happened to me.'

'But it's Paul's fault, is it, that you bailed out on your date with him? And enough of the gutter language.'

'Yeah, yeah, I already heard it from Dad. I get it. Do we have to keep going over it? *Tu capisci?*'

'Ooh, so it was a date.' Mum tickles me. She's practically cackling.

'Are you twelve? The sooner you get back to work, the better. You need adults around you. You're turning into Matty when you should be getting ready to turn into Nonna.'

'Oh, shit, I nearly forgot,' says Mum, conveniently adopting my gutter language. 'Nonna! She's expecting me to pick her up for lunch. Want to come for a drive?'

'No, thanks,' I say. 'Take Tommy with you though, that game is killing me. I do have to focus, you know?'

She calls my brothers as she grabs her handbag from the kitchen bench. 'Cat, ask Paul to move his car, please,' she says.

'Not gonna happen.' I cross my arms and turn my nose up. Even I know I'm the posterchild of pure brat behaviour, but I can't make myself care.

'Going to, not gonna. All right, I can't be bothered arguing. Matty, run downstairs and ask Paul if he'd mind moving his car, please.' She gathers up Tommy from the game. He barely protests, knowing he'll be seeing the woman who maintains a temple in his honour of chocolate and lollies.

I go to the bathroom to survey the damage. *Not too bad. Not great, but not terrible.* I mean, yes, these yoga pants need to go to God, but apart for some dust in my hair from under the house I haven't come off too badly. The monstrosity of a pimple has receded, and my eyebrows are holding their shape from their last interaction with the brow bar. I give my face a quick scrub and pull a hairbrush though my hair. Despite my best efforts at gentleness, my eyes fill as the brush tears through the mini-dreadlocks I've accidentally cultivated at the base of my neck. I give up on the hairbrush; this is a job for conditioner, and that's a job for tonight. Shame I didn't think of it this morning when I spent ten minutes polishing each individual tooth in my mouth with the new electric toothbrush my orthodontist gave me for 'graduating'. Pretty crappy graduation gift, really, considering the gazillions of dollars my parents spent there, and the hours upon hours I spent flat on my back being tortured.

Bathroom ablutions, check. I yank off the hideous grey yoga pants and pull on some jeans. Comfort, be damned. My singlet is unadorned with those insipid logos that everyone seems to love having plastered all over themselves. We're done here. My transformation is complete. The self-loathing for giving a you-know-what about how I look in front of a Neanderthal is next level, even if said Neanderthal is the hottest of the hot.

Back in the living room the paper lies waiting for me. *Ugh, issues. Ugh, dying planet. Ugh, asylum seekers. Ugh, the patriarchy. Ugh, beautiful walking surfer god under my feet, literally.*

As if on cue, the banging starts up downstairs again. How am I supposed to concentrate with all this noise? Mum's car appears at the corner, and there's Nonna perched in the front seat. As they pull into the drive she looks up and I wave. Matty races up the stairs to reclaim his seat in front of the video game. I hear Mum and Nonna moving up the terraces under the stairs, the entrance specifically built for Nonna so she could avoid the steep staircase. Dad did offer to build a pulley system for her to get from the street to the house. Imagine Nonna, perched on a little metal bar, being hoisted over the balcony railings. We laughed; she didn't.

I kiss her on both cheeks as she comes through the door. She walks straight to the dining table and gathers up all my newspaper articles that I've separated into sections. I take them off her, somehow without snatching, fold them neatly and slip them into my issues folder.

'Nonna, want to see my Italian?'

'Why do you need to learn Italian?' she says. 'You're Australian. It's a waste of your time. I didn't come here and learn every word of English just for you to spend all your time learning Italian.'

It's an argument we've been having since Year Nine when I chose to study Italian of my own free will, as opposed to the school insisting on it. It's one of her many paradoxes. In her eyes, we, her grandchildren, are Australian to the point of '*Aussie, Aussie, Aussie, oi, oi, oi,*' but when Tommy tells her that Italy is in the running for the World Cup, she's all '*Viva L'Italia,*' never mind the fact that she's never watched a footy game of any denomination in her life. That's not accurate. She goes to Matty's every game, sitting in Dad's crusty old ute. She used to insist that Dad change ends each quarter, so she'd be right in front of him in the goal square until Matty threatened to stop playing.

'Mama, please don't start this again.' Mum's already endured this argument through her own education. 'You know why. She gets extra points for university by doing Italian, and anyway, we want her to have a connection to her cultural heritage.'

'Cultural heritage? Pftt.' Nonna crosses her arms. 'All your ancestors did was struggle for a better life, which we got, by coming here.'

'Oh, Nonna,' I say. 'Where's your patriotism? I'm going to need your help this year more than ever in my life, so I need you to get over yourself.'

She tells me to watch my mouth. I hand her the Italian novel we've been set. She hasn't read it and sneers at the title. Why do I put myself through this? Well, as Mum says, if I can win an argument with Nonna about the novel then I'll completely smash any assessments. Still, I'm not looking forward to spending the next eight months arguing with Nonna over whatever I write about that book. If I see it as an ode to war, she'll see it as a crisis of faith. If I see it as a metaphor for the universality of religion, she'll see it as a love story. If I see it as a love story, she'll see it as pornographic trash that I should not be reading.

I'm not just doing Italian because I'll get extra credits for my entrance score, although that's a definite advantage, or because it's an easy A for me. I could argue that I'm doing Italian because it's the language of my direct ancestors. But the unsexy truth is I really, *really* love sending Nonna into blind fury by intentionally mispronouncing words with strong Aussie yobbo strine in my accent, and by Italianising words by adding a vowel to their ending, like calling my brothers *le dicki*.

Italian is one of those subjects that, for the past eleven years, I could coast through without an ounce of effort, and I need something this year that won't feel like it's trying to kill me slowly. Em is like that with maths and science. She just turns up to an assessment and can wing her way through it, busting out anything above a ninety with time to doodle with boredom while she waits for everyone else to finish. I'm putting myself through science and maths not because I love them but because I know I need them to have more options, but ugh. Mum and Dad just can't understand why I have to work so hard to get half decent marks in maths. It was a hideous feeling, being the only one in my group of friends who fought for As when everyone else was piling them one on top of the other without a care in the world. It used to get me really down, which I was brainless enough to tell one of my teachers who then mobilised the wellbeing program around me. Hello, endless cups of tea with the school counsellor and her furrowed brow. At least she was generous with her chocolate stash.

School is all about self-esteem. Well, performance and then self-esteem. At the Year Ten subject selection meeting the coordinator told me, 'A brain like yours, Caterina Kelty? Work hard and you could do medicine.' I remember Mum and Dad exchanging glances, probably thinking about how weak my stomach is, how I vomit in sympathy with my brothers. 'The important thing is you don't waste your potential.' Potential, potential, potential. From the time we walk through the doors we're told relentlessly that not only are we expected to succeed, but we're entitled to success, and that every possible resource is there to support us to fulfil our potential. The teachers are there to nurture and massage every high grade.

This year? I need the highest possible marks. I don't have a choice in the matter. My school has such an amazing name, and something like an almost perfect university acceptance rate. Imagine being the only one in my year level that misses out on a place somewhere amazing? I have no plan b; I don't even want to consider a plan b. It's university for me or nothing. So, hello Italian and the boost to my entrance score.

'Coffee, Nonna?'

She murmurs in assent. She's settled herself in the living room, fidgeting in her oversized handbag for her glasses, my Italian novel beside her. I watch her from above. I know this routine so well it's immortalised into my brain. First, she puts her hand in and uses her sense of feeling. Then she mutters in Italian and peers in, nose crinkled into a frown, while her hand continues to rummage. Then she'll curse God above and upend her bag onto the carpet. She'll extract her glasses, put them on, and return everything to her bag with a self-satisfied hum.

I make three coffees: one for Nonna, one for Mum, and another for me. Mum eyes me off.

'How many coffees have you had today?'

'Dunno, maybe three?'

'I don't know, not "dunno" and I'm pretty sure that's your fourth. Put a sugar in it and take it down to your dad. You've had enough. Make one for Paul too.'

'I don't know how he likes it.'

'I know how he likes it,' says Matty. 'On the beach with a blonde, fake or real, doesn't matter.'

'Matty…' Mum purses her lips.

'Who has coffee on the beach?' says Nonna. 'Why would you?'

'Good one,' I high five my brother as he passes me in the kitchen. 'I'll make it, but Matty can take it downstairs. I'm not their slave.'

'Don't worry,' says Mum. 'I'm getting lunch ready anyway. Matteo, go and see what time Dad and Paul want to eat.'

'Matty, wait,' I say. 'Mum, stop! Don't even think about it, he's just here to work, why would he want to have lunch? That's too big a deal, even for you.'

'It's lunch, Cat, not a royal wedding. I can't feed my husband and let his assistant starve, can I?' says Mum. 'Matty, off you go.'

Matty takes the four steps down to Mum and Dad's room and goes into their ensuite. I'm about to tell him to close the door to give himself, and more importantly us, some privacy when his voice booms through the house. 'DAD! LUNCH! WHEN?'

Mum, Nonna and I simultaneously screech at him and it's a wonder that between his yell and our shrieks we're left with a pane of glass anywhere in the house.

'I could have yelled,' says Mum. 'Go outside, walk down the stairs and speak like a human.'

'What kind of animal will Caterina's *ragazzo* think you are?' shouts Nonna. 'Show some class, Matteo. You're not a barbarian. Stop acting like one.'

'Nonna! He is not my boyfriend! He's just some *proprio un bischero* that's helping Dad.'

Mum's mouth is open. Nonna stares past me.

'He's standing right behind me, isn't he?' I say, in Italian. They nod and Matty cracks up.

'I'm guessing she didn't call me anything particularly flattering?' Paul asks Matty.

'She called you baby daddy,' says Matty.

'You're such a turdburger!' He shoots across the room out of reach to avoid my lunge.

'I was just coming up to say hello.' Paul kicks off his work boots and stands in the door, pausing until Mum waves him in. He says hello to her and asks how she is. It's like he's read a book about how to get parents on side. He looks at my grandmother then looks at me expectedly. I sigh. *Best get this over with.* Nonna will make him sorry he ever crossed this threshold.

'Nonna, this is Paul, he's working with Dad,' I say. 'This is my grandmother, Mrs Marea.'

'*Ciao, signora.*' He shakes her hand. My head nearly snaps off my neck.

'*Ciao, Paolo!*' Nonna fires off in Italian, asking after his health.

His mouth drops, and then he smiles. His smile is next level. I mean, after two years of orthodontic treatment mine is good, but he could be in a toothpaste ad. Nine out of ten dentists agree, hottest of the hot. He holds his hands up in mock surrender. 'Uh, *mi dispiace*, is that right? I only know a couple of words.'

'It's wonderful that you have the respect to make an effort,' says Nonna. 'Not many people do. Do you learn Italian at school like my *principessa*?'

'Wow, Nonna, so now I'm a princess when ten minutes ago I was a smart mouth.'

She dismisses me with a wave of her hand.

He sits beside Nonna on the sofa. He tells her he left school three years ago, that he's about to finish his carpentry apprenticeship.

Any minute now Nonna will start shooting her death glares, won't she? She'll do the maths and protect me from the evil intentions of an older man hellbent on destroying my future. Instead, she sits there, nodding and asking questions that give the appearance of her being interested in everything he says, and the scary thing is I honestly believe that she's genuine. She's making a real effort not to drop Italian words in her sentences. And damn him to hell, he's being very respectful and has impeccable manners.

There's the banging of Dad's work boots on the stairs.

'So, you've met Paul, Mum?' asks Dad. 'He's giving us a hand with the cellar; the Dirty Three aren't much chop in the building game.'

I roll my eyes. 'You don't think it's time you stop calling us that, Dad?'

'*Piacere?*' Paul turns to my grandmother. He's completely stuffed up with the pronunciation, but Nonna takes his outstretched hand.

'I am very happy to meet you too.'

Paul walks across my living room and bends to pull on his boots. 'Marry him,' Nonna says to me in Italian. I have a family full of comedians.

'I'm sorry?' Paul lifts his head from where he's crouched.

'She said "what time would you like to have lunch?"' says Mum.

'In around forty-five,' Dad follows Paul down the stairs, Tommy behind them, swinging on the railings. No wonder that kid's constantly crying at the bottom of the stairs.

'He's a good person,' says Nonna. 'He has respect. Never give your heart to anyone with no respect.'

'Are you kidding me?' I throw my arms out in exasperation. 'Not even a week ago you gave me a headache, expressly forbidding me to even consider having a boyfriend. Now you're telling me to give my heart to some shithead that's here to work with Dad? That you've known for less than two minutes?'

'Not a shithead. You're the shithead if you think he's a shithead.' She points her finger at me as I snigger. Shithead sounds hilarious coming out of her mouth. 'You could do a lot worse, *principessa*.'

'That's the other thing, Nonna. Stop with the *principessa* crap. I'm not a child. Anyway, this is a ridiculous conversation.'

'Who are you calling ridiculous?' Nonna positively bristles. If she were a cat, her tail would have bushed, and she'd be clawing my eyes out. As it is, the vein in her temple is throbbing.

'Nobody is calling anyone anything,' says Mum. 'Enough, Cat!'

'Me? What about your mother?'

'I cannot believe the mouth on this one,' Nonna says to Mum. 'If she were my daughter, I'd be ashamed. If I ever spoke to my grandmother like this, I would have been hit with a belt and locked in the cellar.'

'Well, her father is building a cellar right now. I'll make sure he puts a decent lock on it.'

'No need for threats, people,' I say. 'Nonna, all these years of you nagging me to tears has finally paid off. I've decided you're right. I intend to embrace a lifetime of celibacy. Thank you.' I curtsey and go upstairs to the kitchen.

'Celibacy is for the old,' Nonna calls after me. She's certainly changed her tune. It only took a couple of garbled, mispronounced words in Italian.

'How's that for ironic,' I say to Mum from the kitchen. 'She's on my back about studying hard so I can be independent and now she's marrying me off.'

'That's the patriarchy, Bella,' says Mum. 'And you thought it was bad when she wouldn't let you in the street when the boys were out riding their bikes.'

12

I'M lying on my bed trying to read and failing dismally at forgetting that the hottest of the hot is beneath my *freakin'* house when Mum knocks on my door.

'Lunch, Bella.'

There's my beloved family, all gathered around the dining table, you know, the heart of the home, where laughs are shared, problems halved, all that crap. A tray of Nonna's lasagne forms a centrepiece, cut into neat grids. It's surrounded by platters of chicken, bread rolls, salads and cheeses. A water jug and a bottle of red wine bookend the table. Dad's at the head, Nonna to his side. Sandwiched between my grandmother and my mother is Paul. Paul GD Lightwood. The only seat left for me is opposite him. I sit and look around the table.

'I wonder…'

'What?' Matty hates being left out of any potential grain of conversation, no matter how flaky.

'Hey, do you think if maybe it's possible, if perhaps, we might be Italian?'

Dad laughs.

'I'm serious,' I say. 'This is like a scene straight out of a mafia movie. We're being so stereotypical it's offensive.'

Mum takes Paul's plate and serves him a slice of Nonna's lasagne.

'Thank you, Mrs Kelty,' he says.

'Actually, it's Marea,' says Mum. 'I never changed my name, but please, call me Angela.'

'Thank you, Angela.' He takes a bite. He turns to Nonna, his eyes wide. 'This is incredible.'

'It's nothing,' she waves him away, beaming. She's had half a mouthful of red and she's blushing like a schoolgirl in a musical.

Lunch is pretty much our standard casual performance. My brothers are tearing at food with their bare hands, our Nonna slapping them, we're talking over each other with mouths full. Dad teases Nonna, she pretends she's offended, she barely restrains herself from hand feeding Tommy, he barely restrains himself from letting her. Mum and Dad do their nausea-inducing lovestruck eyes at each other before stopping mid-sentence to reprimand each other or any of us. The only difference is the tall, uber-good looking, muscly surfer god at the table.

He looks completely at ease. He's bantering with my brothers, asking Mum about her work, complimenting Nonna on her cooking.

I'm about to have my third serve of lasagne when she shoots me a dagger and uses her head to gesture to the salad. She doesn't give my brothers the same treatment; Matty is onto his third piece with no recriminations; they're growing boys is her classic defensive fallback. Anyway, if we're being sexist, it's a well-known fact that a girl who pretends not to eat is a massive turn-off to the opposite sex and so I lift the spatula anyway. 'Paul?'

He doesn't hesitate, holding his plate before me. As the lasagne lands on his plate, a splodge of tomato sauce flicks and hits him square in the middle of his t-shirt. I couldn't have aimed it better if I tried.

'I am so sorry.' I lean across the table, taking the mineral water and dipping a serviette before pressing it to his chest. The water soaks through and under the heel of my hand I feel the ridge of his abs. *Oh good lord, how many sit ups make these possible?* 'This should get it out, but I can wash it for you?' *Who even am I?*

'Honestly, it's fine,' he laughs. 'For food this amazing I don't care if you marinate my clothes in it.'

'I get the feeling you're not too precious about getting grubby, Paul?' asks Dad. 'You're in the wrong industry if you don't like getting dirty.'

'Yeah, absolutely, I have no problem with getting dirty,' he says.

Matty kicks me under the table.

'Same with Cat.' He waggles his eyebrows at me.

'Real funny.' I sit back in my chair and send a hard kick his way, missing. 'Dad, you should see Paul's car. It's nothing like yours, it's spotless. You could eat dinner off the floor.'

'Yeah, you could catch a third world disease from your car, Dad,' says Matty.

'It's "developing country", you tool,' I say to him. 'Third world is offensive. As are you. But yes, Dad, your car is a health hazard.'

'And that's why my *principessa* will be a doctor,' says Nonna.

'You're going to do medicine?' Paul puts down his fork. 'Wow!'

'Not without a decent score in Year Twelve maths, she's not,' says Dad.

'Dad! We've been over this: if I work hard, I'll get the marks. But maybe, yeah. Depending on my marks, it'll be law or medicine, that's the plan.'

'Either way we'll be covered,' says Dad. 'She'll be able to write prescriptions or having a lawyer in the family will come in handy if anyone ever sues us because their building collapses.'

Mum and Nonna do the sign of the cross, Mum laughing, Nonna deathly serious.

'What about you, Paul?' Mum tops up her glass of red wine. 'Did you always want to be a builder?'

'Not especially. Believe it or not, I was looking at architecture too, right up until, well, I ended up getting pretty average marks.' He shrugs, looking down at his plate. He takes a sip of water. 'A friend of the old man's offered me a carpentry apprenticeship and that was that. I didn't have a lot of other options really. But it's been all right, overall. Not at all like I expected, and I got to stay here and not have to move to the city. But as you know, Mrs Kelty.' Mum frowns. 'Sorry, I mean Angela! But yeah, a lot of the stuff down this way is still pretty stock standard. Not too many people are willing to take a shot at making their house anything other than a three-bedroom, two-bathroom box. Which is why I'm so happy to be working on this place.'

'This is a family home in every sense of the word.' Mum beams with pride. 'We designed it and built it. We dreamed about it all the years we spent staring at skyscrapers. We wanted to see either the ocean or the country from every window. We found this block and here we are.'

'This house, it's good now, but it was trouble,' Nonna says. 'The neighbours complained.'

'Complained? About what?' Paul says. 'You haven't blocked anyone's view?'

'"Out of character" believe it or not.' Dad shifts in his seat. 'Funny, given it was the people with the asbestos hot boxes who don't even live here. Arseholes.'

'That's a bit shit. This house is the bomb! I just love the way it flows across so many levels.' From his position at the dining table, he has a view of the whole house. 'But it's still a home, it's not just a fluid expression of space.'

I crack up laughing. 'A fluid expression of what?'

'Ignore her.' Mum puts her hand on his shoulder as he blushes. 'You know your architecture.'

'Not really.' Paul grins, and for some unknown reason, Mum, Nonna and I all simultaneously reach for a glass of water. 'I read up when I found out what job Mick needed me for. I found an article profiling this house. Just like I memorised some Italian, *signora*, but I hope I did a better job on the architecture words.'

The afternoon drifts on. No one is in a hurry to leave the table, and even Nonna seems to have forgotten her usual afternoon routine of panicking that she won't be home before dark. Dad is as relaxed as I've seen him for weeks.

'I reckon it's knock off time.' He pours himself a drink. 'Thanks to Paul, I think we might even be able to finish this summer.'

'We'll smash it,' says Paul.

'Come have a look, Mum.' Dad leaves the table and helps Nonna from her chair. She reaches for her plate, but before she can collect it, Paul has it stacked on his and clears Mum's plate too. He walks around the table collecting the remainder of the dishes. Nonna's eyebrows practically lift back to meet the soft dowager's hump she's cultivated at the top of her spine.

'It's okay, the kids have got it.' Mum tries to shoo him away.

'By "kids" she means Matty and Tommy.' I hand Matty the pile of dishes.

'Not fair!' He shoves it towards me.

'Matty…' says Mum.

He balances the cutlery haphazardly and carries it across to the kitchen bench where he dumps it with a clatter that makes my teeth clench. He jumps the stairs to the living room and fires up his new game.

'Does that look like the dishwasher, dipshit?' I say to his retreating back.

'Cat!' Mum calls my name like I'm the one abandoning the unclean dishes. 'Just leave it; I'll take care of it. I can't listen to you two squabbling for another second. Tommy, go play with your brother.'

'It's all good; finish your wine.' Paul turns to me, the plates still stacked in his arms. 'Lead the way, *principessa*.'

'You want me to stab you in the eye with a fork?' I brandish one of the two Tommy didn't throw in the sink. He follows me around the bench into the kitchen. Mum's at the dining table, cradling her glass in her hand, staring out the window, a half-smile.

'Your family is awesome,' he says. 'Your mum is so easy to talk to, she's a TV mum.'

'Well, with a bottle down she's certainly something.'

We stand side by side at the sink, scraping plates and stacking them in the dishwasher. I rescue salad scraps from the bin, and he gives me a confused look.

'I know it's disgusting, but Nonna keeps them for her chickens.'

'No worries,' he says.

The bench is clear, the dishwasher stacked.

'That's it?'

'Yep,' I say. 'Thanks so much for your help. Matty and Tommy would have left me to it all by my lonesome.'

'No worries.' He shakes his head. 'I said that already, didn't I? You must think I'm such a dumb tradie.'

'We don't use that expression in this house,' Mum interjects from the dining table. 'I'm married to a tradie, you may recall.'

'Yes, but look who your tradie's married to.' Paul winks. 'Must be the smartest tradie on the planet.'

I punch him in the arm.

'What was that for?' He rubs his arm.

'Oh, don't pretend that hurt,' I say. 'You're tougher than that, a big, strong surfer tradie. Since when do tough guys make cutesy jokes with old ladies?'

'Watch yourself, Caterina,' says Mum. 'Who are you calling old?'

'Can I call you Caterina?' asks Paul.

'Only if you want a punch in the face instead of the arm.' I swing a soft punch towards him, and he catches my fist. His hand moves down mine until our fingers interlock. He doesn't take his eyes off me.

'So, why'd you leave the party? Was it that bad?'

Nonna's head appears in the kitchen window. Startled, I drop Paul's hand. She's light on her feet when she wants. Her face is flushed from either the exertion of climbing the stairs, or from the spectacle of her granddaughter and a handsome stranger *abbracciando*, or canoodling in Matty-speak.

'Ready, *bella mia*?' she says to Mum.

Mum's brow furrows as she considers the glass in her hand.

'I can take your mother home,' says Paul, 'I only had half a glass.'

'Are you sure?' Mum's gleeful tone doesn't quite match the question. In her mind, she's already cracking open another bottle. 'Mum, happy for Paul and Cat to take you home? I'm okay, but it's summer, you know? *Poliziotti* everywhere.'

'I'm very grateful to you,' says Nonna to Paul, patting his cheek.

'No problem, *signora*. Just let me know when you're ready.'

Nonna holds her handbag in both hands low against her hips. She couldn't be more ready. She's determined to get home before dark, never mind the fact that dusk is still hours away and her house is less than a fifteen-minute drive. She kisses Mum on both cheeks and calls out to the boys. They bound up the stairs like puppies and I feel a swell of love for them. There's no prepubescent self-consciousness in these two when it comes to their grandmother; their faces are as full of the adoration they felt for her as when they were toddlers. If the beach is my happy place, Nonna is theirs.

'Can I come too, Paul?' says Tommy.

'Nope,' I say.

Paul shrugs.

'Sorry, mate, your sister's the boss.'

He starts to whine before Nonna holds his face in both hands. In Italian, she tells him to back off and let me have some time alone with my *ragazzo*. I roll my eyes and stick out my tongue.

'What did your grandmother say?' Paul asks me, quietly.

'She said she likes Cat's tits in that top,' Matty says, and Nonna clocks him over the back of the head with her hand.

'*Diavolo*!' He laughs and takes her arm to help her down the terraces under the stairs. I can hear Nonna giving Matty an almighty serve in Italian, a soliloquy that rolls off her tongue like high-pitched automatic gunfire, but she is completely and utterly wasting her breath. He's laughing all the way to Paul's car.

<h1 style="text-align:center">13</h1>

HOW surreal. I'm sandwiched between my grandmother and Paul GD Lightwood in his car. His hand rests on the gearstick beside my right knee, and on the underside of his forearm I see the faint blue of his vein. The glass of wine I had with lunch must have really gone to my head because I'd love to lay my fingertips against it just to feel his pulse. Nonna's handbag is sticking into my hip, so I shift slightly towards Paul. It doesn't go unnoticed.

'Caterina!' Nonna hisses under breath.

'What?'

'You know what,' she says in Italian.

'I honestly don't, Nonna.'

'Be like your mama, not your Nonna,' she says. 'First education, then babies.'

'Oh, for the love of God,' I say in English.

Paul clears his throat. He grips the steering wheel with both hands. 'What's up?' he says.

'Believe me, you don't want to know,' I say.

'I was just telling my granddaughter to make more of an effort to help her mother.' She smacks my leg. 'I'm sorry, it's so rude, I sometimes can't find the right words in English so it's easier to speak in my language.'

'That's fine,' he says. 'I think it's so cool you're all bilingual. I bet it comes in handy when you don't want people to know what you're saying.' He's barely hiding a smirk.

We arrive at Nonna's and as usual she refuses to let me walk her to the door. Instead, she kisses me on both cheeks. 'He's a good person, I can tell,' she tells me in Italian.

'He works for Dad. It has absolutely nothing to do with me.'

'You think I'm stupid, that I don't see things? I see everything, Caterina.' She taps me on my temple. 'Use your brain. Remember your future. Now tell him I'm saying, "study hard."'

I turn to Paul to translate.

'She says you're an arsehole.'

'Caterina!' Nonna shrieks. 'Paolo, I said no such thing. Thank you for driving me home. If you're smart, you'll let this one walk.' She shuts the door and skulks to her front door. She turns to wave, and that's Nonna done and dusted for the evening.

'Man, that was a first,' says Paul. 'I'm going to have to learn Italian, aren't I?'

'You don't trust my translation skills?'

'That would be a no. Want to enlighten me?'

'Now, that would be a no,' I say. 'It's boring anyway, "work hard, Caterina, remember your future, Caterina." Yeah, yeah, yeah. As if I'm not.'

'Honestly? Be glad someone gives a shit,' says Paul. He's holding the steering wheel in both hands and I see his jaw clenching.

'There's giving a shit and there's driving me crazy,' I mutter. 'Bring on next year when I don't have to hear this again and again and again times infinity.'

As the road turns towards Batter's Cove late afternoon sun fills the car. I adjust the visor, blinded.

'So, you're really going for medicine?'

'Or law, I haven't decided.'

'Isn't being a doctor or a lawyer completely opposite?'

'I haven't figured that part out yet; I just need to get good enough marks for both.' I shrug. 'I don't have a choice, really.'

'What do you mean, you don't have a choice? Sounds like you have all the choices.'

'No, I meant I have to get good marks, so I have a choice. It's a bit complicated, but basically the better my marks, the more options

I'll have when it comes down to working out what course I'll do.'

'I might be a tradie, but I know how uni selections work,' he says. 'But why law or medicine? Is that what you even want?'

'I want the marks,' I say. 'I'm smart, I might not be one of those super-intelligent robots at school that could easily get into medicine without even trying, but I know how to work hard. Law's been on my radar forever, but then my careers teacher said I could probably go for medicine. I don't know. It's full on. Be glad you're a tradie; you don't have to think about all this stuff, there's no pressure on you.'

'Sorry, what? You don't know anything about me or my life. You're a kid, you don't even know a hint of pressure.'

'I'm a kid?' I turn to glare at him. 'You're what, three years older than me? Good one, Grandpa.'

We pull into the driveway and Paul yanks on the handbrake.

'Your castle, *principessa*. Tell your old man I'll see him tomorrow and thank your mum for lunch for me.' He stares straight ahead through the windscreen.

'It's *prin-ci-pessa*,' I say as I leave his car, even though he absolutely nailed the pronunciation.

14

'I'M about to have one of those vapid teenage angsty existential crises,' I yell up the stairs to Mum.

'If you're going to have a crisis I'm going to need some bolstering.' She moves from languid-slow-lunch-mode to full Olympic-gymnast-mode. She leaps from the lounge, cartwheels to the kitchen, snatches up a new bottle of red, backflips to the sofa while removing the lid with her bare teeth. Okay, so I might be slightly exaggerating, but it's time for an existential crisis. I take a wine glass from the cupboard and sit down opposite her on the sofa.

'That's a strange choice for a water glass,' she says.

'Are you kidding me? We've been having wine with meals since we were newborns.'

'The meal is long over, and anyway, you don't solve problems with alcohol.'

'You do realise you're being completely hypocritical right now, don't you, Mum?'

'What problem am I solving? It's been one of those lovely, simple, relaxed afternoons that make the work slog and juggle all worthwhile. Anyway, you're missing an extremely valid point, Cat.'

'And what point is that, Mother?'

'The difference between you and I, Cat, is that I'm an adult and I can do what I like. You, however, are not. Not yet. Until then, our roof, our rules.'

'Ugh! Such a hypocrite! I'll be an adult in less than a month.'

Dad comes through the sliding door. He takes my glass out of my hand and fills it with Mum's bottle of red. I look up at him

82

gratefully, until he takes a long, pointed drink. Nice. Parenting 101: always present a united front, even if you've missed the context.

'Paul go home?' he says.

'Yep.'

'Did you ask him to come in?' says Mum.

'Nope. He had to go, so off he went.'

'We're going to get started early tomorrow,' says Dad. 'This was a good move, bringing him on, Angela. He's a cluey kid. A lot more switched on than I was at that age, that's for sure.'

'Hear that, Cat?' Mum cocks an eyebrow. 'He's a looker, and a thinker, that one. Your daughter was just about to tell me about her impending crisis, so drink up.'

'Is it just me, or does it strike you as strange that a Neanderthal builder guy just spent the day with our family? He didn't once act like a Neanderthal, did you notice? What's his story?'

'Actually, it strikes me as strange that the daughter of a builder could be such a snob,' says Dad. 'Why would you call a builder a Neanderthal? When was the last time you saw me dragging my knuckles along the ground?'

Mum smirks from behind her glass. 'I don't know about knuckles, but I think it's high time you drag me back to your cave.' To my eternal mortification, she snuggles into Dad on the couch with what can only be described as a horny giggle. I keep down three serves of Nonna's lasagne. It should be splattered up the wall like a crime scene.

'I think you're missing the point, children,' I say. 'Focus! You're my parents. Aren't you even a bit concerned about this flip flop? You don't think it's all a big act, the nice guy?'

'What does it matter?' says Dad. 'He's just here to work, isn't he, unless you like him?'

'Ooh, Bella, you like him,' croons Mum.

'Seriously, are you twelve? And even if I did, which I don't, shouldn't you be forbidding me to have anything to do with him? Aren't you worried about my moral virtue?'

'Are you one hundred and twelve? Your moral virtue?' says Mum. 'I didn't realise we were back in Elizabethan times. What's the big deal? He seems like a good kid.'

'He's not a total shitbag, I admit it,' I say. 'But that's what I mean. How weird, he turns up, works with Dad, he has lunch with us, and then drives Nonna home. Don't you think that's the most bizarre thing ever?'

'Not really,' says Mum. 'I think it's great. He's obviously not just here for the build. It's not the end of the world if you have a boyfriend, Cat.'

Dad darkens slightly. For all his modern-day male feminist vibe, when it comes to his daughter it's clearly still a struggle for him to fight his inner chauvinistic pig.

'You know what?' Mum continues, 'don't let your preconceptions stop you getting to know someone who is actually a good guy.'

'What preconceptions?' I ask. 'I know this guy. He's the leader of the ultimate pack of sexist dipshits.'

'Easy, cowgirl,' says Dad. 'You don't know him. He's been through so much shit and still his boss didn't hesitate before sending him my way. Maybe the Batter's Cove rumour mill isn't the best place for you to get your information.'

'What shit?'

'That's his story. He'll tell you if he wants to. I'm just saying.'

'And I'm just saying he's here to work with you, it's got nothing to do with me.'

'Come on, Cat,' says Mum. 'You can't tell me you didn't have a good time today?'

'I'm serious. Do you really think I have the headspace for anything or anyone right now? I have goals, you know. They're a bit deeper than a cute guy working at my house.' I realise too late that I've used a word other than Neanderthal to describe Paul, but my parents don't seem to notice.

'Bella, you're 17. It's summer. Have some fun for a change. It won't kill you.'

'It's easy for you to say, Mum, you're not the one stressing about your future.'

'Jesus, Cat, just relax a bit, will you?' says Dad. 'You're going to give yourself a stroke before the school year even begins.'

Mum places her hand on his arm.

'You know we're proud of you. There are no words to express how proud we are, aren't we Mick? We know you're under a lot of pressure from school, from us, from yourself, but that's why spending time with someone who's not caught up in all the ra-ra will be good for you.'

In many ways my parents are opposites and have completely different outlooks. My mother is a university-educated architect, and my father is the tradie who barely finished high school. Yet, my mother has a relaxed, optimistic, trust in the universe personality, while Dad is more of an analytical, control-freak workaholic. I wonder who I take after?

'Yeah, maybe,' I say. 'If I see him around, maybe we'll chat, I dunno.'

'You're going to see him; he'll be literally under your feet. Next time he's here, see if he wants to go for a walk,' says Mum.

'A walk? Now who's Elizabethan? Why would I do that and why would he want to go for a walk?'

'Or maybe the movies, whatever.' She waves her hand. 'The worst thing that could happen is you'll have a new friend.'

'No, the worst thing that could happen is you end up an uneducated, unwed, teenage mother,' mutters Dad.

'Jeez, Dad!'

'Don't be ridiculous,' says Mum. 'He's just spent the day watching you use a nail gun. Anyway, they won't do anything on a walk, and even if they do, Cat's smart enough to use protection, aren't you, Cat?' Mum winks at me.

Dad puts his face in his hands. 'I don't think this is a conversation for me.'

'Mum!' I'm enjoying this even less than he is. My reflection in the window shows my face is as red as the tomatoes I feel like regurgitating. 'Let me get this straight – I'm too young and immature to join you in a casual glass of wine but you're happy for me to walk on the beach and have sex with any guy who comes to lunch? Surely HR would have something to say about the boss' daughter sexually harassing the staff? This is so insane and backwards it's not even funny.'

'Cat, it's your existential crisis. We're just here for the entertainment value.' She gives me a mock cheers with her glass.

'I'm glad this is all such a joke to you, Mother. I'm going for a walk. Solo.'

'I don't think so,' says Mum. 'Paul's back.'

15

THE clifftop path cuts through the bush that follows the meandering coastline, the trees twisting overhead in sections. A northerly wind bounces off the cliffs, howling through tunnels and rock pockets like a submerged whistle. It's warmer in the trees' shelter and I'm borderline sweaty in my puffer. Paul walks to my right, allowing me the full width of the narrow path, keeping space between us. His work boots struggle to gain a grip in the path's soft, sandy banks. Earlier, when we were walking along the street, he suddenly took my arm and shuffled me to his other side, mumbling something about it being rude to walk on my left.

'I have no idea what you're talking about,' I'd said.

'A gentleman always walks on a lady's right.'

'You're a gentleman? Who knew? But what's the point of being on my right?'

'In the olden days of horse and carts, it would stop you being splashed by a muddy puddle. Now, if a car comes sideways around the corner, they'll hit me first.' He shrugged. 'I mean, we'll both probably be dead, but I'll die first. I'll make the bigger mess of their car.'

'That's gratifying, and don't think I'm not appreciative, but I'm a feminist,' I said. 'I can't let you get cleaned up for me. I'm also competitive, so I think I'd like to trash the car more than you.' I'd tried to move back to his left, but he was having none of that and promptly pulled me back. The muscled tone of his bicep bulged from beneath his shirt.

'Hey, Paulie, it's beer o'clock!'

We'd walked past the pub, Paul's friends at an outside table strewn with beer glasses, empty and full. One of the Neanderthals was on his feet, waving his glass with the carelessness of the drunk as he spoke, sloshing beer everywhere. Music was thumping and as the songs turned over a girl leapt to her feet and started dancing.

'Go in if you want,' I'd said, 'not that you need my permission, of course, but if you want to, go for it. It's up to you.' My voice strained a little in my attempt at casual.

'I couldn't think of anything worse,' he'd said. We paused to let a car pass, puttering along at the speed limit. Paul's friends were calling his name. He pointed to his ears.

'I can't hear you,' he mouthed and followed me into the walking track, the coastal scrub swallowing the pub's noise.

At the Gap lookout, the ocean stretches to the horizon. A sign warns of the unstable cliff face. We're out from the trees' protection, hammered by the wind; I brace myself against its onslaught. Far below is the Gap's narrow beach, the black remains of a bonfire smearing the white sand. Paul leans his elbows on the timber barrier, looking out beyond the surf.

'You don't think the strong, silent type is a little overrated?'

'If I'm silent, I can't stuff up, can I?'

'Why? What would you stuff up?'

'Stuff up anything. Everything. You're very intimidating.'

'I'm intimidating? What about you?' I cross my arms.

'I'm not the one with the house, the family, the full-on school, the rich friends.'

Here we go. I'm a Stuck-Up Bitch because of where I go to school, and there's a perception that we're rich because of our house. Obviously, we don't live in poverty but it's not like we spend our evenings rolling around in cash, and we don't wipe our bums with $100 notes instead of toilet paper.

'That's not me at all,' I say. He raises one eyebrow. 'Anyway, you're the intimidating one. You're Paul Lightwood.'

'Well, yes, that's my name, Caterina Kelty, if we're going with full names. I'm happy you know it.'

'Oh, don't give me that false modesty. You know exactly who you are, the impact you have on people. Girls. That makes *you* intimidating.'

'Okay, so we're both intimidating,' he says. 'You're also patronising, you know that?'

'I'm patronising? You called me a kid. Can't get more patronising than that, can you?'

'You're right.' He runs a hand over his head. 'I shouldn't have said that. I remember how much it used to piss me off when people called me a kid.'

'You're patronising me right now,' I say. 'Are you going to ruffle my hair and pinch my cheek?'

'That's hilarious.'

'Yes, funny was exactly where I was going with that one. You're making me very confused, Paul Lightwood.'

'I'm making you confused, Cat Kelty?'

'Yes, you are. Suddenly you're working with my dad at my house, and then from out of nowhere you ask me out, then you ignore me at the party, then you have lunch with my family. You were a massive hit. Even my Nonna likes you, and when it comes to me, she doesn't like any single one of your species.'

'My species?'

'The male species. Anyway, that doesn't matter. You can see why this is confusing, yeah?'

'When you put it like that,' says Paul, 'I'm completely confused. You know what? You have it all arse around. Here's where we are from my point of view. You ready?'

'This should be good,' I mutter but I step forward and rest my elbows against the railing.

'First, Mick asked my boss if he knew anyone willing to get on the tools for the summer, and he asked me. I didn't even know it was your house. And it was just a party. Anyway, I've wanted to ask you out for a long time.'

'What?'

'Forget it.' He pulls his hood up over his head.

'You wanted to ask me out? Since when?'

'Last summer I wanted to but let's face it, you are younger than me.' He turns to me, a half-smile. 'Anyway, last year I was in a pretty messed up place, but that's a story for another day. And your old man scared the crap out of me last year.'

'Really?'

'Your dad still scares the crap out of me. He scares the crap out of all of us. We all know that Mick Kelty's daughter is out of bounds. You have no idea what it was like just to see if you wanted to go to a crap Gap party. I should be up for some sort of medal for that, just saying.'

'And your second point of confusion? That's right, the party, where I ignored you. Not sure how you came up with that conclusion, given it was you that left me there. That was a bit shit, really, taking off like that. And the look on your face when you thought I was trying to cop a quick feel of your bum, Cat, which I wasn't. Your dad just offered me a job.'

'I think I like it better when you're the strong and silent type.'

'Can you let me finish? Please?'

I open my palms. 'Go for it.'

'Thank you. As I was saying, you have a pretty messed up idea about me. I'm not saying that I'd have a crack at a stop sign, but I've done things that I'm not very proud of, I admit that. And I've probably been with more girls than I'd want to count.'

'Now you're just bragging.' I roll my eyes. 'As if I didn't know that. Every summer you have a different girl in your car. You have a different girl every week, every day. Anyway, it's fascinating to hear about your love life, but do you have a point?'

'Yes, I do. My point is I want to be with you, but not like I want to.'

'What?'

'This is all coming out wrong,' he says. 'You're so different to anyone I know and not just because you treat me like shit. You're tossing up between being a freakin' doctor or a lawyer.'

'What are you actually saying?'

'I'm saying you're funny and you're smart. Of course, you're beautiful but it's more than that with you. I saw you at the Pav at New Year's and thought about talking to you then but kept away. I had a few drinks in me. I knew I'd be seeing you at your house and needed to look your old man in the eye. Anyway, you're no New Year's hookup. You are more, so, so much more than that. You're not like other girls.'

'Umm, you know that's not the compliment you think it is?'

'I'm not finished. Then the next day, I'm hungover like a dog, and there you are at Sadie's, giving me nothing. It was obvious you had no idea that your dad had hooked me up with the job and it was also obvious that you weren't happy about it.'

'I was just surprised, that's all,' I say. 'And you were flirting with me. You know you were. "*Can I buy you a drink?*"' I lower my voice in imitation of his.

'Oh God,' he puts his face in his hands. 'I was not. But yeah, okay, I was, I admit it. But I need to be smart here, not be me, but be *me*. I work for your dad. And all I want to do right now is kiss you.'

My mouth dries and I swallow hard.

'You want to kiss me?'

'I don't want to stuff up with Mick.'

'Yeah, I get it.' I shake my head.

'No, not just Mick. I don't want to stuff up with you, Cat. I don't want to do anything that will mess things up. I want to hang with you and your family at your house, I want to know you better.' He nudges me with his shoulder. 'You need to know that all that shit you think you know about me? That isn't me.'

'Wait, what?'

'What you said about me on the way to the party? None of that is true. Okay, some of it is, but what other people say about me? That's not the way I see myself. Does that make sense?'

I think about Isabel calling me a Stuck-Up Bitch, Mum's

blathering about losing myself in stress, Nonna's hysteria about me ruining my future by way of unwed teenage motherhood, the endless school diatribes about maximising my potential when I don't even know what my potential is. A lump rises in my throat. Maybe I've been really unfair in how I've perceived him. The realisation hits me hard and I'm glad the railing is here for me to lean against.

'Yes,' I say. 'It makes perfect sense. Actually, I'm still confused. What do you want from me? Wait—let's be clear about something before you answer that. Don't go assuming anything just because I want to kiss you too.'

'You do?' His entire stance lifts and there is a smile behind his eyes.

'I do.'

'No, wait, let's try something new for me,' says Paul. 'Friends zone. No more talk about kissing. No more punching me in the arm because it freakin' hurts. Friends. I work with your dad. You and I are mates. That's it. What do you think?'

'Mates.' I shrug. It makes sense, but man, I want to kiss him! I wish he'd never said anything about kissing me, because all I can think about is exactly that. But he's right; he'll be around the house all summer. Kissing will make things so much more awkward.

'Start over?' Paul holds out his right hand. 'Hi. I'm Paul.'

'Cat.' I take his hand and shake it. His palms are a mass of callouses.

His hand slides down mine until he grips my fingertips with his, staring down into my palm as if he's reading it.

'Fuck it,' he says, and kisses me.

I kiss him right back.

His lips are soft but fevered. He tastes faintly of cola as his tongue pushes against mine. My heart goes on a rampage and my mind evaporates but not before my instincts kick in, sending a hand to cup that jaw, his stubble raspy. My other hand grips his hoody and it's the only thing that's keeping me upright, as I'm on my toes, teetering, clinging to this adrenaline-inducing balance of soft and hard. He kisses me in a way that I've never been kissed in my life, and it is the closest thing to magic I have ever experienced. I would bet anything and everything that nobody's ever been kissed like this in the history of kissing.

'Cat!' he pulls away and he's panting as if it took all his will to sever the kiss. 'I'm so sorry.'

'I'm not.' I move towards him, my hands outstretched.

'I mean it.' He turns away, shaking his head. 'I want to be friends.'

The word is a slap, and it isn't the wind that makes me bitterly cold. I jam my hands in my pockets and turn my back on the ocean to walk down the path. 'Sorry I'm such a shit kisser.'

'That's not it,' he starts, but I wave him off.

I force each step further away. 'Friends it is. I'll be seeing you. Mate.'

I don't care if he can't hear me.

16

'JUST calm down, Cat, it will be all right.' Mum's bent over the package of books on the dining table.

'Tell me something, Mother, when has anyone ever calmed down just from being told to calm down? Is that the most helpful thing you can say at this moment? Calm down? It'll be all right? How will any of this be all right? I'm already so far behind and I still don't even have the right books!'

'Cat, I'll sort it out. Go take a coffee to your dad and Paul, I'll ring them up and sort it out.'

'I'm not a goddamn waitress. Tell the boys to do it.' All I've seen of Paul this morning after yesterday's kiss was a wave from downstairs and that's more than okay with me. Although, that kiss was pretty much the sole focus of all my thoughts last night, and this morning.

'Oh, for the love of God,' Mum mutters and picks up the phone.

'Yes, hello, my daughter's Year Twelve textbooks have just arrived, and the order is wrong. Yes. No. Order number 46305. Yes, Caterina Kelty. Thank you, I'll hold.' She taps me on the shoulder and points to the coffee machine. 'Go,' she mouths before turning her back to me.

I grind the beans and inhale their scent. Normally, that smell of fresh coffee calms me, and the sound of water moving through grinds is soothing. Not today. Nothing's quelling my anxiety.

'Look, that's really not good enough. She can't wait another week for them and given this is the second time the order has been wrong I think you can do a bit better for us than that. Yes, I realise we're out of your standard delivery zone, but that's hardly our problem, is it?

The school brings a very clear commercial outcome to your business, so what can we do here? Yes. Yes. What's the address? What time? We're a two-hour drive so I need more flexibility from you than that. And your name? Perfect, thank you. See you then.'

'They've got them?' I ask.

'Yes, in stock. We'll return these and get yours. Shit!' she slaps her forehead. 'I completely forgot. I'm taking Tommy and his friends to the movies.'

'Well, that's hardly a priority.' Dumbfounded, I stand at the doorway holding two cups of coffee.

'It is to your brother. Come on, let's go talk to Dad.'

Downstairs in the garage, Dad takes a coffee from my hand and places it on the workbench. He's grubby and sweaty and as he rakes his hand over his face to wipe away sweat, he leaves a streak of sawdust. 'Sorry, Bella, I have to wait here for the electrician,' says Dad.

'Are you freakin' kidding me? Do I mean nothing to you people?'

'What are we going to do, Mick?' says Mum. 'She needs her books.'

'I can take you, Cat.' Paul leans against Dad's workbench, passing a hammer between his hands. 'If it's okay with you, Mick?' He still hasn't looked at me.

'Are you sure? That would be freakin' awesome.' I don't know how I'm not crying.

'It's a two-hour drive, we'll give you some money for petrol,' says Mum.

'Don't even think about it.' Paul rests the hammer on the workbench. 'It's all good.'

'They close at five, but they're going to wait for you. Still, I wouldn't hang around,' says Mum.

'I wouldn't mind swinging past home for a quick shower.' He's covered in builder's dust, glue embedded into his boardshorts. 'I'll go home and get changed then come back and get you.'

'No, that's too much driving back and forth,' says Mum. 'Cat, you're pretty much ready to go, aren't you?'

'Honestly, it's fine, I'll just come back.'

'You're doing us all a huge favour, Paul. I can't listen to Cat's booklist drama for another second. Cat, run upstairs and get a jacket. Grab your booklist too. Make sure they have everything you need. We're not doing this again. Stand your ground if they mess it up. Mick, give them some cash. You kids can get some dinner in the city.'

'You sure about this?' I ask. There's going to be two hours there, two hours back and one amazing, rejection-filled kiss between us.

He finally looks me in the eye.

'Come on Cat. It'll be fun.' Paul smiles, shrugging.

'You're a lifesaver, mate,' says Dad. 'Cat, move it. They say they'll wait, but let's see what happens if you don't make it there by five.'

17

I'M putting on my seatbelt when Paul puts his hand on mine.

'Listen, Cat. My house, my family, they're not like yours.'

'What do you mean?'

'Nothing. I'll be as quick as I can.'

In town, we pull up in front of a weatherboard house. There's a white picket fence with a gate underneath a rose-covered archway. Paul leads me up a path flanked by roses in bloom. I reach to sniff one and find it's unscented. Paul opens the front door and calls out.

'Mum, Dad?'

We move towards the sound of a television at the end of a hallway with doors on either side. I glimpse a perfectly made bed drowning in throw cushions and porcelain dolls. Paul takes my arm, and his palm is hot and sweaty through my sleeve.

'Look who's decided to grace us with his presence, love,' says a deep voice as we enter a living room. Paul's dad, I assume, is in a pale yellow and beige tartan recliner, feet extended, in front of a TV sitting within a huge entertainment unit. Every shelf is filled with hundreds of ceramic figurines. There are cartoon characters next to southern belles, queens and princesses next to horses.

'Mum, Dad, I'd like you to meet someone,' says Paul. 'This is Cat.'

The recliner lurches forward so fast I'm surprised it doesn't tip, and a huge hand is advancing towards me. I accept it and my hand disappears. He's massive; taller even than Paul, and twice as wide. His frame fills the room, but his smile is genuine. He rocks on his feet, his hands on his hips.

'So, you're the reason this idiot has been smiling so much, then,

97

are you? Nice to meet you. Cat, is it? That short for Catherine?'

'Nice to meet you too, Mr Lightwood.'

'Mr Lightwood is my dad, or was, since he's long dead, the old bastard. Call me John.'

'Nice to meet you, John.'

'And this here is the missus, Paul's mum, Lorraine.'

I turn and leaning against the kitchen bench with a cleaning cloth in her hand, stands a slight woman, even without considering her in comparison to the magnitude of her husband. She moves around the bench and takes my hand.

'Welcome to our home, Catherine. I'm sorry it's such a mess, we weren't expecting company.' She nods pointedly at Paul.

'It's Cat, Mum, and we're just popping in. I'll have a quick shower, and we'll go. You okay?'

'Of course, she is,' his dad says. 'Lorraine, put the kettle on. What's your poison, love?'

'A water would be great, thank you.'

'I'll be two minutes.' Paul's voice is low as he brushes past me and heads back down the hall.

'What are you two kids up to?' John settles his enormous frame into a chair at the table. 'Sit, sit, make yourself at home.'

'Well, we're going to the city to pick up my books for school.' I sit on the edge of one of the timber dining chairs, its back hard against mine. 'The first half of my books didn't arrive, and now they've sent me the wrong ones.'

'You're still at school?' Paul's mum places a glass of water on a coaster of garishly bright coloured shells and slides it before me.

'Yes, my last year. Year Twelve.' I say my school's name and the thin lines of her eyebrows raise.

'Fancy,' she says. 'The boys went local, and they did just fine.'

'No point spending all that money on tradies,' John says. 'Jeez, that seems like a long time ago, doesn't it, love?'

'A lot's happened.' Paul's mother stares down at her hands, gripped as if locked in prayer.

'You live nearby, love?' John asks.

'No, we live in Batter's Cove.'

'What does your old man do, love?'

'He's a builder. You might know him. Michael Kelty?'

'Mick Kelty's your old man? That high end job? Thank him for taking on our dickhead. I don't know your dad well, but I've only heard good things.'

'Well, that's a relief,' I say. 'You're a tradie too, is that right?'

'Yep, a sparky. I'm the smart one.' I can't even begin to imagine Paul's dad moving through the roof spaces of a house, let alone fitting through a manhole. 'Hang on, Mick's married to that lady architect, that right? You going to follow in the family business?'

'No, Dad says if I go into construction, he'll disown me.' I grin. 'I'm going for either law or medicine.'

'Law or medicine,' Paul's dad whistles. 'Hear that, love? Our boy's landed himself a future doctor or a lawyer. Not bad for a dumbarse, hey love?'

I blush. If only he knew I was a future doctor or lawyer that his son didn't want to kiss.

'Cat, are you ready?' Paul's in the doorway in jeans and a white t-shirt, his hair damp.

'May I use your bathroom?' I ask Paul's mother.

'What lovely manners. It's the third door on the right.'

There's a doll on top of the toilet wearing a bright red dress, another southern belle, this one hiding a spare toilet roll under her abundant skirt. The sink is a traffic jam of soap, and the hand towel is covered with embroidered roses. I'm too scared to use it so I shake the water off my hands and dab off the excess on the underside of the embroidery. I return to the living room.

'I have one word for you, Paul Lightwood. Jailbait. Mark my words.' Paul's mother has her finger in the air, her lips pressed.

'Mum! Relax, there's nothing happening. I told you. She's the boss' daughter.'

'That's exactly right, Paul. She's the boss' daughter. You

remember that.'

'Calm down, love, they're all right. Look how happy she makes your son. If he had a tail, he'd be wagging it.'

Paul spots me in the doorway, his face as red as the toilet doll's gown.

'I'll see you later, Mum. Dad.'

'Nice to meet you both.' I give a strange wave that's more like jazz hands.

'You're welcome any time, love, maybe get this big dickhead to bring you over on Sunday for dinner? What do you say?'

'That sounds like a plan, Mr Lightwood, thank you.'

'I told you, none of this Mr Lightwood rubbish.'

'Okay, thanks, bye.'

Paul practically drags me down the corridor by the hand.

18

'I'M so sorry about that.' Paul tugs his seatbelt across his torso to click it in. 'I showered as quick as I could. I was in such a rush to get us out of there I'm still wet under these jeans.'

'No, it was fine, parents are my thing.' I wish I were game to look at how they might be clinging to his thighs. 'Parents love me, all my friends say so. But I don't know that any of my friends' mothers have ever called me "jailbait". That's a first.'

'Oh God, I can't believe you heard that.' He shakes his head. 'That's just Mum, don't take it personally. She's hard work. But now you know why I like hanging around your place so much. Here, let's get some tunes happening.'

Music fills the car. My legs tucked up under me, I lean against the door, watching the fields fly past the window. His hand keeps the beat of the song, tapping against the steering wheel.

'I love this,' I say. 'Who is it?'

He names a band I have never heard of before. 'You like? Your old man would too. They're on almost every surf movie soundtrack. I saw them live a couple of years ago, they were phenomenal.'

'Phenomenal?'

'Phenomenal. Don't ask me to spell it.'

'I won't.' A small grin tugs at my lips, and I relax into the car seat's embrace.

We talk about everything and anything: music, movies we've seen, holidays, everything but that kiss at the Gap lookout. I thought it would feel awkward, sitting in his car, but there's no stilted conversation. It just flows like the steady rhythm of a heartbeat.

101

Paddocks turn to houses sprawling on either side of the freeway as far as I can see. We turn into an industrial estate and pull up in front of a double story warehouse. A man paces in front of a reception desk, and spotting us, he flings open the door.

'Caterina Kelty? Your mother said you'd be here by five. I was supposed to leave here ten minutes ago.'

'Calm down, mate, her mother said she'd be here when she gets here,' says Paul. 'And this is your stuff up, not ours. Do you have her books ready to go?'

'No need for abuse, *mate*.' He crosses his arms across his chest. 'I'm doing you a favour so you might want to watch how you speak to me.'

'You're doing us a favour?' Paul shifts his weight forward, his shoulders back.

'My books?' I interrupt before the male standoff continues. I don't think the wiry frame of the administrator would do well against the guy who battles waves for fun.

He bustles behind the reception desk and lifts a box.

'Here.' He holds them out to me, looking over my head at Paul in the doorway.

'Thank you. I'll just check everything's here.'

'They're all there, I assure you.'

'Forgive me, but since we're here because I still don't have the right books four months after I ordered them, I'm going to check.'

He sighs and shifts his weight from foot to foot as I pull the books out of the box, checking them against my booklist.

'Are we done?'

'Yes, thank you. You've been so generous and helpful.' A hint of facetiousness comes out in my tone.

'Look, I'm here, aren't I? I shouldn't be, but I'm here. I don't get paid to put up with smartarses.'

'Who you calling a smartarse, mate?' says Paul as he steps up to my side.

'I think he's calling me a smartarse,' I say. 'I can't imagine why?

I'm quite lovely. Anyway, sir, again, thank you. I'll be sure to tell my school how wonderful this experience was. Have a nice evening.'

'What a dick,' says Paul as we walk back to his car. 'You handled that like a boss. I just wanted to punch him in his smartarse face.'

'Such a dick,' I agree as we both take our seats. 'And thank you. I'm not normally good with confrontation. But I have my books now, I can get moving, and I'm not going to let someone like that get to me. Did you hear that? I have my books!' I hug the box to my chest.

'Pass them here.' He takes them off me and I put my seatbelt on. 'Man, they're heavy! And what, this is only half of them? How are you going to carry them to school every day?'

'I'm stronger than I look.' I pretend to flex my muscles.

'Yeah, nah,' he says, 'I think we better put some meat on those bones. You hungry?'

'I'm starving.'

'What are you thinking?' He leans back to put the books behind us, beneath the car seats.

'I don't know, maybe something Asian-y?'

'Asian-y? Hmm. Let's head into the city. Are you thinking something we can't get at home?' The car hums to life with a turn of his keys.

'You're not suggesting that Batter's Cove is lacking in diverse dining opportunities, are you? How dare you, Paul Lightwood.'

'Have you ever had a good pho at the pub?'

'*Pho* sure I have. The best pho in my life was at that pub, almost as good as their chicken parmas that aren't an insult to my heritage *at all*.'

'Not a fan?'

'Are you kidding? It's as close to Italian food as the plastic pizzas in the frozen food section of the supermarket. Let's pho. You know a good place?'

'I do. *Pho* real.'

We park in a seedy-looking carpark at the back of a busy shopping strip teaming with Vietnamese restaurants. The backs of the stores are covered with graffiti and the footpath is strewn with ingrained chewing gum, mottled black. I grip Paul's t-shirt. He glances down and takes my hand. So much for no handholding. I cling as we pass a line of people entering a pub.

'I know it looks dodgy but trust me.' He leads me into a restaurant. 'You're about to have the best pho of your *pho*-king life.'

The smell of hot wok hits my nostrils, making me salivate to the point where I thumb the corners of my mouth to check for drool. While we wait for a table, I notice that the restaurant is lined with small tables for two along the perimeter walls and large round tables fill the middle. The kitchen is separated from the restaurant with a high bar where food appears as if by magic and is whisked away to waiting diners just as quickly. Loud, clanging music from two speakers hanging from opposing corners accompanies the hiss and sizzle from the kitchen. We sit at a table topped with white butcher's paper under a faded poster of a Vietnamese fishing fleet. Beside it is a giant copy of the menu. Prices are handwritten on top of masking tape that do little to hide the former prices. A roll of absorbent paper serves as napkins and a caddy of sauces in a mix of plastic and stainless-steel sits against the wall.

'It'd better be good, because the decor really isn't floating my boat. The pub wins out in the design stakes, but I'm a little biased there, aren't I?'

'Why biased?'

'It's one of ours. Well, not ours, we don't own it or anything. Mum's firm designed it, and Dad's team built it. Sorry, I thought you knew that.'

'Actually, I think I did know that. I remember them building it, so much better looking than anything else around. Like your house. That makes total sense.'

'Still, what a wasted opportunity for something cool,' I say. 'Mum and Dad were so excited, kept going on about date nights and being able to walk home like when they lived here in the city.' It didn't take them long to realise they were barking up the wrong tree. No chance of having something fresh, light and gorgeous. No chance of even getting a decent coffee. No, it's surf and turf and crappy chicken parma all the way.

A pair of giant steaming bowls of fragrant broth are placed before us. Paul sprinkles his liberally with chilli and bean sprouts, wielding chopsticks like he was born to do so. Noodles slip through mine and the hot liquid splashes all over me.

'I'm so glad your mum's not here.' I tear off a napkin. 'So much for my lovely manners.'

'Mum wouldn't even drive down this street, let alone step foot into a place that's making something other than meat and three veggies.' He emphasises his point by expertly manipulating his noodles.

I swallow the dismal mouthful I managed to coordinate between my chopsticks. It's the most delicious pho I've ever had in my admittedly limited experience. It's fresh, light, the noodles soft in my mouth. I accidentally swallow a chilli and the heat moves in slow motion through my body, making my eyes water. I take a sip of water and laugh. 'So, here's a question for you.'

'Do your worst.' He places his chopsticks across the rim of his bowl and gives me his full attention.

'Why'd you get so fired up at the book warehouse? You looked like you wanted to fight that doofus.'

'Did I?' he raises his eyebrows. 'I wouldn't have touched him. I wouldn't need to. Guy like that? He would've backed down real quick.'

'So, what, you were trying to intimidate him?'

'I sound like a real meathead, don't I?' Paul looks down at the table, his pointer finger doodling on the paper tablecloth. '"I'll fight, till from my bones my flesh be hacked."'

'What?' I tilt my head.

'Nothing, just a quote.' He scoops a mouthful of noodles and follows the bite up with a slurp of his broth.

'It's Macbeth,' I say.

'I know.' He mimics my tone of astonishment, his voice high.

'But I'm not someone who's into fighting.' His eyes meet mine. 'It's just, when someone comes at me with an attitude like that, they see the car, the dumbarse tradie? I don't know. I don't like it.'

'Why do you care what some random thinks?'

'I don't, not really,' he says. 'I didn't like the way he spoke to you. Your mum said for you to stand your ground, and here's where you're really going to think I'm coming in with a saviour complex or something like that, but I kind of think that if you're with me, you shouldn't have to take shit from some little prick by yourself. There's nothing worse than feeling like it's you alone out on a ledge. Anyway, you going to eat that rice paper roll?'

'It's so good, but no, I can't. It's all yours.' I slosh what feels like another litre of pho into my lap as I scoop up the last of the soup with a flat spoon. I'd sigh with contentment if a food baby wasn't making its presence known by squeezing against the waistband of my jeans.

He takes the roll and plonks it in his mouth, then drains the remnants of his bowl.

We wait to pay next to a giant fishtank teeming with lobsters.

'You still hungry?' Paul says.

'Are you kidding? I can barely walk.'

'You sure you can't squeeze in some gelato? It's just up the road.'

The Italian in me perks up at the thought of gelato. 'How do you know all this?'

'Three years of trade school,' he says. 'Once a month for a week I'm up here, doing nothing other than scoping out good food. You're gonna love me when you go to uni.'

I feel the flush move across my face. We walk along the street back to the car. Red lanterns swing from awnings and fairy lights adorn windows.

'You know what, forget the gelato. I'd love a decent coffee, one I haven't made myself. Can we do that?'

'Hardly a challenge. Let's do it.'

We drive across the city, the skyscrapers lit up against the dark sky, helicopters weaving in and out. We walk into an Italian cafe with a wall full of pastries. The staff call to each other in Italian. A giant coffee machine takes up a slab of the marble bar. Our reflections grin at us; I look so happy I could slap myself. I order for us in Italian and the barista unashamedly flirts with me until an older gentleman stands beside him, admonishing him. '*Che bella coppia!*' He raises his right hand, his fingers touching, a wide smile across his face. He adds a cannoli to our order, free of charge.

'What's he saying?' Paul whispers into my ear.

'We're a beautiful couple.' I roll my eyes.

'I wish,' Paul mutters, his voice low, and when I look at him, he busies himself with cutting the cannoli in half.

Paul's headlights illuminate the dark. We're the only car on the highway, the city lights dwindling behind us. The music is low, and he sings along so softly I can barely hear him. My eyes drift closed.

<h1 style="text-align:center">19</h1>

I'M sitting at one of the inside tables at Sadie's with the newspaper while Matty and Tommy play pinball. Matty uses his whole body to move the small silver ball through the obstacles, standing on tiptoes, his arms spread like an eagle across the top of the glass. It's a stretch for him to reach the buttons on the side to move the levers, and he lurches from left to right, twisting at the hips. Through the window, I see the surfers emerge from the bush track. Like a school of fish, they cross the road and come into Sadie's. I just referred to them as surfers, not as the Neanderthals. This is a strange development.

Paul leaves the pack and drops into the seat beside me, Ant close behind. He calls out to Sadie, ordering himself a burger with the lot.

'Hey, Cat.' He reaches behind me and grabs a surfing magazine, so close I can feel his chest against my shoulder. He smells of sea and salt. If I turned my head there'd be centimeters between our mouths. I look down at my phone.

'Hi, guys! You want a burger? Chips?' says Paul.

Tommy shakes his head, but Matty leaps at the offer for a burger like he hasn't eaten for days. Ant sits opposite and calls out the same order.

'Why don't you guys actually go to the counter and order like normal people?'

'Sadie knows we're going to pay,' says Ant with a shrug.

'That's not what I mean. It's called respect and basic manners, something you Neanderthals would know nothing about.'

'What are you talking about, Neanderthals?' says Ant. 'We're the model of respect. Look it up in the dictionary, you'll see a picture of us. Isn't that right, Paulie?'

A woman walks past the window, weighed down with a boogie board, a beach bag and a bucket and spade. A beach towel drapes over a shoulder. She has three small children with her and as she pauses to shepherd them along, she drops her towel. She bends to pick it up and Steve stands behind her, thrusting his hips rapidly. The four Neanderthals outside with him laugh.

I spread my hands, gesturing at the foolery outside, and raise my eyebrow so high there's a chance I've given myself an aneurysm.

'You're right. You guys are *the* model of respect and decorum. It's a crime against humanity that you haven't been nominated for a community award.'

'That was just really bad timing,' says Ant. 'You can't judge all of us from the one dickhead.'

'I don't see any of those guys outside telling him off.' I cross my arms and lean back in my seat.

'They're not his mother.' Paul flicks through the magazine. 'We're not responsible for anyone but ourselves, so I don't know why we cop your Neanderthal crap.'

Sadie places orders on the table, complete with a side of chips, on the house.

'You're the one they all look up to,' I say. 'That makes you King Neanderthal.'

'Cat, stop hinting.' Paul bops me on the nose with a chip. 'You can be my Neanderthal Queen.'

I shake my head and look out the window.

'Wind's turned.' Paul grins like he's just won a prize. 'We're hitting Miller. Come for a surf, Matty?'

Matty nods enthusiastically, the one time in his life electing not to speak with his mouth full. His legs are swinging on the seat like a toddler. As he shoves another handful of chips into his gob, possibly more delicious because they haven't come out of his pocket, Paul taps my thigh under the table. 'Matty, you're with me,' says Paul. Matty high-fives him.

'And me too?' says Tommy.

'No way in hell are you surfing Miller Point,' I tell him. 'You know how dangerous that beach is. Mum and Dad would kill you. And they'd kill me if I let you go in.'

'Please, Paul?' He pulls out the puppy dog eyes that do laps around Nonna.

'Why are you asking Paul? You think he's the boss of you? *I'm* the boss of you, and I just told you, you're not going. It's too dangerous for Matty, let alone you.'

'Shut up, Cat,' says Matty.

I point a chip at him. 'Say that again and see what happens.'

He gives me a look, *that* look, but thankfully turns his attention to the remnants of his burger, scooping up every crumb.

'You coming too, Cat?' asks Ant.

'I'll come, but I'm not surfing.'

'No, you won't. I don't need a babysitter,' says Matty.

'No, you need a keeper.' I lean across the table and wipe his mouth with a napkin. 'You don't own the beach; I'll go where I want.'

'You surf, don't you, Cat?' asks Ant.

I shake my head.

'But you're a local! Haven't you ever had a crack?'

'At the risk of offending present company, not that I give a rat's how offended you are, in a place like this, surfing is the most sexist of pastimes of all the sexist pastimes,' I say. 'I'm completely uninterested in being objectified while trying not to die off the reef.'

'Sexist? That's bull,' says Paul. 'The surfer with the most world titles is a woman.'

'Yeah, but she has balls, so it doesn't really count,' says Ant.

'*Grazie mille, Antonio.* That's what we call "Exhibit A".'

'You're a dick, Scampo,' says Paul. 'Come on, plenty of girls surf.'

'Whatever.'

'Seriously? That's not an argument,' says Paul.

'Do you really think I'm going to waste my energy arguing with white crayons like you?'

'White crayons? Ahh, because we're useless, I get it. Come on, Cat, we're just getting started.'

'Give me that magazine,' I say. 'This is the highest selling surfing magazine in the country, isn't it? Let's look inside, shall we? Let's see how women are represented.'

I flick through the pages. He doesn't need to know that I spent an hour last night looking at that magazine for my issues assignment. He's been almost stroking it like a pet.

'Ooh, look, we're twelve pages in, no women. Hmmm. Interesting. Let's flick the page. Oh look, here's a woman, oh wait, it's a woman's knees. Charming. What else do we have? Oh, this is a new angle, an ad for a travel company. "*The ultimate wedding gift.*" Here's a woman, sipping a cocktail all alone on her honeymoon, watching her beloved surf. How romantic.'

'Yeah, yeah.' Paul's shifted in his seat to pass Tommy some chips, and his thigh leans against mine. I do my best to ignore it.

'Hang on, I'm sure there's more.' I keep flicking to find the article. 'Here we go – a woman at the forefront of professional surfing, dating another professional surfer, and his perception of her. They haven't even asked for her opinion. That's equality right there.' I flick a few more pages and clap my hands with glee. 'Boom!' There's a beach, the water blurred, and the focus of the image is a muscular woman covered in oil, wearing dental floss where her bikini should be. 'Maybe I'd be more inclined to give it a try if I thought I wouldn't be objectified like this.'

'You think too much.' Paul puts the magazine back on the shelf.

'And you don't think enough. I hope you have seven daughters just to give you a smidge of karmic retribution.'

'Careful what you wish for, Cat.' He winks at me.

'Wait, what? No, not me!'

'Wow, way to make the dad of your seven daughters feel good. Thanks a lot.' He stands, pushing his chair back into place. 'Are you coming to Miller or not?'

'Such a charming invitation, how could I refuse? I'll meet you there.'

'Okay, see you soon. Matty, let's go get your gear.' They walk to the door, Matty with a skip in his step to keep up.

'What about me?' says Tommy.

'You can walk with me,' I say as we follow Paul and Matty.

'I don't want to walk with you,' he whines. 'I want to go with Paul.'

'Well, I don't want to walk with you either. Just for that, you can go with Paul, and then you can stay home, ungrateful little shithead. Matty, make sure you ask Mum or Dad – don't just disappear, and make sure you put on your seatbelt. And listen to Paul.' He flips his middle finger at me.

As we leave Sadie's, I tug Paul's wrist. The two boys continue ahead on route to Paul's car.

'Paul, wait. Matty's not as good a swimmer as he thinks he is,' I say. 'This is a really bad idea.'

'Cat, he'll have a ball. I'll be on him,' says Paul as he puts his hand on my shoulder.

'He'd better be. If he's not, Nonna will make you into *passata*.'

20

IT'S hard to believe that only yesterday the ocean was still. The wind has shifted, blowing straight into the sea, carving perfect ribbons of waves through the omnipresent rips, but doing nothing to abate the heat. My hair is a wet tangled mess on top of my head, and I can feel some loose ends dripping down my back.

The water was almost biblical when I swam two minutes ago, although, I don't think what I did could ever be described as swimming. It was more of a roll into an oncoming wave at knee height. I mean, I can swim, but I'm no match for the strength of these waves.

I can't believe I can even put a toe in the water after last summer's almighty dunking. I'd had literally no idea which way was up. Not a clue. The ocean was trying to kill me, I swear it. The waves ripped my elastic clean out of my hair. It wasn't just my hair elastic that was missing. I lost my top in that hammering. Mortifying!

This summer, exposing myself isn't something I have the time or headspace for. Especially when Paul GD Lightwood is on the beach. When the waves are up, I'm not leaving the shoreline. I've also said farewell to the type of bikini that deserts a girl when she needs it the most. Mum gave me the best set ever for Christmas. This top isn't going anywhere. A nuclear bomb could go off right here on the beach and there'll be nothing left but the cockroaches and my skeleton, still wearing this top.

Even though Miller Point sits on the other side of the Surf Beach, less than a five-minute walk, it could be in the middle of nowhere. It's unmanned, not a red and yellow flag in sight, which keeps the families away, and so it's popular with walkers, surfers and fishers. Today, it's too hot for fishers and walkers. I sit at the base of the sand dune and count fifteen surfers and body boarders bobbing on the water, lined up out the back like kids waiting for the school bus. My brother's on his board next to Paul, and even from here I can see Matty's mouth going a gazillion miles an hour.

The surfers love it for the reefs and rips that create pockets in the water for waves to form. Or something like that, anyway. At low tide, reefs are exposed, a kilometre of jagged rocks down the length of the beach. They're slippery and prone to errant waves that scrape the skin off limbs. I have scars on my leg to prove it. It's Miller's reefs and the rips that make anything other than a splash in the paddles a no-go zone for me. Dignity be damned. That, and the spectre of the sharks beyond the breakers which only last week attacked a surfer at a beach less than half an hour away.

Matty looks so little next to the guys, and among the waves he's but a speck. I mean, if the waves can smash a big guy like Paul into a sandbar as effortlessly as swatting a fly, what could they do to Matty? Still, Mum or Dad must have given him permission to bodyboard here. Maybe it's safer being on his stomach rather than standing on a board, trying to balance. Paul's supine, his head swivelled towards the horizon. The waves move in lines across the water, so defined and thick they look superimposed. They're big, far too big. They descend on my little brother. The air leaves my chest.

The first simply rolls under him. Paul has a hold of Matty's arm rope, keeping him close. Two surfers take off on the same wave, grappling for position, pushing and shoving each other out of the way. One takes off; the other falls forwards, sucked down beneath the wave, his board high in the air. The leg rope goes taut, then the board cuts down just as the surfer emerges coughing up seawater and it hits him square in the face. Blood gushes and streams through his fingers. He stumbles to the shore holding his nose with one hand, his board under his arm.

Out the back, Paul is pushing Matty forward on his bodyboard, facing the beach, setting up for a wave. The size of it sends me to the water's edge, waving my hands above my head in a way that is so embarrassing. Matty is absolutely going to kill me, but what can I do? It's like I'm out of my own head. My brother balances precariously on the tip of the wave, just for a moment, and then plunges down its face. He's gone in the tumult of foam and white water, but there he is, bouncing across the surface as the wave bellows its way into shore. He reaches me in the shallows, lit up, eyes wide. 'Did you see that?'

'That was the freakin' worst.' I yank his arm rope as the water splashes up my legs.

'What are you doing?' He turns to paddle back out. 'Let go, you fuckwit.'

'You're the fuckwit. And you're not going back out there.'

'Yes, I am, let me go!'

'They're too big for you, shithead!' I pull him to the shore.

'You broke my nose, you freakin' loser!' The surfer has the other guy by the throat, blood pouring down his face; he snarls and there's blood in rivulets between his teeth.

'Get your fucking hands off me!' He punches him, a hard undercut to his side. We hear the thud of his fist against wetsuit and then they're down in the shore break, punching and wrestling. The whitewash is bloodstained, the splashes of pink against the white turn to rust against the sand. A surfer rides a wave right into them, jumping off his board and pulling them apart, shouting obscenities.

'Matty, that was awesome!' Paul appears in front of us, his board under his arm. He raises his hand in a high five, but I move between them.

'That was anything but awesome!' I yell. 'I don't give a shit if you're a fuckwit who wants to kill himself but keep my brother out of it.' I grab Matty by the arm and drag him out of the water.

Like a toddler, he pulls all his weight against me.

'What are you on about?' says Paul. 'We had him. He just had a wicked wave.'

'Yeah? How are you with him when you push him down a freakin' eight-foot wave? Do you realise how that sounds?' I turn to

Matty. 'We're going home.'

Matty flings his arm out of my grasp.

'I'm not going.' He drags his bodyboard out of the water, rips off his arm rope and flings it all on the sand, his lower lip trembling.

'Listen, I'm sorry I yelled at you,' I say, 'but there's blood in the water, those tools are fighting, and you take off on a massively big wave and disappear. I might have panicked a bit, but you're too little for this.' I move closer and put my arm around him but he flings me away, turning his back on me.

Paul's shadow consumes me.

'Have you finished calling me a fuckwit?'

I cross my arms across my chest. The remnants of a wave breaks across my ankles and my feet sink into the wet sand. I step back, the sand relinquishes its grip, and the space left behind fills with water.

'Have you finished being a fuckwit?'

'Cat, I *was* watching him. The boys were watching him. He knew to stay on the centre line and to keep it steady while it broke. He was fine. Hey Matty, were you scared?'

The disloyal little traitor shakes his head.

'Let's go back out?' Matty grabs his board and pushes past me into the shallows.

'Too easy, mate' Paul says. 'Listen, you're a smart chick but you don't know everything. The way you were all yelling and hysterical, you could put your brother off the water for life.'

'I think I know everything? Don't call me a chick and don't you dare tell me how to behave. He's my brother, not yours.'

'Jeez, Cat, I know that. Do you really think I'd let anything happen to your brother?'

'Whatever. The ungrateful little shit can drown for all I care.' My feet crunch the sand with each stomp.

When I reach the point, I realise I've left my towel, thongs and dress at the base of Miller's dunes. I either have to hang on the beach and wait for Paul to leave, or I get to do a walk of shame through the streets of Batter's Cove in my bikini. *Freakin' awesome*. I'm tossing up between getting home as fast as my tender feet on the asphalt will let me when I see my mother waving to me, Tommy digging at the sand at her feet.

21

'YOU'RE a vision.' I sink down beside her on her beach towel. 'Tommy, I left my stuff at Miller, can you please run and grab it for me? My striped towel and black dress? They're just at the bottom of the dune.'

'I'm not your slave.' He flicks sand over his shoulder.

'I'll give you ten bucks,' I say, and he's off like a shot, racing around the point.

'You look like a Roman goddess,' says Mum, 'but one of the tragic ones. What's wrong? Have you been crying?' She strokes my cheek, her eyebrows sinking together.

'I just had a fight with Dad's shithead tradie and your shithead son.'

I tell her about seeing the surfer's nose splattered all over his face, about Matty nearly drowning on a monster wave, the fight, about Paul speaking to me like a toddler. Mum lets me speak without interrupting, which must be causing her physical discomfort. 'And that's my suckhole life,' I finish.

'You like him.' It's not a question.

'Seriously, Mother, that's all you took from that whole thing?'

'It's pretty obvious, Cat.'

'It is not!' I bury my toes into the sand.

'What's not?'

'This isn't a TV show, Mum,' I say. 'My problems aren't going to be all sorted within thirty minutes. And anyway, he doesn't like me like that. We've talked about it. We're mates. That's it. And even if I did. Which I categorically don't, even if he's not *completely* the airhead deadshit I thought he was.' I'm rambling and shake my head as if that will help me clear my thoughts. 'Anyway, he's a grown man nearly twice my age. Would you and Dad really be that comfortable with him being Dad's minion *and* my boyfriend?'

'Didn't he say he's not yet 21? You're 18 next month. You're not that bad at maths, Cat. Anyway, you just said you're friends. You're not planning on marrying the guy any time soon, are you?'

'Funny.' I'm borderline spluttering. 'Did you miss the part where I said he doesn't like me like that?'

'Cat, he likes you, that's a given. He wouldn't have driven you around the countryside for four hours to pick up your books if he didn't. He wasn't doing that as a favour.'

'Yeah, well, maybe.' I flip over onto my front and bury my face in my crossed arms. 'But that was before I called him a fuckwit.'

'So, apologise when you see him next, no big deal.'

'You didn't see his face.' A hot flush of shame crosses me. 'Maybe I went a little overboard.'

'I know you love your brothers, it's beautiful that you're such a good sister but it's not your job to mother your brothers; it's mine. You're 17-turning-18. It's your job to have a wonderful summer with a super-hot surfer boy.'

'Mum!' I jerk my head up and stare daggers at her.

'What? I might be ancient, but I'm not dead. He is gorgeous with a capital G. Those shoulders…' She pretends to fan herself down.

'Yeah, well, as fun as this conversation is, it's all pretty much theoretical now anyway.'

'Oh, Cat, the way he looks at you? Your little beach tantrum won't put him off. But what do you want? You're the one in control here. Do you want more than friendship with this kid?'

'I don't know. I mean, clearly, he's a walking god. He's more than that though, Mum. He's smart, he's funny. He's sweet. He can use chopsticks. He freakin' quoted Shakespeare at me!' Mum raises an eyebrow. 'If my friends were here, they'd be telling me to go for it. But doesn't that make me shallow and unfocused?'

'I know you don't want to hear this from me, but two things, Cat. Number one – it's perfectly okay for you to fall in love. Some might say mandatory, in fact, and number two, it's okay to fall in love and be sexually active. As long as you're smart.' She gives me a pointed look.

'Mum! That's not what I'm talking about at all! Why do you have to turn everything into a sex-fest?'

'Curiosity about sex is natural at your age,' says Mum. 'Add in someone like Paul? Curious wouldn't even come close.'

I shake my head and hide my face in my hands, wishing the tide would come and wash me away. I want to hide my entire body.

'If sex is something you feel ready to experience, and you have a partner who is respectful, kind, and you trust, then sex can be wonderful. Transformational even. But honestly, at your age it can also be awful, humiliating, and uncomfortable. I don't want that for you. If Paul's the right guy, then make sure you are in the context of a consensual relationship and use protection, protection, protection. Be crystal clear with each other about what you want, and what you don't.'

'Please stop talking, Mum. I'll join a convent if you keep talking. I'm not sexually active. We've barely even been orally active.' The humiliation of Paul pulling away from that incredible kiss at the Gap lookout stabs me right in my chest.

'What?'

'Yeah, I knew that was coming out wrong even as I said it. Anyway, this is the most ridiculous conversation in the history of ridiculous conversations. I have so much more I need to think about. I can't be distracted, not now. I've worked too hard. And anyway, I told you, we're just friends.'

'Stop overthinking everything, Cat.'

'Weird. Paul said the same thing, about me thinking too much.'

'He's right. You're giving me anxiety, and I'm the parent here, not you. I order you to calm down before you give yourself and me ulcers. Meanwhile, have a look at this creep.' She juts her chin over my shoulder. A toddler sits scooping sand in front of a man sprawled in the shade of a sun tent, openly ogling me while the kid fills a bucket.

'You all right there?' Mum shouts and eyeballs him until he looks away, but not before he metaphorically strips the meat from my bones.

I can't put a name to this. I'm not uncomfortable, that's not the right word, even though that's what's used in every freakin' self-defense workshop we do at school, and I'm not really scared either. What is it? Why does a sleaze like Creepy Dad over there make me wish I was invisible? It's like that bus driver we had, he'd be a stone statue for everyone except the Year Nine girls. He was all happy and cheery for them, until a parent complained that he made their daughter feel uncomfortable. There's that word again. Good on her for sticking up for herself. When I told Mum about it, she went off, and believe it or not was angry at me for not saying anything about it when it was my turn to be the focus of his attention. Then she and Nonna had a massive fight because Nonna said it was a woman's lot in life and to just look down and ignore it. Mum wasn't on board with that, at all.

'Thanks, Mum.'

22

I'M in the bathroom inspecting my sunburn when Mum screams. I pull a towel around me and race to the laundry door to see Mum running across the grass, Tommy chasing her with the hose.

'What is it with this family?' I yell, and then Tommy turns the hose on me. I clasp the towel tight against me. 'Dipshit! I'm naked!'

'Well, that's just gross.' He squirts me again.

I scream, my hand shielding my face as Mum sneaks behind him. She pounces. As he falls to the ground she wrestles the hose off him, drowning me in the process. Nonna has come out onto the balcony and sees me in the backyard wearing only a towel. I swear her hackles rise.

'Caterina!' she yells in Italian, 'your *ragazzo* is here. Get inside and put some clothes on!'

I look at Mum, my eyebrows raised. She lets go of Tommy, squirting his back. 'He's downstairs with Dad getting organised for tomorrow,' she says. 'Nonna's right. You're too old for running around in the nudie.'

'Why'd you scream like that? I thought you were being attacked!'

'Why are you still standing here in a towel? Go inside before Nonna collapses from shame.'

I scuttle inside, leaving a trail of wet footprints, and back into the bathroom to grab some moisturiser. As I bolt between the bathroom and my bedroom, I hear Dad, Matty and Paul on the stairs. I close my bedroom door behind me and dive for my wardrobe. I pull on some underwear and the elastic's abrasive. I slather myself in moisturiser, my skin drinking it like water. I don't even remember the last time I burned like this. I consider my failure to burn as one of my lifetime achievements and wear it as a badge of honour. My skin feels too tight for my body, but as I slap the cool cream across my skin, I feel it relaxing into itself, the lobster-vibe decreasing.

I find a black singlet dress in my cupboard. It's a little short, covering the bare minimum, which will send Nonna into a tailspin, but it's the only piece of clothing I have that won't feel like sandpaper against my skin. I run a brush through my hair, and it falls down my back in a chocolate river, as Mum used to say when I was little. The hair against my sunburn feels like razor wire, so I scoop it up into a ponytail high on my head.

Everyone's out on the balcony and chatter flutters on the air. Mum sees me in the doorway and asks me to grab the steaks Dad has marinating in the fridge. Paul, talking to Nonna, looks up at me and winks.

'Let's eat outside tonight,' says Mum as I carry out the steaks. 'It's such a beautiful night. Paul, you're staying for dinner, aren't you?'

'I'd love to. That's if suicidal fuckwits are welcome?' He flashes me a cheeky grin and I shake my head, trying not to smile as I wait for the blush to recede from my cheeks.

'What?' Dad jerks his head to Paul as he takes the steaks from me.

'Long story for which our charming daughter is going to apologise,' Mum says. 'Oh, you didn't have to do that!' she adds as Paul hands her a bottle of wine.

'I came prepared,' he says, 'but do you mind if I impose just a little bit more and use your shower? I haven't had a chance to go home and change.'

'Of course,' says Mum, 'no imposition at all. Use the kids' shower. Mick's just going to run Mum home, and then we'll eat.'

As Nonna does her farewell tour, kissing us all goodbye, I remember my bathers are in a sandy pile on the floor. God knows what else I've left in there.

'Hang on a minute.' I push past Paul. 'I'll just make sure Tommy hasn't left it too feral.'

'Me? I haven't even been in there,' says Tommy. 'It's school holidays. I'm stinkin' it up. I haven't brushed my teeth for days.' He puffs his chest out as if permanent morning breath is an achievement to be proud of.

In the bathroom, I scoop my bathers into one of the wet towels I left on the floor earlier and toss the bundle into the laundry basket. I slide my toiletries into the top drawer. How much does this guy need to know about me?

'Is it presentable?' Paul stands in the doorway, his face bemused. 'You remember that I live in a mansion, don't you, with servants and shit?'

'It's all yours.'

I go to move past him but he puts his hand on my shoulder. I can't tell if the heat is from him or from me, but it feels like we could send smoke signals.

'We good?'

'You're good, I'm the absolute opposite.' I shrug, disappointed when his hand leaves my skin. 'I'm sorry I yelled at you. You're not a fuckwit.'

'Well, that's the nicest thing anyone has ever said to me.'

'I'm trying to apologise.'

'Cat, it's fine. I'm sorry it scared you, but honestly, Matty had a ball out there.'

'I know, I just get a bit overprotective sometimes. Curse of being a big sister.'

'He's lucky he has you looking out for him,' says Paul. 'But he's got me too. He had the full lineup looking out for him. Tommy's got me too. And so do you, Cat.'

'I've got you?'

'You've got me. Have I got you?'

The doorway feels too small for this conversation. Paul's eyes never leave mine and the openness in them makes my heart ache.

'You're going to have to define 'got' for me,' I say.

'Got is a little something like not yelling at me.'

'I make no promises.'

'I'll take it.' He leans down and softly kisses me on the cheek, his lips right near the corner of my mouth. I could turn my head, just an inch, and they'd be on mine and I flush a red deeper than any sunburn. I feel his breath hot against me and as he straightens, we lock eyes and it's like I can't look away.

'Now where are the salad servers?' Mum screeches from the kitchen and Paul almost hits the roof in his rush to move away from me. Smooth, Mum, and immaculate timing as always.

'I'll get you a towel,' I say, opening the linen cupboard beside the bathroom. 'Do you use two? I use two, one for my hair, but do you need two?'

'One is fine, thank you.'

'There's face washers in the bottom drawer.' I point towards the vanity. 'And there's soap in that cupboard. Do you need a toothbrush? We have spares, but they're just manual. Mine's electric. For my braces, you know. My old braces, obviously. They're gone now.' If only I could wire my mouth shut to end this torrent of verbal embarrassment.

'Thanks,' says Paul. 'All good.' He stares at me, and I realise he's waiting for me to leave.

'Oh, sorry, enjoy. Don't worry about how long you take, Matty's a shocker and we have an amazing hot water system. It never runs out. You want the door shut? Of course you do, you're not a total exhibitionist, or are you?'

'Thanks. Cat, I think I can handle it from here.' He pulls the door shut, closing me out.

Ugh, good one, Cat. So sophisticated. I tug at my hair, eyes rolled. Why am I such a complete tool? The door flies open.

'The towel?' he says.

Holy crappola, I'm still holding it. I just about throw it at him, then all but run into the kitchen. A task is what I need, a super important task to focus on so I don't think about the naked beautiful walking surfer god in my shower. My shower. Naked.

'Cat, can you please get the plates and cutlery while you're in there?' Mum calls out.

Bless you, mother of mine, you always come up with the goods when I need you to. I set the table and take out glasses and the water jug, as well as some wine glasses. Mum eyes me off as I place a wine glass at each setting, except for my brothers.

'Don't even think about it, Mum,' I mutter. 'We're Italian, remember? It's not like I'm going to neck the bottle and vomit all over my shoes.'

'You can have half a glass.'

23

AS it turns out, I have more than half a glass. Mum's right; it's a beautiful night. We have dinner on the balcony: Dad's steaks, salad from Nonna's garden, some corn grilled on the barbecue and slathered with lime juice and butter. The jasmine from the neighbour's garden sits heavy in the air, Paul's beside me, and he smells so good it takes all I have not to bury my face in his chest just to inhale him.

After dinner, Mum asks Paul if he's ever tried an affogato. He shakes his head, so I go inside to fire up the coffee machine. Mum sends Matty inside with clear instructions to stack the dishwasher. He dumps the plates on the bench next to the sink.

'Oi!' I say. 'I heard Mum. Stack the dishwasher. That's that shiny thing under the sink there. Oops, sorry, forgot who I was talking to. Matty, my darling brother, the sink is that other shiny thing on the top of the dishwasher with the magic spout that when you flick the knob water comes out.'

'You're the knob.' He disappears downstairs. The 'ping, ping, ping' of a godforsaken video game starts up. Tommy races downstairs after him, and then the dulcet tones of their fighting drifts across the evening.

As the coffee machine hums, I open the freezer and thank the stars above. Mum has bought some ridiculously expensive vanilla ice-cream. As I spoon it into the shot glasses, I spot the limoncello that Nonna gave Dad for Christmas. I turn off the coffee machine and top all the glasses with limoncello instead. The balls of ice-cream float and bob in the liquor, a pale concoction with the slightest hint of yellow.

'Good call,' says Dad as I carry them out.

'I thought it'd look like coffee, like tiramisu,' says Paul.

'Change of plans.' I take my spoon and carve through the ice-cream, letting the liquor marble. There's the sweet tang of citrus on my tongue, the headiness of the alcohol. It's summer in a shot glass.

Paul dips his own spoon into his serve and his face lights up. 'Man, this is the bomb. How have I never had this?'

'We had this every night on our honeymoon.' Thankfully, and totally out of character, Mum leaves it there. I don't think I could stomach a honeymoon story.

We sit on the balcony, music in the background, our mouth full of the heaven that is the combination of lemon and vanilla. The sun sets into the ocean and it's all feeling a little too Hollywood in its perfection. When Paul rests his hand above my knee, it's definitely out of the friend zone.

'What time are you kids heading out?' Mum says.

'What?'

'Beach party?' says Paul. 'We talked about it this morning?'

'Oh, that's right.' Between the night sky, the heat of my sunburn, the alcohol coursing a little too fluidly through my veins, and let's face it, the hot guy making the invitation, I feel like going to a party. Or at least, being anywhere Paul is.

'I need you to come,' Paul says. 'I need to prove to your parents that I can take you to a party and bring you home again. So, no sneaking off this time. Deal?'

I look at my parents. Mum nods and there is pride in her eyes.

'Go have fun,' says Dad, 'but put on something decent first.'

'What do you mean? What do you call this?' I gesture to my dress.

'That's a headband.'

'Oh, Mick, don't be ridiculous. Let her wear whatever she likes,' says Mum. 'She looks fine.'

'She looks beautiful,' says Paul and he strokes his thumb over my knee.

'You ready to go?' My stomach flutters.

He nods and rises from the table. He goes to clear the limoncello glasses, but Mum tells him to leave them. He kisses Mum on the cheek and shakes Dad's hand.

'Thanks for dinner,' he says. 'What time do you want her home?'

'Midnight,' says Dad.

'One thirty,' says Mum.

'Mum's the boss.' I kiss them both on the cheek.

24

'TODAY has been one of those super-awesome, perfect days of summer.' We walk along the dark beach. The tide is out and the water lapping sounds a long way away. It almost feels irreverent to speak in the perfection of the night.

'Totally,' says Paul. 'My favourite part was when you called me an ignorant fuckhead.'

'I said no such thing. If you're going to quote me, at least do it properly. And I do believe I apologised. Am I still not forgiven?'

'I'd forgive you for anything in that dress.'

'What?'

'Nothing, and yes, I forgive you, I'm just playing with you.'

'Hey, here's a question for you,' I say. 'I want a male opinion.'

'This could be dangerous, but okay, hit me.'

'Do you think girls ask for it?'

'Ask for what?' he says. 'Is this about that school thing you were talking about with your mum? The patriarchy?'

'Yep, that's the one.'

'You changed your mind on global warming or drowning kids?'

'Not yet, I haven't decided, but what do you think? As king of the Neanderthals?'

'I'm still a Neanderthal? Seriously?'

'Okay, sorry, as a walking surfer god, what do you think? Do girls ask for it?'

'Do I think girls ask for it? Absolutely not. Any man who hurts a woman is the lowest of the low. It's never a girl's fault if she gets abused but I can't say that I don't think that girls can sometimes put themselves in positions where they are at risk.' He crosses his arms. 'That's just the shitty world we live in. It's fucked, but it just is.'

'At risk?'

'Yeah, like I think it's shit that you can't walk home through Batter's without your parents worrying about your safety. Watch it.' A wave races up the sand, and we step quickly out of its path. 'That's why I didn't blame your dad for giving me a serve for not taking you home that night of the Gap party. Promise me you'll never walk on this beach at night on your own.'

'But if I do, if I wear this dress, you'll forgive me?' I don't know if it's seeing how easy it was to hang with Paul, how he slotted in so effortlessly around our family dinner table, how he was so open, or how he seems to give a flying you-know-what about me, but my hands are shaking and I want to prod at him, at us, like a bruise. 'So, you like my dress?'

'I do. I think so,' he says. 'I can't see shit, it's so dark tonight.'

'I have another question for you.'

'Okay...'

'What did you mean by "I've got you"?' I stop walking and let my feet sink into the sand.

'What do you mean, what did I mean?' he says over his shoulder.

'You know what I mean,' I say, unmoving.

'Did I mean what you know I mean?' He stops and turns to me. 'Will you say it on a beach or with a leech?'

'Forget it.' I cross my arms to hug myself and keep walking, my gait clunky and ungainly as I sink into the sand.

'Cat, wait,' he says. 'I'm only playing around. What exactly are you asking me here?'

'I'm...' I bite my lower lip and hug myself tighter.

'You're...' he prompts, taking a step towards me.

'Here's the thing,' I say. 'You said "I've got you, Cat".' I deepen my voice in a gruff imitation.

'That's what I sound like?'

I keep going, not wanting to lose my momentum, or more

accurately, to not chicken out. 'You also said that about my brothers, and I don't want to walk around thinking there's something happening that's not, but it feels like something's happening, that's not just you being the muscle who protects me from the dangers of Batter's Cove to keep my dad happy.' I pause to take a deep breath. 'Is something happening, Paul, with you and me? That's what I'm asking you.'

'Cat.' My name rolls off his tongue slowly, and he runs a hand across his head.

'I know you said friends, but I've got to tell you, this doesn't feel like friends.' My legs are trembling; it's like I have pre-exam jitters. 'You put your hand on my knee. Does this feel like friends to you?'

'No, it doesn't.' He comes to a stop, and crosses his arms, body turned towards the ocean.

'Do you want to kiss me?' I swallow hard at the memory of our 'just friends' chat at the Gap lookout turning into the most incredible kiss of my life. I want more of that, even if it comes with a side of rejection.

'Do you want to kiss me?' He looks at me sideways.

'Not if you see me as just the boss's daughter. Paul, is it all in my head? Can you answer me that?'

'You are the boss's daughter.' He puts an arm around my shoulder and propels me along the beach.

'You still haven't answered my question.'

'That's because I don't have to.'

'That's not fair.'

'I'm sure your parents and teachers have told you this, Cat, but life's not fair.'

I stick my foot behind his ankle and expecting a mountain I use my whole weight to push against his chest. He yields so readily that gravity takes me with him and the next thing I know he's flat on his back on the sand with me lying on top.

'Jeez, Cat,' he says, 'buy me a drink first?'

I scramble to my feet, my hands pushing off his shoulders, trying not to think about how freakin' good they feel. 'Don't patronise me.

I'm not up for being played with.'

He sits up and pushes off the sand to return to standing. 'Man, I knew I'd stuff this up. I'm not playing you, Cat, not by a long shot. I want to do the right thing by you.'

'What does that even mean?'

'I told you that day at the Gap lookout. It means I'm a selfish prick, really. There are a million guys out there that would be better for you than me, but, well, fuck them. Of course I want to kiss you.'

'So just kiss me.'

He takes my face in his hands. He kisses my forehead, my nose and then tilts my head to kiss my chin.

'That's not what I meant.'

'You're so bossy. I'm getting there.' The crash of our lips leaves me suspended in the night sky, tethered to the ground by his hands on my face. If he let go, I'd either float into space or I'd crash to the sand, more than possibly with my eyes still closed and my tongue still hanging out. He breaks away and I desperately wish he hadn't.

'So, what is this?'

'*This* is simple. *This* is something. Since I saw you at Sadie's I've been fighting in my own head. I can't stop thinking about that kiss at the Gap lookout. This is insane but...' Paul grabs my hand. 'Fuck all the reasons I shouldn't say this, I want you to be my girlfriend. Is that clear enough for you? That's what I want. But is that what you want? For us to be together?'

'Yes.' My voice is patchy and breathy, like he stole the oxygen from my lungs, and my thoughts crash, like my mind can't keep up. 'Wait, so, you're officially my boyfriend?'

'Officially. Want me to sign something? Or should we just seal it with a kiss?'

'Not yet,' I say. 'I have another question.'

'There's a surprise.' He tugs me by the hand until we sit side by side on the sand.

'You said you've been fighting in your own head, since New Year's?'

'Oh, that…'

'Is it me? You think I'm stuck up too?'

'What? No!' As easily as lifting a sheet of paper he moves me to sit on his lap. I'm eternally grateful for the darkness of the beach because in broad daylight… In my headband dress, as Dad called it… Let's just say he'd have a full, uninterrupted view of something that doesn't need viewing. 'I mean, you sure as hell are far too good for this place, and for a shit-for-brains tradie like me, and you've got a temper on you that's freakin' terrifying, but the crap in my head is all me. Or it's all you, but it's not you.'

'I know you're speaking English here, but I have no idea what you're saying.' The sand under my knees retains the day's heat. I break the surface and the cool grains move under my fingernails.

'There's so much I want to tell you but there's also so much that I don't want you to know.' His hand leaves my hip and I feel rather than see his hand go up to rub his head. 'It feels so complicated when it should really be simple.'

'Just tell me.'

'Okay, here it is.' He pauses, his fingers twirling the ends of my hair. I wince as it pulls.

'Hang on a tic.' I reach behind me and tug out the elastic, releasing the ponytail. He smooths my hair as it slides down my back.

'None of this is helping me focus.'

'Sorry, am I too heavy?'

'Are you kidding? I have surfboards heavier than you.' His arms come around me and I'm sandwiched between his knees and his chest, his chin resting on my head. 'I know why I've been holding back, which really, I haven't. I can't get over how quickly I've felt so sure of this, of wanting to be with you.'

I run my hand up and down his forearm, my fingers encircling his wrist.

'That's one thing. The second thing is harder for me to get my head around, but do you ever feel trapped by other people's crap? Like they can't cope if you're not a certain way?'

'Have you met my Nonna? She's nothing compared to school. Then there's my parents, driving me crazy.'

'Man, Cat, they just want what's best for you. They want you to have options. I'm a chippy because the old man lined that up for me. I live here because this is where I've always lived. It's not only that, but it's also this life, the working, surfing, drinking, chicks, drugs, it's all bullshit, and I'm just so sick of it.' He sighs heavily. 'The only thing that means anything in all of it is surfing and working, and even work, up until I met your old man, work was just something I did. Surfing is different, that feels like it's the only good thing I do, for no reason, with no expectations, even though you think it's for redneck, sexist racists. One day I'll get you to understand that.'

'Good luck with that one.'

'What I'm trying to say, the reason I told you I wanted to do the whole friend zone, take it slow thing with you, was because you make me want to be better. I'm not such a dipshit that I know if I didn't go that way I would've done something to mess it all up before it even started.'

'So, we're out of the friend zone?'

'You are my girlfriend, remember?' He kisses me. Then again. Then again. And in between his kisses I wonder how it is even remotely possible that I live in a world where there aren't fireworks being set off all over Batter's Cove at this moment.

We're interrupted by dull footfalls coming down the stairs at the top of the beach. From the Lifesaving Club's flickering light, we see Isabel and a couple of girls are off their faces, stumbling, clutching each other and shrieking.

'Want to skip the party?' Paul asks.

'Sounds good.' I could lay in the dark like this forever; Paul's chin resting on the top of my head, the soft skin of his bicep under my cheek, his hand trawling up and down my arm from my collarbone to my fingertips and back again, over and over.

'Remember at the lookout, when I told you that last year I was in a bad place?' he asks. 'I freakin' hated myself then. I think I hated myself right until the point where I went to your house that first time, hung out with you on your balcony, met your family.'

'You mean when you ate all my avocado toast? That made you feel good about yourself?'

'I literally stole food from the mouth of a babe.'

I slap him lightly on his arm.

'Don't be objectifying.' I make a mental note to tell Em and Sal that the hottest of the hot called me a babe. 'You're the walking surfer god, you can't tell me any different.'

'I'm happy you've moved on from calling me a fuckwit but I'm not just a surfer, you know.'

'You missed the "god" part in that,' I say. 'I almost feel sorry for you, what a cross you must bear. You can't help the impact you make.'

'There's only one person I want to make an impact on, and it's my girlfriend, now that it's official, and it's time to take her home.' He bodily lifts me off his lap and onto the sand. He stands and holds out his hand. 'Let's go, beautiful. I can't let your parents down again.'

'Ugh…' I take his hand.

He lifts me to my feet and hugs me, his mouth against my neck.

The streets are quiet as Paul walks me home. We have the roads to ourselves, and houses are in darkness. Every now and then, the glare from a television reflects through a window. We hear quiet voices from a balcony and a glowing cigarette is all we can make out from the street below.

My sandals have rubbed a blister across the back of my heel. It's the first time in weeks I've been in shoes that have more than a scrap of rubber. My skin's still on fire, and my eyes are tired. Still, the night feels light, and the stars are right on top of us. The day's heat is replaced by a breeze that cools my scorched skin.

When we get home, Mum and Dad are still on the balcony nursing wine glasses, sitting in the glow of citronella candles.

As we reach the base of the stairs, Paul tugs at my hand to stop me. 'I can't believe I'm saying this, especially after what, a couple of weeks? But it feels like there's nothing more important to me than you, and far out, all I want is for you to feel the same way about me.'

He kisses me on the cheek and calls out to my parents that he'll see them tomorrow, then takes off in his car.

'Did you have a good time?' Mum asks.

'The best,' I say. 'It has now transpired that I, in fact, am officially a beautiful walking surfer god's girlfriend. How do you like that?' I kiss them both and go to bed.

25

I'VE just finished inhaling a mango on the deck when Paul's car turns into our driveway. He waves up at me, then goes straight under the house to talk to Dad. Five minutes later there's the slap of thongs on the stairs. Paul grabs the railings on either side of his body and swings himself right up the next set of three stairs, taking him to the balcony where I'm sitting, surrounded by folders, notebooks and novels, and covered in mango juice.

Paul's feet are a shock of white against the tan of his legs. A large vein stands on each, blue against his pale skin. Hair stands at attention on each toe.

'Oh, thank God, you're not perfect! Your feet are truly hideous,' I say. 'Can you put your boots back on?'

'And hello to you too, Cat.' He leans down and kisses me on the cheek. 'Where's your mum and brothers?'

'Don't know, don't care.'

'Coffee?' He takes the seat opposite me.

'That would be fantastic. No sugar for me, thanks.'

'As if I didn't know you're sweet enough.'

'Yeah, I can tell by that peck on the cheek.'

'I'm a gentleman, remember?'

'Yes, and now you're sitting as far away from me as possible.'

'Just enjoying the view,' he grins and dances his toes across mine under the table.

'How are you going to cope with no swell?'

'We're going off Sueys.'

'That's because you're a bunch of bright sparks,' I say. 'Have fun smashing your tiny, unformed brains.'

Sueys is the nickname of a local point of interest, shortened, delightfully, from Suicide Rocks. It is a deep channel in the rock face high above sea level, carved by high tides, pocketed with underwater caves. Rock fishers love it, ignoring the safety sign that stands sentinel on the beach. At least once each summer, sometimes twice, a fisher is swept off the rocks by an unexpected wave, sucked into an underwater cave where he remains until it's safe enough for some poor search and rescue person to retrieve him, or what's left of him. It's always a him, by the way. In all the years of annual bombardment by news helicopters it's never a 'she' that's been caught unawares.

'You're coming too,' says Paul.

'Thank you, but no thank you. I have work to do, as you can see. And Suey's and I are not even remotely *simpatico*.' I emphasise the last word with staccato syllables.

'Quick coffee, and then let's go?'

'Coffee, yes, Sueys, no.'

Paul follows me into the kitchen. He leans against the bench, his hands on either side of his hips. I bend to open the cupboard beside his leg, gently nudging him out of my way with my hip.

'Excuse me.' I retrieve two cups. As I stand, his arms wrap around me and he pulls me against him, his legs stretched so we are the same height, chest to chest, face to face. I put the cups down on the bench and slide my hands under his t-shirt, up his back, spreading my fingers across his shoulders.

'Well, hello, Paul, what are you up to on this beautiful day?' Mum's voice cuts across the kitchen. Paul's arms drop and I leap back in one super-human move.

'I'm just making coffee,' I say. 'You want one?'

'So that's what you're calling it, "coffee",' says Matty. 'Right. Good to know.'

'Hey, Matty, you want to come jump off Sueys with us?'

'Yes!' he says.

'Can I go too, Paul?' Tommy says.

'No way are either of you jumping off Suicide Rocks,' I say. 'Tell them, Mum.'

'No way in hell are either of you jumping off Suicide Rocks,' Mum deadpans. 'You're both too small.'

'Come on, Dad was doing it when he was five,' says Matty.

'What was I doing?'

'Jumping off Sueys as a preschooler, apparently,' says Mum.

Tommy starts clambering all over Dad, Mum opens the fridge, berating Matty for the teeth marks in the parmesan, which he strenuously, ear-piercingly denies.

'Let's go.' I grab Paul's hand, forgoing our coffees in favour of escaping my family.

AT the top of the cliff, the bush gives way to a car park for the world's dodgiest boat ramp. As old as Batter's Cove, its wedge of concrete peters off into the ocean through a tiny inlet of zig-zagging rocks. The only people game enough to use it are weather-beaten, shrivelled old men with wizened faces and little boats with engines that seem too big for the vessels they propel.

Every now and then a tourist tries their luck, reversing a trailer only marginally narrower than the ramp, their wheels butt-clenchingly close to the edge where a two metre fall awaits. That's when the community spirit of Batter's Cove really comes to the fore with the clifftop filled with spectators, some with deck chairs and eskies, laughing, shouting words of encouragement and derision.

The air's still today, the water has barely the slightest ripple all the way to the horizon. The tide has receded, doubling the size of the beach, exposing the long flat expanse of rocks that usually lie submerged. Everything has a white glare from the sun. The air feels like I could stir it. Paul's hand is on my shoulder, the rough of his thumb moving across my collarbone, and I'm about seventeen seconds away from purring.

We walk down the boat ramp, the sea a perfect shade of tourist postcard blue; it could be photoshopped. As I squint into the horizon, a gazillion diamonds reflect off the surface of the water. The tideline is a hundred metres away from where the boat ramp's concrete abruptly ends. The sand is hard underfoot, the heat baking it like concrete. Our feet barely make an impression as we walk. In the distance, fishing boats scatter across the deep water between Australia and Antarctica, today as smooth as a sheet of cardboard. In front of us, the coast curves and the farms on top of the cliffs look as yellow as the sand. In a few short months they will be as green, according to my Nonna, as the hills of Italy.

We cross the Bay, Nonna's favourite beach. It's a small beach with a gentle slope where Tommy and I watch the sunset most nights, and calm, sheltered water, favoured by families dragging both their kids and their mountains of beach paraphernalia. The Bay is also where the lifeys deliver their training programs for little kids. As we pass, some lifeys are dragging huge paddleboards to the water's edge, shooting dirty looks at anyone, man, woman or child who dares move to the water or across their path.

It's a beautiful beach, despite the behemoths in their red and yellow uniforms. On the edge of the dune, I see Nonna's spot. It's where she and my grandfather always sat, long before I was even born. I never met him, but through Mum's stories and a photo in Nonna's bedroom, I can see it in my mind's eye – my Nonno in his work pants, rolled up to below his knee, the top button of his long-sleeved shirt undone in a concession to the heat. The two of them on matching yellow striped beach towels, sitting upright under a beach umbrella, also striped in yellow and white with fringing around the canopy.

Nonna kept that umbrella, although one of us carries it for her, and it now lives permanently in our garage. I picture Nonna sitting there, watching us pass, and she would not be impressed – me a good catholic girl, wearing a lime green bikini with denim shorts, Paul wearing even less. He's holding his thongs, chest bare, t-shirt tucked into the top of his board shorts, flapping against his thigh as he walks. The weight of his t-shirt on the super light fabric of his board shorts drags, pulling them down below his hipline. The juxtaposition of his tanned torso and the white of his hip bones startles. His abdominals descend in a deep v. It is actually offensive how good he looks, and I have to admit walking beside him feels pretty amazing in a shallow, superficial, vacuous way. Every female gaze on the beach follows him. We pass a group of young mothers watching their kids play in the shallows and they look me up and down, wondering no doubt, what kind of charity case the living god deigns to support with me by his side.

'What?' says Paul.

'What, what?'

'Your face.'

'What about it?'

'You just looked really angry for a second there.'

'Really?'

'Really.'

'Hmm, weird.'

He takes my hand and he's leaning over me, kissing me in full view of the entire beach, mean mummies and all. Nonna would be apoplectic. The thought tugs the corners of my lips into a smile.

'Better?'

We pick our way across the rocks. They're covered by a furry sea mat of lichen that are dry to the touch but slimy and slippery below the surface. They're laced with mollusks, tiny cone-shaped shells that dig into the flesh of my feet. Rock pools are everywhere. When we were kids, Matty and I would spend hours out here at low tide looking for blue ringed octopuses, excited yet terrified at the thought of finding one, picking over each individual rock pool, lying in the larger ones, warm as bathtubs from the sun.

We reach the end where the rocks form a small, flat platform and beyond lies, well, nothing, just the undertow that could drag me out to a platoon of sharks waiting to tear me apart. Paul's friends say hi to me and give him some sort of convoluted secret handshake. If I weren't scared shitless by being at the edge of the rocks, I'd roll my eyes. Directly below us, where the rocks end, is the sheer drop to the water, still, tranquil and sun-glinted. It could be a suburban swimming pool if it weren't on the most dangerous stretch of coastline in the whole freakin' country.

'Coming through!' One of the guys launches off the rock, dropping and landing with a large splash that doesn't even reach the lip of where I'm standing.

'You want to go first, Cat?' Paul drops his t-shirt and thongs in a pile on a rock ledge.

'You've banged your head against your surfboard far too much,' I say. 'If you think I am jumping to my death you are out of your freakin' mind.'

He laughs and walks to the edge, turning to me. He grins that perfect smile, then backflips into the air. My breath catches as he disappears beyond view. I peek over the edge and see him treading water. He wipes the ocean from his face and behind him, it's dark and still, barely a ripple from where he submerged. Bubbles float around him, reflecting the sunlight.

'Come on, Cat.'

'No way.'

He dives deep, before scrambling up the rock face on all fours like a monkey, using his feet and his hands to grip and pull himself up and over the edge. He wraps his arms around me, and his hands are freezing against my back. I rear back.

'You're so cold!' I put my hands flat on his chest, pushing away. It's like trying to push the cliffs; he doesn't yield.

'Yeah well, you're so hot.' He kisses my neck before releasing me.

'Get a room,' Ant yells, then runs hard across the rocks. He pushes off the cliff edge on one foot and somersaults through the air. The thwack of skin hitting water is matched by our audible winces. Ant climbs out, and a red smear reaches from hip to shoulder blade across his back. One of the guys, Tom, slaps it, and the handprint stays white before fading to mottled red.

'Ya dick!' They wrestle to the edge of the rocks, Ant bracing his whole body before flinging Tom over. Ant wobbles, corrects his balance, overcorrects and then dives into the water. As he surfaces for breath, Tom pounces on him, pulling him back below.

Beside me, Paul's lips are salt crusted.

'And you wonder why I call them Neanderthals,' I mutter as the two boys wrestle each other back to the cliff face.

'That's not very nice. They think you're the best.' He wanders across the rocks to chat to Cavey.

'Come on, Cat,' Ant says, wiping his face of salty water. I've found a perfect spot, a rock ledge that could double as an armchair, and I'm nestled into it, the sun at my back, the rocks still cool from the night. He pulls me to my feet, ignoring my protests. 'Let's go.'

I'm dragged to the edge. My throat tightens and I'm covered in a layer of sweat.

'You're gonna love it.' Ant nudges me forward. Droplets from his wet hair land on my bare skin like needles.

'Don't push me.' I look down into the water.

'Of course not,' he says.

'What if I land on the rocks?' Tears cloud my vision and the ribbon of the road far above the beach wavers.

'You won't,' he says. 'I'm coming with you.'

'I got it, Scampo.' Paul takes my hand and I grip it with both of mine.

'Sorry, mate, I didn't mean anything,' says Ant.

'Don't let go of my hand.' Paul's eyes never leave mine. 'We've got this.'

'You sure?'

'On three.' We're standing side by side and far across the Bay there's a car at the lookout. The sun glints off it, a giant blinding light. 'One, two…'

'No!' I shout, but I'm laughing, and as I hear three, I'm in the air and it seems like a lifetime that I hover in space before the water is all around me and my mouth is open and I'm happy. Light reflects off a million bubbles. As I gasp for air in the sunlight, Paul is still holding my hand.

I let go, kicking towards the wall and hear Ant cheering my name from above. Paul grabs my foot and pulls me under, and then pushes past me to reach the wall. He clings to the side and gestures for me to go first. I make sure my bikini is where it should be and start climbing. I hate the thought that he's looking directly up at the place where the sun doesn't shine, but I'm more conscious of the boys at the top with a perfect view straight down. Paul must have the same thought: he scrambles up the rock face past me. When I reach the top, he holds out his hand. He grabs me and for a moment I'm hovering mid-air again as he pulls me to stand on the rocks. My legs manage to keep me upright despite my trembling.

'That was amazing.' I wrap my towel around my waist and grab my sunglasses.

'Let's go again.'

'Never again as long as I live.' He laughs and flips off the platform.

The thrum of my heartbeat roaring through my ears fades. I stand facing the sun, my eyes closed behind my sunglasses, feeling my breath return to normal. They snap open when I hear a high-pitched giggle.

26

'YOU'RE *sooo* out of control, bitch!' Isabel Scuzzbucket and some random girl pick their way across the rocks.

'Hey, guys!' Isabel moves her way around the Neanderthals, air kissing some, hugging others. As Paul pulls himself up and over the cliff, she takes off her dress and arches her body against the sun, making sure everyone has a chance at a good look at her. Her bathers are pulled up too high and she giggles as she puts her pointer finger between the bikini and her butt, flicking it back to where it should be.

'Hey, Paulie!' She runs her hand down his arm. 'Ooh, goosebumps!'

Ignoring her, Paul steps across the rocks to stand behind me. His arms come around me, crossed against my chest like the safety barrier on a rollercoaster and he plants a gentle kiss on my cheek.

'No, stop!' Tom flings Isabel's friend over his shoulder, full Neanderthal style, her shriek the aural equivalent of stepping on Lego with a bare foot.

'Aww, they're such a cute couple,' purrs Isabel. She drapes her arm across Cavey's shoulders and points at Tom and her friend. 'Aren't they just adorable, Cavey?'

'So adorable,' he says in a monotone, his hand sliding down to rest on her backside.

'Oh, shit, look who's coming,' says Ant.

A convoy of lifeguards have deserted their post and are striding across the beach towards the rocks.

'They think they're cops now? Stuff that!' One of the Neanderthals runs and jumps off the cliff, shouting obscenities all the way down.

'This area is off limits.' A lifey steps across a rockpool.

'Yeah, what are you going to do about it?' says Cavey as he, Paul and Tom walk towards them, arms crossed.

With the boys distracted, Isabel takes the chance to be her pleasant self. 'What are you doing here, Kitty Cat?' She looks at me over her sunglasses, head tilted.

'I live here.'

'You don't normally slum it with us locals though, do you? Where's all your rich friends? Have they dumped you?'

'Oh, that's so sweet. You're concerned about me!' I say, putting a hand to my chest. 'But it's quite pathetic. How much real estate am I taking up in your brain? You never cross my mind.'

'Why don't you just go have sex with a book?' she spits, all the vomit-inducing sweetness gone.

'Is that really the best you've got?'

'You're just jealous!' She's shouting now.

'Of you? Hilarious! Why would I be jealous? What do you think you have that I could ever want in a gazillion years?'

'Your "boyfriend" is happy with what I've got.' She puts her hands on her hips.

'Whatever.' I grab my shorts. 'I'm so not interested in sharing any more oxygen with you.'

'You're full of shit,' Paul says, his voice low.

I spin, my mouth dry. He's staring at Isabel, his glasses pushed up onto his head. Behind him, Cavey and Tom are arguing with the lifeys, all of them throwing their arms around, chests puffed like a lion standoff in the savannah. I walk past them towards the beach. Thongs slap behind me.

'Man, that's not going to end well,' says Ant as he jogs up beside me. 'Cavey would die before backing down to those dicks.'

'You think?'

'Meanwhile, you were awesome. I can't stand that skank.'

'Yeah, I can tell you guys don't like her,' I say, 'that's why you let her hang off you and you take turns giving her love bites. And that's not a judgement on her; I'm not into slut shaming. That's on you guys for hanging out with someone who is just a vile human.'

'Not me; I'm a good boy. Ask my Nonna. You okay, though?'

'I'm fine. I've been dealing with that loser all my life. I can't believe we were ever friends. This time next year I'll have forgotten she even exists, and she'll still be getting treatment for the disgusting disease that one of you guys give her. And boom, just like that, here I go slut shaming. The patriarchy's a hard taskmaster, hey Ant.'

'The patriarchy's the actual worst,' says Ant. 'It does my freakin' head in.'

We crack up laughing and the animosity and tension that had been building up inside me dissipates.

'Here comes Paulie, wait up,' says Ant.

Paul jogs up to us and takes my hand.

'You okay?'

'Again? I've already been over this with Ant. I'm fine. F-I-N-E.'

'We're back to spelling things out for the dumb tradie, are we? That's a good sign.' He flings an arm across my shoulder. 'Let's go back to yours. We'll see you later, Scampo.'

'Yeah, okay, see you, Cat. See you, Paulie.' He disappears into the sand dunes.

'Quick swim?' I ask. We dump our stuff and swim out past kids in their floaties.

'Come here.' He pulls me against him. Underwater, my legs wrap around his waist, and he bobs in the water, easily taking both our weight, steady and anchored.

'We should stay like this all the time.'

'That sounds like a plan,' he says. 'I might drown, but it'd be worth it.'

I lay my head on his shoulder, my cheek against his collarbone, looking at the sand dunes rising above the beach like skyscrapers. Little kids clamour up on all fours, then once at the top, they sprint down, their bodies unable to match gravity as they lose control and tumble to the bottom, often with a mouthful of sand, their eyes grit-filled and rubbed raw. A couple of fishing boats dot across the horizon line but out this far, we're all alone. Paul's skin is cold beneath mine and so smooth it should be illegal. I run my hand across his chest from shoulder to shoulder, then, my palm flat, my thumb follows the trail of hair from the base of his throat to the top of his abs. He grabs my hand.

'Do you want me to drown?'

'You could think of worse places to die.' I nod towards the distant outlines of ancient volcanoes. 'It's so beautiful here. Look – you can see where South America ripped away from Australia.'

'Gondwanaland.' Paul laughs when I gape at him. 'Told you I'm not just a dumb tradie.'

'I never said you were,' I say. 'First Macbeth, now this. I just didn't think you'd be a geography nerd.'

'I'm no nerd,' he says, 'but I liked it. It was cool, learning about how the cliffs and channels make waves.'

'Me too,' I say. 'I thought about keeping it, but preferences, and all that.'

'Didn't you want something that's just for fun, not just about your entrance score?'

'Isn't that your job?' I tickle under his chin.

He grabs my waist and tosses me. I scream, taking in a mouthful of ocean water. I emerge laughing and swim back to him, pushing my hair back off my face. We turn back to the shore, me swimming, Paul trudging through the water.

'Hey, Paul,' I say, 'what's with Isabel?'

'Absolutely nothing,' he says. 'She's full of shit.' I feel the sand under my feet as he takes my hand.

27

'HOW cool is this?' Paul leans forward to look through Mum's telescope.

'Yeah, very cool for a decorative item, fairy lights and all. Kinda like you.'

'Well, that's not a very nice thing to say. But I'm glad you think I'm cool.'

'And decorative. Don't forget decorative. You're not completely terrible to look at.'

'Stop, you're making me blush. It looks brand new. Doesn't it work?'

'It did, originally.' We gave it to Mum one Christmas. It cost Dad a bomb and was so powerful that we could see people picnicking on a beach hundreds of kilometres away. 'We could literally see people's food spread out on a rug, if you could lip read, we would have known what they were saying, it was that clear. And it had this super-cool night sky feature.'

'What happened?' Paul frowns.

'Tommy happened. He messed up the settings and no one's been able to figure it out since.'

'I did not.' Tommy flops onto the sofa.

'Let me have a crack; I love this stuff.' Paul uses his pinky to lift a hideous pair of boy jocks off the telescope. 'These probably aren't doing it any favours. They yours, Cat?' He flings them at me.

I scream and duck and they land on the floor at my feet.

'Hey, Matty!' Tommy calls, 'Cat and Paul are playing with your undies.'

'I'm not playing with anything,' I say. 'Ugh, so disgusting! Matty, pick them up.'

My phone rings and I scoop it up.

'Sal!' I run upstairs to my bedroom, phone clutched to my ear. 'Tell me everything!'

'Everything? Everything is as boring as ever,' she says. 'I miss you so much!'

'Ugh, same here. I miss you too, you have no idea.' I quickly yank up my doona and sit on my bed.

'I don't believe that for a second! Em tells me you're seeing someone.' Sal's panting, and I know that she's either on a run or simply pacing up and down as she chats to me. 'You're not just seeing someone – you have a boyfriend! Oh my God, Cat! And not only do you have a boyfriend, you have the ultimate boyfriend! A walking surfer god! I nearly died when she told me. Your texts are so shit! Em had to tell me everything but I want to hear it from you. All of it. Don't hold back. Tell me everything. Everything!' She squeals and her excitement for me makes me miss her even more.

'Look, just picture every summer rom com you've ever seen, and that's basically it. There's even the evil villain.'

'Miss Scuzzbucket, your arch nemesis, I presume? I hope you're not letting her get to you. Anyway, forget her. What's he like? What about his friends? Are they your friends?'

'That's pushing it.' As we've crossed paths more and more, we've settled into what could never be called a friendship, that's too much. At first, they were awkward around me, clearly uncomfortable and contrived, like their mothers had told them they'd better be on their best behaviour. 'I think they've moved from complete obliviousness of my existence, to tolerating my presence through to maybe even saying "Cat? Paulie's chick? Yeah, she's all right, for a Stuck-Up Bitch."'

'Ooh, so once a Neanderthal, always a Neanderthal?'

'Oh my God, yes.' I adjust the pillows behind my back. 'But, and believe me, this hurts to say out loud, I'm seeing another side to them.'

They're the group of mates I've witnessed from afar for years, vulgar, undoubtedly, but also funny and intensely loyal. 'There's Ant,' I continue. 'You'd love him, Sal, he reminds me so much of JB. He's considerate, friendly and easy to talk to. Just a nice guy, you know? Then there's Cavey, older, cagier. He calls himself Paul's best friend, but there's something about him that I can't quite get.'

'What do you mean?'

'He reminds me of the sheepdog in the old cartoons,' I say. 'He's hard to read, he barks every now and then to keep the sheep under submission and to ward away predators. And I get the feeling that he really, really doesn't like me.'

'Who wouldn't like you?'

'Right?'

'Maybe he thinks you're stealing his best friend,' says Sal.

'That's a bit dramatic for a fling, don't you think?'

'According to Em, it's more than a fling. She thinks you're going to get married and have his babies. Little beautiful walking surfer gods with firecracker tempers.'

'Wow, it's not like Em to exaggerate, is it?' I roll my eyes. 'Trust me, it's a fling. How's it going to work when school goes back and we're doing five hours of homework a night? And you really think a beautiful walking surfer god isn't going to get sick of hanging out with a boring schoolgirl?' The muscles in my legs feel tight, the tendons in my knees straining. I uncross my legs and shuffle to sit on the edge of my bed. 'Did I mention the beautiful walking surfer god thing? Sal, he has girls throwing themselves at him everywhere he goes. Even the mums on the beach check him out, and then I get these looks like "girl, what the hell is he doing with someone like you?" Anyway, what about next year when we move to the city?'

'Cat, stop.'

'What?'

'Next year is next year. We'll worry about that then. And enough with the self-deprecation.'

'Self-deprec-nothing. I'm serious, Sal, you remember this guy?

He's next level. He's one of those annoying beautiful people that's as nice on the inside. Ugh.'

'You're next level, Cat. It's so shitty that you don't see it.'

'Whatever. Enough about me, tell me about you, what have you been doing? How's Char?'

'Char is amazing. Let's just say you're not the only one indulging in a spot of sexy time between holiday homework.'

'Sal, you and Char were sexy timing long before holiday homework.' I smirk. 'You almost needed surgical separation at the end of year assembly.'

'True, and I regret nothing.'

Suddenly, Tommy runs into my bedroom, cheering.

'Cat, Cat, he did it!'

'Did what?'

'Paul got Mum's telescope working again, come see!'

'Tommy, say hello to Sal. Sal, hold on, I'll put you on speaker.'

'Sal! When are you coming over?' Tommy takes the phone from my hand and almost sits on me in his excitement to talk to one of his favourite people.

'What? He's there now? He's at your house?' says Sal, her voice tinny through the speaker. 'Tommy, get your sister to go bask in the glory that is her boyfriend. Cat, tell him Em and I want to meet him, especially since we're his babies' non-biological aunties.'

'Ha ha, very funny. Say hi to Char for me. Love you! Miss you!'

'Love you too. And Cat? Enough self-deprecation. Seriously.'

In the living room, Mum is peering through the telescope flanked by Matty. Paul's at the base of the stairs.

'You really did it.' I put my arms around him from behind, my hands looping under his arms and up to grip his shoulders. From where I'm standing, I'm actually looking down on him for a change. I lean forward to kiss his cheek, his stubble against my lips.

'Not bad for just a fling, hey?' He moves out of reach.

'You heard that?'

'I heard. You have a decent set of lungs on you, and your door was wide open. Is that really what you think?'

'I dunno…'

'You dunno? She who knows everything?'

'Umm…'

'Well, let me make this really simple for you, Cat. For me? Asking you to be my girlfriend? It's not just a summer thing. Or a fling.' He turns to face me. His jaw clenches, pulse surging in his throat. 'What is it to you?'

'It's not a summer thing,' I croak, my throat thick and to my eternal horror I feel tears lurking. 'It's a scary as you-know-what thing. It's a confusing as you-know-what thing. I look at you, I look at me and on paper it doesn't make sense.'

'I get it. The smart AF doctor slash lawyer and the dumb arse tradie, but Cat, let's just go for it. Forget what it looks like on paper.'

'That's not what I mean. You're gorgeous, and I'm… well let's just say I don't stop traffic.'

'I'm not even going to give that one airtime. You're beautiful to the point of dangerous. Full stop. I know that's not what's going on here.'

'Okay.' My face is hot and I can barely look him in the eye. Out of all the excuses how freakin' pitiful and pathetic of me to vomit out that tired old cliché straight from the patriarchy rulebook.

'What doesn't make sense to you?' His gaze is unwavering, and I know that he deserves a proper answer, but where do I start?

I'm feeling all the stupid feels. It's a happiness and a certainty and a lightness that could let me float into the stratosphere, but it's also not. It's his certainty that throws me because I've had that. I've had a plan since I don't know when. Work hard. Get into uni. Move to the city. With him staring at me like this, my whole plan feels wobbly, like its cemented in jelly rather than concrete. He just fits so easily here in my house, with my family, even when he hugs me with that squeeze across my shoulders. He just fits. He's so Batter's Cove, but Batter's is my past. Where do I fit?

He's still staring at me, waiting for an answer.

'It's just a bit overwhelming, sometimes, you know?'

'I get it, but I don't want to stop this thing we've started. Do you?'

'Are you freakin' kidding? This has been the best summer.'

'And it's just the start.' He drops his head into my chest, his arms around me. I tilt his head back and kiss him.

'Woooo, lovers,' my brother yells as he runs past us down to the living room. We jerk apart and I feel the flush spread across my face.

'That's enough, Tommy,' Mum says as we come down into the living room. 'But seriously, guys, do I need to keep a bucket of water on standby?'

28

THE sky's heavy with clouds and the storm belting into the shoreline obliterates the view. The wind hits hard, the gums doing a highland jig. A blanket of rain covers the road, filling the potholes.

I'm lying on my back on the couch, Paul's lap a pillow, trying to read my Italian text but not getting far *at all*. I keep reading and rereading the same sentence over and over, my notebook on the floor beside me, a pen on alert ready to capture my most insightful thoughts and perceptions. Sadly, they don't extend further than *oh my freakin' God, oh my freakin' God*, caught in infinity as Paul's thumb figure eights its way across the ball of my shoulder and dips into the hollow of my collarbone, around and around and around. A callous, just below his little finger, skims my skin following the trail of his thumb. I hear the scratch of hard against soft, even over the scream of the wind, the rain against the windows, the movie Paul's watching.

I look up at him through my eyelashes. From this angle, he's upside down, but I can't fully see his face past the concave of his abs, his chest like a cliff face under his white t-shirt. I pull my head back slightly. His eyes fixed on the movie, he has a layer of stubble from the underside of his chin along his jawline and up into his hairline. I lift my hand and run my fingertips against him, it goes from soft and smooth to abrasive and back again.

'Read your book.' Paul stills my hand and places it flat on my stomach, his eyes never leaving the screen.

'I am.' I slip my hand out from beneath his to trace his lips. 'I'm one of those talented people who can do two things at once.'

'I'm not.' He returns my hand, again. 'I do have a good memory, though, and I distinctly remember the serve you gave me yesterday when I had the nerve to ask if you wanted to come surfing down the coast for the day.'

'Really? That's not ringing a bell at all.'

'Not even the slightest recollection? Nothing about me distracting you from the biggest year of your life, your complete lack of interest in ruining your future just to sit on the beach and be my official towel holder?'

'Nope, nothing. Weird, hey? Yesterday never happened. I'm drawing a huge blank.'

'Okay, let's try and refresh your memory. What else was there? Oh yes, how a dipshit like me has no idea the work involved in…'

'Shh…' I put my fingers across his lips, 'don't upset yourself by living in the past, beautiful walking surfer god. Harsh words might have been said, but the important part is I forgive you.'

'*You* forgive *me*? For what?'

'For being a distracting, beautiful walking surfer god. You're very distracting, even now.'

'Me? I'm just trying to watch a movie.'

'It's the view. It's like I'm staring into a wall of gorgeous flesh.' I trail my fingers across his abs.

'Yeah, well from where I'm sitting the view isn't bad at all.' He leans down and we're kissing, my textbook forgotten, hell, *everything* forgotten.

'Do you think you could come up for air and give me a hand, Paul?'

Dad's standing on the level above us, hands on the railing.

Paul leaps to his feet, sending me flying onto the floor. He reaches to help me up, and I laugh. His face is the colour of what remains in Nonna's dedicated passata buckets, no matter how hard she scrubs.

'Yes, Mick, Mr Kelty, Mick, no problem, yep.'

'Cat, go help your mother bring in the shopping,' he says to me. 'Nonna's with her, so maybe fix your top first.'

29

'DAD says he caught you and Paul canoodling on the sofa,' Mum whispers as we put away the groceries.

Nonna's at the table, nursing a coffee and talking to Tommy.

'We were kissing, if that's what you mean by canoodling,' I say. 'I don't know why Dad had to make such a big deal out of it.'

'From what he said, I think he handled it perfectly. His first instinct was to throw Paul over the balcony, so I think he did well. That said, I don't know how comfortable I am about them being alone together downstairs where Dad has access to potential weapons.'

'Good point.' I stack the apples in the fruit basket.

'You're spending a lot of time together.'

'And…'

'And nothing! Just an observation, Cat.' She turns to the fridge, a portrait of innocence.

'Anything else you've observed that you'd like to get off your chest, Mother?'

'Well, I haven't "observed" any condom wrappers, so I hope you're "observing" being smart with contraceptive choices.'

'Mum! I'm not talking about this with you.'

'Cat, if you're old enough to canoodle in the living room then you're old enough to have a conversation about contraception.'

'For the love of God, can you please stop saying "canoodle"? And "contraception"?'

'Okay, fine, no more canoodling, but even if you don't want to talk to me about it, you really need to make sure you're having this conversation with Paul. And believe me, Cat, it's a conversation you

158

need to have before you're on the sofa wearing next to nothing.'

'Seriously? You're shaming me now for wearing a singlet top and trackies? Who even are you?'

'I'm not shaming. Why is everything so black and white with you? All I'm saying is you can remember Paul's not your whole life. When did you last speak to any of your friends?'

'Yesterday for your information. Anyway, wasn't it you pushing me out the door to "date" him? Well, now we're dating and you're still not happy. I can never do anything freakin' right around here, can I?'

'Caterina! The way you speak to your mother is a disgrace.'

Here we go. Nonna can't help but stick her unwanted opinions into the conversation. Ugh. *I know where she can stick them…*

'Thanks, Mama, but I've got it,' Mum says. 'Cat, if you're going to throw a tantrum like a toddler go do it without an audience. Go to your room; I'm sick of arguing with you about nothing.'

'It's mutual, Mother.' I grab my puffer from my bedroom and go downstairs.

Paul and Dad are huddled over a pile of timber.

'Can we go do something?' I say to Paul. 'Go into town or whatever?'

'He's helping me get this frame up,' says Dad.

'I thought you weren't working today? So Paul has to work 24/7 like a workaholic too, Dad? Is he contractually obligated?'

'It's okay, I'm happy to help.' Paul frowns.

'Cat, go calm yourself down,' says Dad, 'you're acting like a baby.'

'Funny, your wife just said the same thing.' I turn and walk back out into the rain, yanking my hood down over my head.

30

A MESS of cut out newspaper articles are scattered across my desk chair. I'm sorting them into piles; anything even slightly related to asylum seekers sits on one side of my desk, on the other is anything about the climate crisis. Right in the middle are stories about sexism and that's just too depressing for words. What a downer of an assessment. You'd think they'd want us all uplifted and positive leading into Year Twelve. It should be all peace and calm yet only this morning I yelled at Matty for stealing my pen which was stuck through my top knot.

'What was all that about?'

Paul leans in my bedroom doorway, his shoulder against the door jam, his hands stuffed into the pockets of his jeans. There's a fine layer of sawdust in his hair and a dirty mark across his white t-shirt.

'I'm just sick of my dad being such a workaholic which means you are too.'

'I don't need you to talk for me and I really don't need you to embarrass me in front of your dad like that.'

'Sorry for sticking up for you.' I turn back to my articles.

'When I need you to stick up for me, I'll let you know. I'll give you a hand signal.' He smiles, trying to diffuse the tension coiling inside me.

'I know the perfect hand signal,' I say. 'You want to see it?'

'Don't even think about it.' He moves into my room, and I watch him take it in. It's disconcerting and discombobulating.

Discombobulating. I scribble that down on a sticky note. He meanders across to my bookcase and picks up a framed photo.

'Who's who?' he asks, and I point out Em and Sal. His hands move over the collection of tiny paper cranes Em gave me, the leftovers from her art folio assessment. He holds my jar filled with sea glass to eye level and twists an abalone shell against the light, its mother of pearl shimmering.

'Can I have a go?' He gestures towards the delicately painted Venetian kaleidoscope that Nonna gave me from an Italian trip. 'This is supremely cool.' He turns it slowly against his eye. The glass beads clink – he's so tall I can see their colours shifting in the light of my bedroom window as he holds it aloft. The boys got gift after gift after gift from that trip. Seriously, Nonna had three suitcases, two of which were filled with crap for my brothers. All Nonna bought me was the kaleidoscope and the world's ugliest earrings. He stands in front of the open door of my wardrobe, his eye caught by what Mum calls my gallery, with its art posters, collages I've made from images I like, photos of my friends, my family.

'Man, you look so beautiful here.' He points to a photo of Sal, Em and me. I'm wearing a long black dress, a split up one side revealing my thigh and the most painful heels that should never have been invented, let alone bought. I grit my teeth just thinking about how much they hurt that night. 'Was that your formal?'

'Yep,' I say. 'I didn't look like that for long, though. We pulled an all-nighter at Em's.'

'Who's we?'

'Well, pretty much all of us. There were bodies everywhere. Someone even slept in the bath.'

'Where'd you sleep?'

'I didn't. JB and I were on Em's balcony until the bakery opened, then we jumped on some bikes and bought croissants which I vomited as we were riding back.'

'Nice,' he says.

'I know,' I say, 'I'm classy like that. JB had to hold my hair and he's still traumatised.'

'Who's JB again? Scampo's footy mate, yeah?'

'My best friend. We went to formal together.' I point to the photo of JB and I posing at the foot of the stairs. Mum took a gazillion photos that night before Dad eventually told her enough's enough and took us to the pre-formal party.

'You're just friends? That's it?'

'That's it. We have a pact across our year level: no seeing each other in *that* way unless it's absolutely, positively unavoidable.'

'Really?'

'Is that strange to you?'

'Hell yes,' he says. 'Has it ever been absolutely, positively unavoidable for you to hook up with this guy?'

'We're close, but not that close,' I say.

He turns back to the collection on the wall. 'I love this photo.' I cringe as he looks at me as a cherubic toddler, crouching naked over a sandcastle that's thankfully obscuring my bits.

'Can you believe I actually remember that day?' I say. 'Mum was pregnant with Matty, and I remember Dad held me under the shower at the lookout to get the sand off me. I was throwing a tantrum because I didn't want to go.'

'So the temper isn't a me-thing,' he says. 'Good to know.'

'Well, the Paul-thing doesn't help, that's for sure.' I slide down in my chair, slumped, and swing it slowly side to side. 'But all we do is talk about me; I'm sick of it. What about you? What's your earliest memory?'

He rubs the back of his neck and drops into the grey cotton armchair in the corner of my room. He sits on the very edge of it, leaning forward. 'Probably Mum and the old man fighting.' He presses his lips together and looks down at the kaleidoscope in his hands, turning it gently. 'That, or one of my brothers kicking the crap out of me, or each other.'

'See, this is mortifying! This is exactly what I'm talking about,' I say. 'You know about how I vomit croissants and I didn't even know you have brothers. How many? How old? What are their names?'

'One, Michael. My other brother, Peter, died about five years ago.'

'What? That's horrible!'

He shrugs. 'It is what it is, and now it's one brother, he's pushing thirty and he's on the other side of the city.'

'Do you see him much?'

'Not if I can help it.' He reaches across to my bedside table. 'This isn't the water bottle I bought you that day at Sadie's, is it?'

'It's been through the dishwasher once or twice,' I say.

'You kept it?'

'Of course. You've seen me picking up rubbish on the beach. Do I look like the type of girl that doesn't reduce, reuse or recycle?'

'That the only reason?'

'Maybe,' I shrug. 'But we're talking about your brothers. I can't believe it. I'd die if I lost one of mine.'

'You'd be surprised what you can live with or without.' His gaze doesn't leave the floor. The muscles in his jaw flex.

I rise from my chair and sit on his lap, hands on either side of his face. I kiss his forehead, on the verge of tears.

'Oh, no you don't.' He pushes me away gently. 'I can't survive two run-ins with your old man today.'

'Did he say anything?' I sit on the edge of my bed.

'Nope, we were both really careful to avoid eye contact,' he says with a soft laugh. 'I've never taken so much interest in measuring up timber.'

'Which brings me back to my original question. I know you work for Dad, but you don't have to work all the time if you don't want to.'

'I wish I worked for your dad permanently,' he says. 'I hate the crap I work on. Working with your old man would be the bomb.'

'This is going to sound harsher than I mean it to, but answer me honestly: is working for my dad after the reno one of the reasons we're a thing? I mean, I know there's you and me, but is that another drawcard, maybe not the *main* drawcard, but you know what I mean?'

'Are you freakin' serious, Cat?' He runs his hands through his hair. 'Let me get this straight. You're asking me if I'm using you to get a permanent job with your old man?'

'Are you?' My voice cracks.

'No, Cat. I'm not. I'm helping your dad on the reno, and the fact that you're my girlfriend is a bonus that I didn't see coming. But good to know what you think of me.' He walks out of my room.

I curl into a ball on the bed. In the kitchen below I hear him talking to Mum and Nonna before the sliding door opens and shuts.

31

'HEY Cat, wait up!'

I'm walking along the tideline, turning shells over with my toes. I stop and turn, my hand shading my eyes from the sun. Paul, Cavey, Ant and a couple more surfers lope down the dunes, surfboards under their arms. They're wearing their wetsuits – Paul's pulled up to his waist, his chest bare. *Thank you sweet baby cheesus.* At Paul's grin I almost make a sign of the cross. *Thank you sweet baby cheesus times infinity, I didn't 100% scare him off.*

'You hitting the Point?' Waves are curling beyond the bombora, where rocks meet the open ocean.

'Yep, have a look, it's perfection,' says Ant, *'come puoi resistere?'*

'I'll take your word for it.' Between the rocks, the reefs, the underwater caves and the sharks, the Point is only for the uber-reckless thrill seekers of the world, aka my boyfriend. Will that ever not feel weird to say, even in my own head? A wave curls and breaks, as opaque as a piece of sea glass, the white of its crest spraying into the sky. It looks engineered, and yes, indeed, perfect.

'Go ahead, Scampo,' says Paul. 'I'll catch up.'

'Nah, it's all right, I can wait. The waves aren't going anywhere, hey?'

'Mate. I'll catch up.'

Ant's eyes dart between us. 'Ahh, yep, sorry, yeah okay. See ya out there. See ya, Cat.'

'Have fun, Ant,' I say. *'Non annegare.'* He laughs.

'It means don't drown,' I translate. 'Oh, and Ant, *attenzione agli squali!'*

165

'Don't put that shit in my head, I'll never go out.' He steps onto the rocks.

Paul raises an eyebrow at me.

'Keep an eye out for sharks,' I shrug. 'Just channelling my inner Nonna.'

'He's the shark,' Paul says. 'He has a massive crush on you, but who can blame him? He has a pulse. And eyes.'

'Don't you think you're a little too mature to use the word "crush"? Anyway, he doesn't. We just get each other. We both have grandmothers that drive us crazy. That's not a crush; it's pure sympathy. Maybe a bit of solidarity too.'

'Enough about Scampo.' Paul takes my hand. 'I'm sorry about taking off like I did earlier.'

'Honestly, I don't blame you for taking off. I'm surprised you're even standing here talking to me after I keep being such a fuckwit to you.'

'Hey, that's my girl you're talking about.' He tugs gently at my hand, squeezing.

My stomach flips.

'Yeah, well, your girl is sorry. Your girl is going to stop listening to her inner nasty bitch.'

'What?'

'It's a book. You know, about the voices in your head that whisper horrible stuff to you?'

He looks at me blankly, still holding my hand.

'Anyway, point being, after you left, I had a cry, and then I rang Sal, my unofficial and unqualified head doctor, and her take on me is that given your beautiful walking surfer god status and my lowly school girl status there is a power imbalance that I'm making up for with bitchiness that's actually self-sabotage.'

'Hang on.' Paul tilts his head to one side. He looks over my head, and then back to me. 'Power imbalance? Sabotage? Wait, you cried? You told your friend I made you cry? You *cried?*

'Just a little bit. But I made myself cry by being so horrible to you.'

'Oh man, Cat, that's not what I want to hear.' Paul lays his board on the sand and wraps his arms around me, my face against his chest, the rubber arms of his wetsuit against my bare knees. I breathe the faint coconut of his sunscreen. 'I hate that you cried. I never want to make you cry. Never in a million years.'

'Your abs could make me cry right now,' I say. 'You're like every teenage girl's summer dream come to life. I mean, look at you.'

Paul sits and runs his hand over his head. 'Listen, I think we need to talk.' He sits and pats the sand beside him. 'You keep going on with this walking god bull but honestly it makes me really, I dunno, uncomfortable.'

'What, like you don't know that you're hot?' I slump beside him.

'That's what I mean – when you say stuff like that. It's like when you told your friend that we're having a fling. I don't know how to explain it, but I feel like a piece of meat, like that's all I mean to you, and that's all I have to offer someone like you.'

'Someone like me?'

'This is why I get all up in my head. Of course, I'm happy you're into me. You're beautiful but you're so much more than that, you got me?' He traces the outline of my jaw, then taps me on the temple. 'I want you to see me the same way but if I really think about it, I'm pretty much shit-scared that you won't. That's *my* inner bitch, that's what you called it, yeah? Mine loves reminding me that one day, years from now, you'll be a doctor, or a lawyer, and you'll be telling your friends about the summer you had slumming it with a dumb arse tradie.'

'Slumming it? That's a horrible thing to say.' I bring my knees up to my chest and my feet sink into the sand. 'It's not even close to true, and anyway, did you forget that my dad is a dumb arse tradie? Is my mum slumming it? What do you think that says about my life, my family?'

'I'm stuffing this up,' he says, 'just for a change. I don't mean slumming it, of course that's not what I mean. All I'm saying is, Cat, this summer? Being with you?' He breathes deeply, his eyes on the horizon. 'You're the best thing that's ever happened to me.' He grins and shrugs. 'That's it.'

'That's it?'

'Yep, that's it.' He folds his arms across his knees, gripping each elbow. 'I'm about to choke on all this vulnerability bullshit, so enough with the D and Ms. Time for me to go back to being the strong and silent type. Whatcha got there?' He bites his lip and nods at my hand. In my shock, and utter humiliation in essentially objectifying Paul I'd completely forgotten the stash I'd been collecting.

I open my palm and reveal half a dozen shells, different sizes and shapes. There are shell fragments there too, crushed, and some tiny pieces of aquamarine sea glass. He picks through them and separates two, laying them on his board. 'Perfect,' he says. 'Wait here.'

He jogs down the beach to a fisher, talks briefly to him before they crouch down to peer into a tackle box.

'Thanks, mate,' he calls out as he returns to me. He brandishes fishing line, his eyes shining. He threads a shell onto a piece of line, then the other.

'Which one?' he asks and ties it around my neck, kissing the top of my spine. 'My turn,' he says, and I do the same to him. It sits at the hollow of his throat, and as he touches it, the knot unravels, the shell slips down his chest and lands in the folds of his wetsuit, the fishing line curling.

'Sorry! I'm really bad at knots.'

'That's a relief,' he says. 'I was thinking it might be symbolic, but much better that you can't knot a fishing line. Here, you take care of mine until we sort it out.' He ties it around my neck and the shells nestle against my chest.

'Thank you.' I brush my fingers over them.

'Don't get too attached; I want mine back.' He stands and lifts his board. 'We good?'

'We're good.' I'm beaming, my face feels as lit up as the summer sky above me. Not for the first time, I'm eternally grateful that my braces came off before I started constantly grinning to the point that my cheeks ache.

'I'll come around later?'

'I'll be the one wearing two shells.'

'I'll be the one asking your old man to knot a shell around my neck. That won't be awkward, at all.'

32

'UGH, Tommy, can you just stop?' I put my hand over my brother's to still it. He's been playing the drums with his cutlery against the table for the past two songs and the incessant sound sets my teeth on edge.

'He's all right,' Dad says.

'He's not all right, he's embarrassing,' I say. 'We're in public. Would it kill him to act like a human and not a cartoon character?'

'Calm down, Cat.' Mum hands some cash to Matty. 'Go buy a lemonade for you and for Tommy and get some coins for the games. Two games each, right? I expect change.'

I twirl the glass of sparkling water in my hand. 'This is crap, you know. The law says I'm allowed to drink here under your supervision.'

'I don't think that's accurate,' says Dad, 'and even if it were, maybe I don't want my 17-year-old daughter as my drinking buddy at my local.' He gets up and moves to the bar to chat with some randoms he'll be best friends with before the hour is up.

'Did you see the new family staying next door?' says Mum.

'I saw the cute dog, but I heard a screaming baby at five this morning. Adorable. How long are they down for?'

'Just the weekend. There's three generations in that one house. That'll stop being fun really soon. That poor mother had the "kill me now" look in her eyes. Nothing worse than an unsettled baby when you're away from home.'

'Nothing worse than a baby full stop; they just turn into annoying little people,' I say. 'Look at Exhibit A there. So embarrassing.' Tommy's standing in front of the band setting up, still playing air drums.

'You know what I love best about Tommy's age?' Mum says. 'His complete lack of care factor. You could learn something from him, Cat. Here's a secret for you: everyone's too busy with their own stuff to worry about yours.'

'Whatever. Are you guys going home soon?'

'No, I think we'll stay, hang around, watch the band. I haven't danced in ages.'

'What? You can't!' I splutter water through my nose as Mum cracks up laughing.

'Your face!' She clutches her chest, her head thrown back.

'What's so funny?' Paul leans down and kisses my cheek.

'Nothing. Please excuse my mother; she's too far gone.'

'How was dinner?' he says.

'Let's just say I've had my hot chip quota for the whole year.'

'*Pho*-shame?'

'That's *pho*-real.'

'Yet I'm the one that's too far gone,' Mum says. 'None of what you kids say makes any sense. Pity you couldn't join us, Paul. We owe you dinner. If it weren't for you, Mick would still be crawling in and out through the manhole.'

'You owe me nothing, you know it's what you guys pay me for, right? It's looking sweet now, isn't it? You happy with where things are at, Angela?'

'You've done a beautiful job, the two of you. Mick can't believe how much you've done; he's saying he's months ahead. He never would have been able to get all this done on his own with his team on holidays.'

'Yeah, not much more, and your mother will be ready to move right in.'

'Shhh!' Mum and I say at once.

'Don't say that out loud!' I put my hand over his mouth. 'You want to jinx us?'

'So, not much more, and you'll have your husband back to yourself. How's that?'

'That's an even scarier thought,' says Mum. 'Mick has no concept of relaxing. If he's not fishing, he's pottering, and if he can't find something to do, he badgers us to entertain him.'

'You can't keep a good man down, hey?' says Paul.

'That's what they say,' says Mum.

'Who's they and what do they say?' says Dad. 'Hey mate, how are you? Haven't seen you for ages.' He shakes Paul's hand. 'What's it been, two hours? You all right? Having withdrawals?'

'Hilarious, Dad.' I roll my eyes.

'We were talking about the renovation, Mick,' says Mum. 'What's left?'

'Just all the plumbing, and then we can hang the sheets.'

'That's right, let me grab Cavey.' Paul gestures behind him. I turn, and there's the Neanderthals leaning against the far end of the bar. Cavey raises his beer in hello, then crosses the pub.

'Hey, Cat,' he says to me before Paul introduces him to my parents. 'How you going?'

'We're going good.' Dad shakes his hand. 'I hear you're a plasterer.'

'Have a seat,' says Mum.

'Aren't you guys going now?' I round my eyes at Mum.

'Calm down, cowgirl,' says Dad, 'Cavey, is it? What were you saying?' *Ugh.* They launch into construction chit chat as tables are cleared all around us and more and more people pour into the pub.

'Mum…' The house lights turn down leaving the pub in a hazy darkness, the remnants of the sunset filtering through the windows facing the beach, the coastal bush absorbing the twilight.

'We're going, we're going.' Mum rises from her seat. 'Mick, you ready? Boys, time to go.'

'What about Cat?' whines Tommy. 'How come she gets to stay?'

'I swear to God…' I mutter.

'Cat. Do not walk yourself home, you hear me?' Dad stares directly at Paul.

'I've got her,' says Paul.

'Make sure you do,' Dad says, 'and have her home by midnight.'

'What am I, a pumpkin?'

'Mick, don't start,' says Mum. 'One thirty, guys. Cat, come here.' She pulls me aside and in Italian tells me to keep myself nice.

'What's that supposed to mean?'

'No more than one drink. You're still underage, remember? And any sign of fighting just leave. There's far too much testosterone floating around. Especially this one. It's coming off him in waves.' She tilts her eyes towards Cavey. 'He's a walking ad for toxic masculinity.'

My parents usher my brothers out the door and leave with a final wave as Ant walks in.

'Hey, Cat! Paulie, Cavey. How's it going?' He sidles up to the table to stand next to me.

'Babe, I'm grabbing a beer. You want one?' says Paul.

'God, yes. Thank you.'

'Cavey? Scampo?'

'Yeah, thanks, mate,' says Cavey.

'Jump up, Cat,' says Ant.

Two guys approach our table. They're dressed in the pub uniform of black jeans and polo shirts with the pub's logo. Neither are locals, or none that I recognise anyway. I realise our table's the last one standing in the whole pub.

'I'm so sorry,' I say.

'All good, little surfer girl.' One winks at me, staring just a little too long as he carries the table out the back door.

'Look at you, making friends everywhere you go,' says Ant.

'Very funny,' I say, 'and offensive.'

'Offensive? Because he called you a little surfer girl?' says Cavey. 'Complimenting a chick is offensive?'

'Offensive because it's belittling, and offensive because am I really giving off surfer vibes? God help me. I'm spending too much time with you guys.' They return to collect the chairs, stacking them on a weirdly shaped trolley which needs the two guys to steer it through the door of the pub.

'That seems a bit excessive,' I say, 'too bad if we wanted to sit.'

'Better than having a chair thrown through the window like last summer,' Ant says.

'Yeah, I'd forgotten about that. What's with you guys and fighting?'

'Hey, nothing to do with me, *bella*, I'm a lover, not a fighter.'

'Yeah, yeah.' I laugh.

'Hey, JB tells me you're going for medicine?' he asks.

'That, or law. I still can't decide and it's freaking me out.'

'You'll be right. When are you catching up with him?'

'Probably when school goes back, which totally sucks. I haven't seen any of my friends since school finished. Online just doesn't cut it.'

'That's nice. Hear that, Cavey? We're not Cat's friends.'

'You know what I mean. School friends. Got my back no matter what friends.' His face drops and I lightly punch his arm. 'Someone who's been there for the long-haul, that's all I mean.'

'That's slightly better, but I'll take it. You're not friends with any of the locals?'

'Have you seen the friendship opportunities around here? I don't think so.'

'One of your friendship opportunities is having a crack at your boyfriend,' says Cavey.

I turn to look behind me, and there's Isabel Dillon leaning against the bar, standing right next to Paul, licking her lips and grinning in his face like the freakin' Cheshire Cat. He moves away to speak to the bartender.

'Case in point,' I shrug.

'There's nothing for you to worry about there, Cat,' says Ant.

'I'm not blind; I know she has a thing for him. But I also know he has a thing for me, so I think I'm good.'

'Paulie's into you so bad. Mate, we've never seen him so into a chick like he's into you.'

'*Che bello, Antonio.* You really should be a poet.'

'*Mannaggia*, I'm serious!' he laughs. 'Hey Cavey? Am I right or am I right?'

'Must be. I've barely laid eyes on my best mate all summer.'

My shoulders descend as Paul weaves through the crowd back to my side.

'Here you go, Cat.' He cracks open a beer and hands it to me.

'Good timing, mate.' Cavey takes a long swig of his beer. 'One of the uni try-hards working here just had a crack at your girlfriend.'

'What? Which one?' His eyes traverse the room.

'Nothing happened,' I say as the band starts.

Paul stands behind me, his hand on my hip as we move in time. A familiar guitar riff starts.

'Oh my God,' I shriek. 'It's my favourite! Let's dance!'

'I'm going to need a few more of these.' Paul tips his beer at me.

'Ant, you're up.' I reach to pull him onto the dance floor.

'Woah, Italians don't dance, you know that.' His hands rise in mock surrender.

'Are you kidding me? That's all we do!'

'Not this Italian.'

'Cavey, you in?'

'Yeah, good luck with that.' Cavey takes another slug of his beer, looking anywhere but at me.

'Paul? Seriously? I'm dancing on my own?' I thrust my beer into his hand and move through the throng of people, pushing when I need to until I reach the front of the stage. I jump and bounce and sing and toss my hair and it's hot, sweaty, loud and fun. It's so much fun that it feels almost impossible that I'm surrounded by strangers. The band gets to the chorus and my fist is in the air; I'm singing along with the lead singer who is grinning at me, and I'm grinning at him, and despite my half a glug of beer I feel borderline drunk. As the song ends, the lead singer leans out across his guitar, across his amp and over the stage and high fives me. The drums crash, the bass thuds through the floor and a new song starts. A hand grips mine.

'Can't let you have all the fun, babe,' Paul says.

We're dancing, hands entwined in the air, he twirls me and spins me then as the song changes, he pulls me close. He sings, his voice low in my ear, and it's all I can hear. *Never dare dreamed, ever me, ever you, ever more, your heart my core, my dream come true, my dream come true.'*

'You're the dream.' My stomach flutters. I grip the back of his head and find myself on the very tips of my toes kissing him. A hand taps my shoulder.

'Okay, lovebirds, that's enough,' says a deep voice.

I turn, ready to slap the living shit out of whoever has dared rain on this ridiculously sexy parade and I'm staring into the black-shirted chest of a security bouncer. 'ID?'

'I left it at home,' I say, 'I'm a local, the owner knows me, I'm all good.' I turn back to Paul, but the bouncer moves between us.

'If you can't show me ID you'll have to leave,' he says, his hands on his hips, the sheer width of him blocking out the band above us.

'Come on, mate, she's a local,' says Paul.

'I don't care if she's from Mars,' says the bouncer. 'Out you go. Don't make me ask you again.' His face repeats the sentiment in no uncertain terms.

'This is bullshit, rent-a-cop,' Paul says.

'Don't worry about it.' I push my way through the crowd, trailed by my new burly best mate, face aflame. Standing right next to the door is Isabel Scuzzbucket Dillon.

'Bye, Kitty Cat.' She throws back a shot and whoops. 'How embarrassing for you. I wonder how they knew you were underage?'

'And you're not?' I hiss.

'Not according to my ID,' she giggles and turns her attention to Paul, her hand on his chest. 'Paulie, let's get smashed.'

'Mate, not enough alcohol in the world.' He follows me out the door. 'Eff you very much, rent-a-cop.'

The bouncer crosses his arms and smirks.

'You have a good night, kids.' He stands sentry at the pub door as the Neanderthals come pouring out.

'What's happening?' says Cavey.

'We're kicked out,' says Paul.

'Technically I was kicked out,' I say, 'not you. You can go back in.'

'Not without you,' he says.

'What happened?' says Ant.

'Remember my friendship opportunity? She freakin' told Mr Security here that I'm underage.'

'Hey mate, come on, we're locals,' Ant says to the bouncer. 'Give us a break, will you? Let her back in.'

The bouncer stares impassively back at Ant, then talks into his walkie talkie. Bouncers seem to materialise from the walls as four come to stand beside him.

'Is there a problem here?' one says.

'Not if you let him back in,' says Cavey, his shoulders back.

'He can stay; she can't.'

'It's not enough that you come here from wherever the fuck you came from and take all our jobs? You think you can tell us who can go to our own pub?' Cavey passes his empty beer glass between his hands. 'Just fucking let them in.'

'That's not going to happen, mate.'

'I'm not your *mate*, mate.'

'Come here, Cat.' Paul takes my hand and pulls me behind him, his voice low. I shake him off and move between Cavey and the bouncer.

'Enough! I'm leaving, don't worry about it.'

Ant grabs Cavey's arm. 'Don't worry, mate, let's just go have a good time. Cat, you're all good?'

'I'm fine, go back inside.' I take a few steps away from the entrance and grab my phone from my pocket to check the time. Ugh, it hasn't even been an hour since my family left.

'You're not going too?' Cavey's got his hand on Paul's chest, blocking him from following me. 'We were gonna have a few.'

The bouncers haven't shifted position. I walk towards the beach, flustered, my mind racing, my hands jittery. I shake them, and startle as a car drives past, its wheels flicking up the stones on the side of the road. I didn't even hear its engine over the thumping of my pulse in my head. Paul catches up to me and slings his arm around my shoulder.

'You don't want to go home?' he says. 'That was a bit shit, wasn't it?'

'No way,' I say, 'I need to calm down, I'm so angry. Isabel's hated me forever, but I don't know why she'd go out of her way to do that to me. Ugh. I was having the best time.'

'Me too, never thought you'd get me dancing on half a beer.'

'That was the best,' I say. 'I am so sorry. You sure you don't want to go hang with your friends? Watch the band?'

'No way times infinity. We can see them anytime.'

We walk along the foreshore, the music almost taunting us.

'Have you ever been to San Francisco?' Paul asks.

'Um, that would be a no,' I say. I'm already counting down the days to move to the city, so the thought of being anywhere other that Batter's Cove entices. 'I've always wanted to. Almost every movie I love is set there. There or New York. Have you?'

'Yep. This reminds me of it.'

'Yes, Batter's Cove must take you straight back to the memories of those San Francisco streets.'

'I did all this tourist stuff, you know, rode a bike over the Golden Gate Bridge, went to Alcatraz. It was such a cool place to see.' He tells me about a tour led by an ex-prisoner, that on New Year's Eve the sea breeze carried the sounds of music and laughter and celebration, and it was an extra layer of torment for the prisoners, being so aware of the joy they were missing.

'I'm so sorry, you should be in the pub,' I say.

'That's not what I'm saying, Cat. There's nowhere I'd rather be,' he says.

'What about Cavey?'

'What about him?'

'About him telling you to stay? Telling the bouncers to let you back in? And what's with him being such a racist?' The sky is almost mauve above us in the twilight, the path ahead dark. I stop to kick off my sandals, my hand on Paul's bicep for balance. I scrunch my toes into the gravel of the path. It's almost soothing the way it scratches.

'Yeah, that was weird, all of it. As if I'd rather hang out in the pub. Actually, I'd rather be back on the North Shore of Hawaii, but I'd want you there too.'

Two kids run along the path towards us, trailing sparklers and screaming, two women following them. One gives Paul a slow look up and down and smiles at me.

'Enjoy,' she says as they pass. They both barely conceal their smirks.

'Thanks?' I say haltingly.

'You're home early,' says Mum as we open the sliding door.

'We're going to watch music videos. Is that okay?'

'Of course, just keep it down.' Mum kisses me goodnight. 'Not too late, please Paul.'

Mum's footsteps recede downstairs and her bedroom door closes. I pull my doona and pillows off my bed. I turn off all the lights, and we lie on the floor in the television's glow. I'm a human blanket sprawled across Paul, my cheek on his chest, his chin resting on my head, my doona over us, his hand on the bare skin of my hip, my fingers tracing his biceps. He smells so good, and I have it on good authority that tomorrow, and the next day and the next day I'll be hugging my pillow to my face, breathing him in.

'Find that song,' I say, 'the dream come true one, the one you sang to me when we were dancing.'

His chest and shoulder move against my face as he works the remote.

'You like it? That's now officially our song.'

'I love it.'

The song floats over and around us, his fingers grip my hair, pulling my mouth up to his.

33

'I LOVE it here.' I look up at Paul through my eyelashes, my head resting on my forearms. We're lying on a giant beach towel in a sand dune crater. The sand is soft, and the wind whistles high above us. The king tide woke me before sunrise, as if the waves were belting into the house, yet here, cocooned in the dune's protection, the waves barely make a murmur. It's hard to believe that if I stood, I'd either be blown out to sea or would die of frostbite, whichever came first. Paul's lying on his side next to me, the stem and frond of a bunny tail in his teeth. We're surrounded by them, our hollow oasis amongst plumes upon plumes of bunny tails that wave in the wind. He's threaded some through my hair, and he's using another to draw on my back, bare except for my bikini, willowy bristles as soft as cotton wool. 'You make me want to purr. What are you drawing?'

'Nothing,' he says. 'I'm writing.'

'What are you writing?'

'You can't read?' The bunny tail dances across my skin, so light I can barely feel it.

'Yeah, sorry, you're going to have to spell it out for me.'

'First word, five letters.' The frond moves across my back. 'D. R. E. A.' he says, 'M.'

'Dream.' My eyes close, the sun toasting my eyelids.

'Second word, four letters. C. O. M. E.'

'Come.'

'You've got it. Third word, four letters. T. R. U. E.'

'Dream come true,' I say. And yes, he is. I never want this summer to end, these slow moments. Once school goes back, when

180

Year Twelve starts, what then?

'Never dare dreamed, ever me, ever you, ever more, your heart my core, my dream come true, my dream come true.' He whispers the lyrics into my neck, his breath below my ear, his hand on my lower back, his fingers slipping under my waistband. How is it possible that my skin hasn't turned to butter?

The blossom brushes against the top of my spine.

'Still writing?' I want to grind my hips into the sand beneath me.

'Yep.'

'Let me guess again?'

'Nope, not this time.'

'Why not?'

'It's a secret message,' he says. 'If I tell you I'll have to kill you.'

'Right now, you're killing me anyway. How secret is secret?'

'Not secret at all. It's really pretty freakin' obvious. Let's see if you can figure it out. First word. One letter. You ready?'

He trails a long line down my spine.

'I or l?'

'Since when is "l" a word?'

'Okay, I, first word is I. Right?'

'Right,' he says. 'Second word. Four letters.'

Another long shiver moves down my spine, followed by a wide, slow circumference of my back. Next, he moves from my left shoulder to my sacrum and back up to my right shoulder.

'L.O.V.'

'I'm not done yet.' He moves the bunny tail across my back from side to side. The breath leaves my chest. 'Did you get that last letter?'

I roll over and reach for his face, but he leans back.

'So, we have first word I, second word is brought to you by the letters L, O, V, and?' he says.

'Is it maybe E?' I can barely get the words out.

'Exactly. Last word. Three letters.' The frond moves across my chest and down my stomach. He could be writing the magnum carta for all I know; every nerve across my body feels alight. He looks up from my chest, and his eyes feel like they're seeing all the way through me, through the sand dune and into the Earth's core. His leg crosses mine, the hair of his calves electrified against my ankles. My pulse hammers in my ears and I lick my lips, tasting the sea mist, a grain of sand under my tongue. 'You get that?'

'You love me?'

'I love you,' he says.

Bunny tail forgotten, he's kissing me, and I never want him to stop.

34

'I KNOW I'm going to regret this but if I tell you something do you promise not to laugh?' Paul's piggybacking me to the beach, his arms tucked through my bare legs.

'Not after that,' I say, 'I promise nothing. Give it to me, Lightwood.'

'Oh, so we're going by surnames now, are we? Good to know, Kelty.'

'Stop stalling.'

'Picture this, Year Eleven English and we have to write a poem. I wrote about this walk, from the car park to the beach.'

'Why would I laugh? I love that.'

'I wrote it completely off my head and I got the best mark I'd ever had.'

'I have to read it.'

'No way would I let you read my high distinction Year Eleven poem.'

'Wait, high distinction and you were on something?' I mock-smack his shoulder. 'That's so unfair. Some of us have to work for high distinctions. Maybe I should just take drugs?'

'Don't even think about it.' He hitches me up higher on his back and I lean my head down to breathe in that incredible space between his shoulder and his neck. 'I'm pretty sure the teacher was on something. Want to hear something funny?'

'Uh huh.' I'm distracted. Maybe he could carry me around like this forever, his back hard against my chest.

'She was my English teacher but also the careers teacher, right?

She wanted me to go to uni open days and when I said that wasn't going to happen, she was really pissed off. She tried to make an appointment with Mum and Dad and everything, but you heard Dad.' He drops his voice to mimic his father. '*'No point wasting money on tradies.'* She thought if I put my head down, I could have had a crack. Can you believe that? Me at Uni?' He laughs.

'Of course I can believe that, but why didn't you? I mean your actual teacher was telling you to go for it. What did your mum think?'

'She wasn't keen either.'

'Why not?' I'm incredulous. I can't even imagine turning my back on a ticket out of here.

'She wanted me here.' We reach the top of the dunes where the Neanderthals have gathered. The beach lays out below us, the sun starting its slow drop into night.

'Hello, lovers.' Tom passes Paul a couple of beers. He flips the lids off both, handing me one, pocketing the caps.

Clouds hover, the horizon a luminous thread between the sky and the sea. There are some people surfing the last waves of the day and a trio of teenage girls swim in the shore break, fighting the rip. Their laughter hits me almost physically; I hug my arms. I mean, some of these guys are all right, funny even, but they're not Sal, Em or JB. They're still the Neanderthals, maybe not *complete* Neanderthals, but except for Ant, they're Paul's friends, not mine. Cavey pretty much confirmed that at the pub with the bouncers. I'm just a Yoko to them, and that's fine. I'll have my real friends back as soon as summer's over, but in the meantime I'll have to make an effort. If Paul didn't get on with my friends I don't know what I'd do, how I'd feel. Devastated comes to mind, but it's not even remotely possible to compare my friends to his.

The Neanderthals' aura of confidence that borders on belligerence, their weird combination of aggressiveness and simplicity in the way they live their lives does my head in. It's so perplexing. They're either picking fights with anyone and everyone or they embody a hippy, woo-woo platitude that you'd see on a sticker or a t-shirt. They are completely different to any other group of people I know. All the times I've listened to their nonsensical conversations I've never heard one of them say, 'Man, if I don't get into industrial pharmacology, I don't know what I'll do. Maybe engineering will have to do?'

It's like the future means nothing to them, but sometimes it's kind of refreshing to hang around people not completely preoccupied with what's coming next. This morning, after weeks of getting the timing wrong and missing each other, the stars aligned and I managed to talk to Em in London, and even on the other side of the world she's ahead of me in the Year Twelve prep stakes.

I take a swig of beer and grimace. 'You want?' I say to Paul. I twist it to stand upright in the sand between us.

'Want something else? Tommo, what else you got?'

'No, thanks, I'm all good.' I stretch his hoodie out over my knees, my arms crossed over my shins, my stomach cramping. *Great.* Not that it's a surprise; Em told me she had the angry pixies visiting her in London. Seems that even with all this distance between us we're still in cycle. Sal must be suffering too. I wonder if Charlotte is, given she and Sal have been together night and day. It was Sal that came up with angry pixies to describe our shared time of the month, saying cramps are like nasty little angry pixies using a blunt, rusty machete to hack their way out of her uterus. The way I'm feeling right now I can almost hear the angry pixies' high-pitched evil giggling.

Ant drops to the sand beside me, groaning.

'What's up with you, Scampo?' one of the guys asks him.

'Man, I am so sore. 10K run for preseason footy. I'm too old for this crap.'

'Mate, you're only as old as the girl you feel,' says Cavey. 'That makes me around about sixteen, fingers crossed.'

I flinch, the lingering taste of the beer sour in my mouth.

'Mate,' admonishes Paul, his hand stroking the back of my neck. I shift and pull my legs out from the hoodie, crossing them at my ankles, and turn towards Ant.

'Did you see JB? How is he?'

'He smashed it,' says Ant. 'Man, he's fit. He's training every day. I couldn't catch him. None of us could.'

'No way? That's so good.' I don't add that he's training hard just to get away from his father; it's not my story to tell. Anyway, if JB's town is anything like Batter's Cove, it'd be no secret what his dad is like. I'll never forget the mortification of that time on camp when we were talking about our parents fighting, and I realised that my definition of fighting and JB's were on two different planets. 'He said he was running, but ten kilometres? Amazing.'

'Yeah, he said he spoke to you. Cat, he made it look easy.'

'Great, just one more way for him to show me up this year,' I shake my head. 'He's such an overachiever.'

'Funny, he said the same thing about you.'

'Bull.'

'*Dici sul serio!*'

'*Non riesco proprio a crederci.*'

'Would I lie? He's your number one fan.'

'Actually, that would be me,' says Paul, his hand on my knee.

Music fills the dune, pumping through a speaker, the bass line deep. The girls who were swimming walk up the dunes, wrapped in beach towels, holding their clothes.

'Mind if we hang?'

'Go for it, ladies.' Tom flips the lid of his esky. 'Beer?'

One comes to sit opposite me. 'I feel like I know you from somewhere,' she says, 'where do you go?'

I tell her and she snaps her fingers. 'That's it! You did that *King Lear* workshop in the city last holidays, didn't you?'

'Yes! Were you there?'

'I was, Mel and I both were.' She turns to her tall blonde friend who is grabbing them a beer. 'Mel, come over here! I'm Jay, by the way.'

'Cat,' I shake her outstretched hand. 'So, you're going into Year Twelve, yeah? How's your holiday homework going?'

The three of us compare subjects and holiday homework, finding the overlaps, grimacing in solidarity at the workload expectations, exclaiming at the serendipity of discovering we're all aiming for the same university, if not the same courses. Next year, I could feasibly be having lunch with these girls hundreds of kilometres away from this sand dune, and I grin at the thought.

'Hey guys, can you turn it down a bit?' An older guy, a tourist, crosses the dune. 'We're here for some serenity, not a nightclub.'

'Are you kidding?' says Cavey. 'Mate, you want serenity? What if I knock you out? That enough serenity for you?'

Ugh, here we go. Jay's head swivels from Cavey to the other guy before looking at Mel, eyes wide. I shuffle back a bit closer to Paul and put my hands on the tops of his thighs, palms flat.

'Look, mate,' the tourist says, 'I don't want any trouble, I'm just trying to watch the sunset with my friends.'

'If you don't want trouble, then pack up your shit and go find somewhere else to watch the sunset. This is our beach. Fucking terrorists.'

'Terrorists?' Jay mouths at me.

'It's what the locals call tourists,' I explain.

'Aren't you a local?' she asks.

'Only technically from a geographic perspective, and only for another year, thank freakin' God.' I explain the great divide between me and the rest of the general population.

'Is it like a money thing?'

'It's more like a dickhead thing. My dad's a tradie too, but he's nothing like them, so it's a bit weird.'

'Wow, sounds Shakespearean,' she says, 'so what, are you and your hot boyfriend like living, breathing Capulets and Montagues?'

'Not quite. He's nothing like them either. Anyway, how long are you down for?'

'We're heading back tomorrow,' says Mel, and gets out her phone. 'You have to give us your details so we can catch up when you move.'

'Tomorrow? Bummer! And I'd love that. I was just thinking I was so jealous of you girls hanging out, I miss my friends so, so much. And this is the first intelligent conversation I've had in weeks.'

'Sorry, what?' says Paul, and tickles my ribs. 'The dumb arse tradie not intelligent enough for you?'

'You know that's not what I mean,' I say, 'but you're really bad at girl talk. Like *really* bad.' I smile at Jay. 'Devo you're leaving tomorrow.'

'It's just enough time to check out the hot surfer boys.' She giggles. 'Come on, give me all the intel. Which should we go for? Who should we avoid at all costs? Please tell me they're not one and the same.'

'It depends. Are you into misogynistic racists?'

'Hard pass. Don't think I haven't noticed that you nabbed the number one. Lucky girl.'

'Tell me about it,' I say. 'I keep thinking I'm going to wake up and the hottest of the hot has just been a dream.'

'Awww… that is so, so sweet! I wouldn't be letting him out of my sight. Especially the way that one's looking at him.' She nods her head across the group. Isabel Scuzzbucket Dillon is shooting daggers at me while curled up in Cavey's lap like a cat, her arms up around his neck. 'Even though it looks like she's already landed herself a surfer. Some people are just greedy.'

'Man, she wishes,' I say. 'I think I'm safe.' Paul's grip tightens on my knee.

35

'EWW, Cat, look at this!' Tommy's flipped a giant piece of seaweed and even from my viewpoint at the base of the dunes I can see the flicker of movement as thousands of sand fleas jump, leap and tumble, their hideous little opaque bodies reflecting the sea and the sand.

'What is it?' I yell.

'Come look!'

I get to my feet and pick up the bag of rubbish we've collected. Tommy's found the partially decomposed remains of a fish in a jumble of fishing line. An eyeless cavity is filled with dirty sand. The smell is enough to turn my stomach. 'Man, fishers are pigs,' I say. 'They just leave their crap everywhere.'

'What are we going to do?'

'We can't leave the fishing line,' I say. 'What if a dolphin or a whale or something gets caught up in it? We'll just have to grab the whole lot. Give me your rubbish bag.' I turn his bag inside out, gripping the base of it, my hand encased in plastic. I try not to gag as I reach out, my mouth clamped shut, my eyes watering, and grasp the fish. Something gives under my fingers, and I scream and drop it, disturbing the sand fleas who resume their disco. 'Ew, ew, ew!' I yell, jumping from one foot to the other. I take a deep breath, lift the fish and quickly pull my hand back through the bag, trapping it in a parcel of grossness. I knot the bag and drop it into mine, knotting that too. I toss it up on the beach. 'We'll grab it on the way home,' I say, then use the sand to scrub my hands like I've never scrubbed them before.

'Hey look – here comes Dad,' says Tommy.

Dad's walking up the beach, his fishing rod resting on his

shoulder, tackle box swinging in one hand, a bucket in the other.

'Good. He can take the bag of rubbish,' I say. 'Go grab it, Tommy.'

'Eww, no, you do it.'

'I picked up a dead fish. Don't even think about it.'

He runs up the beach, scoops up the bag, holding it with his arm fully extended, his head turned away.

'What makes you think I want it?' says Dad as he approaches.

'Sorry, Dad,' I say. 'You fish; this line could have been yours, tangling and trapping some poor creature minding its own business out in the ocean.'

'It's not my line,' says Dad, but he lets Tommy drop the rubbish into his fish bucket. We all pull a face at the resurrected smell.

Our shadows are long ahead of us, the late afternoon sun reflects off the water and the sand is hot underfoot. We reach Dad's spot, and he and Tommy climb the outcrop that extends out into the ocean. A wave curls, and I recognise the flash of blue that is Paul's surfboard. Tommy calls out, and Paul waves. Bobbing out the back amongst the pack is Matty.

'Did you know your son was out here?' I say. 'When did this happen?'

'We finished up early.' Dad kneels on the rock to thread his line through a hook. 'And before you have a go at Matty, Paul offered. I didn't know they were surfing here, though. That's just good luck, my Dirty Three all together!'

I walk across the rocks to where a natural gorge has formed, a channel of ocean water crashing through the rocks. I carefully lower myself down and sit with my back against the rocks, my feet in the ocean. There's a perfectly heart-shaped hole in the rock formation above me, framing the sky's incredible shade of blue, deeper than what could ever seem possible. The surfers crest their waves, and as Paul stands, he fills the heart. *How freakin' symbolic.*

I'm surrounded by rock pools, and I turn onto my stomach to peer down into one, my chin resting on my forearms, the rock beneath me as warm as an electric blanket. A world lies beneath me, a city of shells. There's the faintest ripple as my fingers twist and turn, choosing then discarding them. Buried beneath the shells is a perfect piece of sea glass. *Boom!* I jump up to show Tommy and as I step across a rock pool a boulder teeters under my foot, throwing me sideways and down the rock face across the mollusks. Three deep grooves in my thigh fill with blood; it runs down my calf onto the rocks and into the water. The heel of my hand is a swamp of blood too. My hip thumps as I push my hair back out of my face. I turn onto all fours, my sea glass gone, then slowly get up and limp to Dad.

'What the hell?' Dad visibly pales and Tommy bursts into tears.

'I slipped on the freakin' rocks.'

'Can you see? Are you dizzy? Here, sit down.' Dad guides me onto the rocks.

'Look at my leg.'

'That's just a scratch,' Dad says, 'it's nasty, but once you rinse it out, you'll be fine. I'm more worried about your head.'

'Why? What's wrong with my head?'

'Paul, Paul, come quick!' Tommy shouts, 'Cat's hurt!'

'Are you kidding?' I hiss. 'Stop yelling!'

Paul's suddenly standing over me, dripping with sea water, his shadow blocking out the sun.

'Babe, you okay?' Paul's fingers are against my hairline, probing and parting my hair.

'Cat, how many fingers am I holding up?' Dad's waving his hand in my face.

'Paul! Dad, stop it!' I push their hands away. 'I'm fine, I slipped. No big deal.'

'Your face is covered in blood.' Paul resumes his search over my head. 'It's coming from somewhere.'

'Stop!' I rear back. 'I didn't hit my head, just my leg. And my hand is hurting like a mofo.' I turn it towards the sun, and warm blood runs down my wrist.

'Okay, you're swearing, so you must be fine,' says Dad. 'Go clean yourself up; get the shells out of your skin. Tommy, Paul, give her a hand, will you?'

'I'm not a baby; I don't need rescuing.' I stand and as I put my weight through my hip the pain hits me. I buckle, and Paul puts his arm around my waist, holding me steady. I'm wincing, grimacing and covered with cold sweat. I swear I can feel the hair at the back of my neck curling, prickling my scalp.

'Just relax,' Paul says and lifts me into his arms. I balk at the red I have painted across his chest.

'Don't you drop her,' Dad calls out.

'Never,' Paul returns over his shoulder, 'I'm treating her like she's toxic waste.'

'That's beautiful,' I say, 'but it's pretty much true. Your wetsuit's covered in my blood.'

'You say that like it's a bad thing,' he says, then frowns. 'Yeah, okay, that's weird, you don't have to tell me.'

'And more than borderline creepy.'

'Can you stand now?'

I stand in the shallows and scoop the water over my leg. I grit my teeth, the salt stinging, the shell fragments sharp under my hand.

'Let's go in a bit more,' says Paul.

'Why don't you just give the sharks a written invitation?'

'It will take a bit more blood than this, but you did a good job. Look at your face.'

I take off my glasses to look at my reflection. No wonder Dad flipped out. There's a massive smear of blood across half of my forehead. I lean down and scrub my face in the shallows.

'Can I have a look?' He stands before me, tilting my head in his hands.

'No, I've got it.' I pull back out of reach. 'I told you; I didn't hit my head. It doesn't hurt.'

'Will you just let me see for myself? It's not that deep, Cat.'

'Exactly, I'm fine. I told you. I don't need rescuing.'

'Says the girl who I just carried across the rocks.'

I have no answer to that, so I continue splashing myself with sea water.

'Come on, let me kiss it better,' says Paul.

'My head's fine. It's my left hip that hurts, but you better not kiss that in front of Dad. He might feed you to the sharks.' Already my skin is starting to swell with blues and purples.

'I'm kinda thinking it would be worth it, but point taken,' he says. 'Let's just stick with this invisible head injury. There's a scar in your hairline, did you know that?'

'Yep,' I say. 'When I was three, I tripped over Matty and split my head open on the coffee table. Now *that* bled. We had to throw out the rug. Yet another time Matty's caused me grief over the years. Speak of the devil…'

'Look at him go,' says Paul, 'he's loving it out there.'

'I *hate* him being out there,' I say.

'The boys are taking care of him, he's all good. But if it's really stressing you out, I'll go back out, give him another couple of waves then bring him in?'

'Are you sure?'

'Am I sure that I want my girlfriend watching me be a hero out on the waves? That's a yes!' He kisses me and skims across the surface of the water, the sun bouncing off the white foam.

36

'COME on, Matty, Mum's waiting. Can you move it?'

'Two more lives,' says Matty, his body writhing around the freakin' pinball machine. 'Just go, I don't need you to hang around.'

'Nice try, shithead,' I say. 'I'm not carrying all these bottles by myself. I'll wait outside. Hurry up. We've got to get home before they get there or Mum'll kill us. Thanks, Sadie.' I wave to Sadie and as the door opens, I move quickly to make it through. I bump into Steve, the Neanderthal I punched at the Gap party. 'Excuse me.'

'Stuck-Up Bitch.' He pushes past me, shadowed by a guy only slightly taller than him, but much older. He sneers at me, and like Steve, he has a black tooth right in the middle of his top teeth. He takes his time looking me up and down. I put the shopping bags on the outside table.

A couple of minutes later I hear the door open behind me, the bell jangling. I look over my shoulder, willing my brother to appear, but no.

'Hey, cutie!' Black Tooth stands in front of me. Steve leans against the bonnet of a wreck of a sedan with a smashed-in bumper, his arms crossed, smirking. 'So, you're the firecracker that gave my little cuz a black eye, hey? What are you, Italian? Greek? You're a hot chilli firecracker, hey? I like a firecracker. Want to take me on?'

I turn my back on him and rearrange the bottles in the shopping bags, my stomach churning. I will my face to stay impassive.

'What, the little firecracker doesn't want to talk to me? I hear you're into older guys, I'm not your type?'

'Keep walking.' My voice quavers. I clear my throat.

'Yeah, nah, I think I'll just hang here for a while.' He sits opposite me.

I grab my bags and bang on Sadie's window. Matty jolts, startled, then, without sparing me a glance, gives me the middle finger salute. *Matty, I am going to stab you with a fork, I swear it.* I move to Sadie's doorway but Steve beats me to it. He stands in the doorway, one hand across the door jam.

'You're not so tough without your boyfriend around, are you?' he says.

'And look how tough you are.' I'm shaking and it's taking all my strength not to turn and run. 'Are you going to get out of my way?'

'Make me, Stuck-Up Bitch.'

Sadie catches my eye, and one look at my face sends her from behind the counter.

'Off you trot, fella,' she says to Steve, and he slinks his way to his cousin, still sitting at the table, staring at me.

'Matty, let's go,' I call from the doorway and miracle of miracles, he comes out. As we cut across the spare block, our hands full with bags, I hear the low putt of a motor. Black Tooth drives past, windows down, elbow out, Steve in the passenger seat beside him grinning.

'Where you going, firecracker?' Black Tooth calls. 'I won't bite. Not hard, anyway.'

'Who's that dickhead?' says Matty.

'Some loser friend or cousin or something of that other loser,' I say. 'Just keep walking.' They drive past us, then do a U-turn to drive past again, this time spinning their wheels, black smoke pouring from the tyre rims. They roar off down the street.

'I think they're gone,' says Matty.

'Listen, Matty, when I say, "let's go", I mean it. That a-hole could have done anything and you're in there playing pinball, sticking your freakin' finger up at me.'

'How was I supposed to know that?'

'You weren't, but why didn't you come when I asked you? Oh fuck, here we go again.' The car slows beside us, and Black Tooth leans out the window, banging his hand on his door panel in time to some really bad music blaring from the car.

'Leave my sister alone, dickhead,' Matty yells.

'You going to make me, little man?' He pulls the car over and gets out. 'Why don't you go play soccer with your little mates?'

'Matty, ignore them,' I hush. 'Keep walking, let's just get home.'

'What's your hurry, firecracker?' He blocks the footpath.

I jut my chin and swap the shopping bags to one hand and grab my brother's arm with the other. The handle digs into my palm, cutting off the circulation. I clench and unclench my fist, and mutter to Matty to just keep walking. As I pull him by the arm, Black Tooth shoves Matty and he staggers, dropping the shopping bags. 'Not so mouthy, now, are you, little man?'

'Steve!' I yell. 'I know you're no Einstein but this is next level, even for you. Call off your attack dog or you'll regret it.'

'Calm down, firecracker,' Black Tooth laughs. 'No need for threats. I'll be seeing you around, cutie. Maybe we'll go for pizza. Extra chilli, yeah? Be nice to my little cuz and I'll be nice to your little bro.' He whacks Matty on the back and saunters back to his car. We're sprayed with roadside gravel as the car fishtails down the road.

I turn to Matty and burst into tears. I drop the shopping bags and throw my arms around my brother. 'Why aren't you crying? That was so freakin' scary!'

'I know, right?' Matty hugs me tight. I can feel him trembling. 'I was about to drop the bags and run home to get Dad and Paul, but I didn't want to leave you. Man, they are going to flip out.'

'Let's go,' I say, and we run the rest of the way, the bottles banging against our legs. Paul's at the top of the driveway, crouched over some timber. He looks up when Matty calls out to him, his grin dropping.

'What's wrong?'

'This dickhead kept calling Cat "firecracker" and "cutie" and was trying to pick her up and he was going to bite her and then Sadie told them to nick off but they followed us nearly all the way home and then he shoved me and we dropped the bags and then he did two burnouts and we got hit by gravel and then Cat was crying it was so scary and then…'

Paul's eyes widen. 'Someone pushed you? Bit you? Who?'

'Slow down, Matty,' Dad comes out of the garage, wiping his hands on his pants. 'What happened, Cat?'

'We were at Sadie's getting drinks and we ran into that tool, Steve.' I wrap my arms around Paul's waist and he pulls me into the firmness of his body. Sawdust covers my arms. 'He had this guy with him, his cousin I think, who wouldn't leave us alone. I've never seen him before, so I don't think he's local, just a feral with missing teeth. We're okay, but it was scary, and then when he pushed Matty? I didn't know what to do so I just yelled at Steve to back off and then they left.'

'Who's this Steve?' Dad says to Paul. 'Tradie?'

'No, just a local deadshit from town,' I say.

'That fucking little shit,' Paul mutters.

'Leave it, Paul.' Dad shakes his head. 'They had their fun; they'll be long gone. I mean it, mate. Don't do anything that'll come back to bite you on the arse.'

'It's all good.' Squeezing me against him, Paul kisses my forehead then steps away. He unclips his toolbelt and lays it across the timber. 'It's time I took off though, I've just got a few things to do before your family gets here.'

I put my hand on his arm. 'Please don't do anything; they're just dipshits showing off how tough they are. And you should have seen Steve's face when I told him to back off. He'll be freaking out about you. We're fine now, aren't we, Matty?'

Matty nods and crosses his arms.

'Don't stress, Cat.' Paul kisses my cheek. 'I'll go home, have a shower and I'll be back in time for lunch with your family, okay?'

'You promise?' I wrap my arms around his waist, spinning him so he's on the lower slant of the driveway. We're almost, not quite, eye to eye. 'I need you back here, I told you, I can't deal with the second cousins without you.'

'I've got you, babe,' he says. 'I promise.'

37

'AND this is Paolo, Caterina's *ragazzo*.' Nonna pats the vacant seat between us. 'Paolo, you come sit here with me.' He grins, nodding at my extended family, kisses Nonna on both cheeks, Italian-style, then sits beside us, his eyes bulging.

'You're thinking there's not enough food, aren't you?' I say and he cracks up laughing.

There's barely any tabletop visible; it's covered with platters upon platters of food. There's a plate with a mountain of meatballs, three giant shallow bowls each with a different type of pasta, a platter of seafood shines in a glaze of garlic and lemon with capers and parsley drizzled on top, and there's one overflowing with barbecued pork ribs. A steaming earthen tray of baked eggplants sits in the middle of the table and there's a bowl of marinated mushrooms to its side. Paul takes a sweet pepper from the plate, its skin shiny and blistered black from the barbecue, and plops it in his mouth. There's a garden salad the size of a small pony and bread is piled haphazardly in any available gap.

Each table setting has a pasta bowl atop a dinner plate and Paul wastes no time getting stuck in when Nonna gives him the nod.

'Oh my God,' he says, and as he bites into Nonna's homemade ravioli his eyes almost roll back into his head.

'*Ti piace*? You like?' she says, and he nods enthusiastically. 'This is kind of like our Christmas, really, so we make it special. Although Angela wants all the food out at once; we should do *primi*, *pasta* and then *secondi*, but what are you gonna do?'

'Let's just keep things simple, Mama,' says Mum and I catch Paul's eye. Yeah, like enough food to feed a small nation is simple.

199

Nonna's been cooking for days. She would have gone through kilos upon kilos of flour for all this pasta. Amongst the cacophony of people talking and crockery and cutlery clattering I quietly explain to him everything that's on the table.

'Your timing is perfect,' I whisper. 'Everyone's too busy stuffing their faces to give us a hard time.'

'Food like this? I'll deal with any kind of drilling from your family. But remind me, who is everyone? Are you related to all these people?'

'Are you kidding? This isn't even a fraction of my extended family.' There are eleven extra adults around our table. I point out my mum's cousins, Nonna's sister's children and their husbands, as well as my uncle (my dad's brother) and his wife. My brothers are outside on the balcony on the kids' table with what sounds like four hundred and twenty-two rampaging Huns, the offspring of, well, I'm struggling to recall with any real accuracy.

'I'd tell you who's who, but we'd need a whiteboard and some sticky notes,' I say. 'I know it's full on. Thank you so much for doing this.'

'Babe, it's nothing. I'm happy to meet your family. How good is it that you have such a big family and that they all get along, like even your dad's family coming along with your Mum's side. My family can't even do Christmas Day.'

'I think that's more a case of Mum having excellent time management skills.'

'Man, how much does your dad look like his brother?'

'I know, right? Although, Dad claims to be the good-looking one.'

Paul's smile drops when his gaze lands on Matty. 'You and Matty both looked pretty shaken up. You sure you're okay after this morning?'

I swallow my mouthful of pasta. 'It was full on, especially when he got rough with Matty. And when Steve wouldn't let me into Sadie's and she had to rescue me from a slime ball like that.' I shiver. 'How mortifying. I freakin' hate that I had to be rescued from a nothing loser like Steve. I think that's the most embarrassing part of it. I never thought I'd need an old lady to protect me, but I really did. I just felt helpless, you know? I was waiting for that fight or flight to kick in, but it felt like I was frozen.'

'Fight, flight, freeze or fawn,' he says, just as I fork another huge mouthful of fettuccini.

My mouth full, I twist my face into a question mark.

'It's a trauma response. Most people know about fight or flight but there's freeze and fawn too. But you don't have to worry about it. You won't have to deal with any more shit from Steve, he knows not to even step foot in Batter's Cove. Same with his deadshit cousin. It's all good.'

'What do you mean?' I put my fork down on the table.

'I ran into them on my way home. They won't ever bother you or your brothers again.'

'Just like that?'

'I'm pretty persuasive. These ribs are incredible. You want some?'

I open my mouth to reprimand him for evading any further questioning but Mary, my mum's cousin, calls from across the table. 'So, Cat, the big Year Twelve, hey? What's on the cards for uni?'

'Medicine,' says Nonna.

'Law,' says Dad.

I roll my eyes. 'Thank God you're both here to answer anything directed my way.'

'Well, both are pretty amazing,' Mary says. 'What are you leaning towards?'

'I honestly have no idea. All I know is I can't waste the marks. I love the thought of anything social justice-y, so law would be good, but then so would medicine.'

'How are you with blood and guts and gross stuff?' her husband asks.

'Have you met my brothers? I'll be fine.'

An hour or so and a couple of hundred kilos later, the table's cleared, the kids are having water fights in the backyard and the adults are cradling red wine. 'Let's get out of here,' I say quietly to Paul as he helps me place cheese platters down the middle of the table.

'No way,' he says. 'I saw that cheesecake in the fridge.'

'You can't still be hungry,' I say. 'Anyway, that's for later. Let's go to the beach, have a quick swim, make some room for that cheesecake, yeah?'

'I'm pretty sure I'll sink,' he says, 'but okay, let's do it.'

If any of the adults notice we are slinking away they don't say anything. We walk through Batter's Cove, the streets crowded with parked cars. As we pass a yard, an elephant of a man snores in a hammock and I can't help but laugh.

'Siesta time. I bet he's Italian.'

'I could go a siesta,' says Paul, 'especially if it means I get to wake up next to a beautiful Italian goddess like you.'

'Words like that could get you in some serious trouble,' I say. 'Anyway, if you were Italian, you'd be pinching my cheek right now.'

'On it.'

'Good try, but that's the wrong cheek.'

'Is it?'

'Hey, Cat, hey Paulie!' Ant calls out from the pub's outdoor courtyard. '*Com'era il pranzo?*'

'Completely over the top,' I say. 'We're going for a swim; it's that or die.'

'I can imagine,' he says. 'Nonna caught up with yours at the supermarket, sounds like she was bringing out all the big guns.'

'Next level,' I say. 'She freakin' hand rolled cannoli.'

'And I'm all for it,' says Paul. 'No complaints here at all.'

'Good timing, hey mate.' Ant leaves the table and walks over to us. 'No way you'd have outrun the cops now, hey?'

'What?' I turn to Paul. 'What's he talking about?'

'Nothing, he's exaggerating.' Paul gives him a hard look.

'What happened, Ant?'

Oblivious to Paul's posturing he continues. 'Nothing, just Paulie kicking the shit out of two losers who deserved it. I can't believe those dickheads gave Paulie's chick a hard time.'

'Paulie's chick? You know I have a name, right?' I turn to Paul. 'Tell me what happened.'

'I told you, nothing. I ran into them when I left your place earlier.'

'Can you please define "ran into" for me?'

'I saw them, I told them to fuck off.'

'Yeah, with your right hook,' Ant laughs.

'You punched them?'

'Mate, do you ever shut up?' Paul says to Ant. 'Cat, I know you're not going to like it, but they're lucky I didn't kill them, I was so angry.'

'Yeah, he had one by the throat while he was laying into the other one, you should've been there, Cat, it was awesome,' says Ant. 'The boys were all there ready to jump in and help out if we needed to, but Paulie had them both down for the count, until some woman driving past went crazy and threatened to call the cops.'

'Scampo, it's always a pleasure catching up. Let's go, babe.' Paul takes my hand as we follow the beach track through the scrub. 'Don't be angry, Cat. I know what you're going to say, that you don't need rescuing, that I can't go around punching people, but the thought of those feral fuckers bailing up you and Matty? I wasn't going to let that one go.'

'That's not what I was going to say at all. It's actually, I don't know, kind of thrilling. No one's ever punched anyone on my behalf. It's all very medieval, really, isn't it?'

'Medieval? So you're not going to go off your head at me?'

'Not even close. This is so embarrassing, and I'll never admit I said this as long as I live, but I think I like the idea of you defending my honour. Duels at sunrise and all that. It's borderline sexy.' *And it freakin' is.* I tug him towards me by his shell necklace, the twin to mine, and kiss him, big time, so he knows just how sexy it is.

'You just keep surprising me, don't you, Cat? I might just keep punching people if I'm going to get a reaction like that.'

'Don't even think about it,' I say. 'Let's go for a swim. I have another reaction I want to give you. I'm thinking something medieval.'

38

'COME on, how much longer?' Paul and I are walking the back beach at dusk. 'We haven't seen anyone else for ages. Who's going to see it from here?'

'Just around the next point,' says Paul, 'there's a stash of wood in the tea tree.'

'How do you know that?'

'Cavey's old man cut down a tree on that farm there.'

'Where?'

'Here.' He drops my hand and sprints up the dune.

'You want a hand?' I yell as he disappears into the scrub. I slide my hands up my sleeves and hug myself; there's only the slightest wind moving the tea tree and the line between the sea and the sky darkens with the encroaching night. I'm just starting to worry when Paul's outline emerges, his arms filled with slabs of timber. He uses his hands to dig a shallow round bowl in the sand and sparks fill the air as fire catches.

Paul sits heavily on the sand, pulling me down to sit between his knees. His chin rests on the top of my head, his arms crossed in front of me. I lay my hands on his forearms. The hair on his arms stands on edge, pale against his tanned skin. I run my fingers over them, pushing them against their natural grain and feel him visibly tremble against me.

'How is it that the hair here is longer than what you have on your head?' I reach a hand overhead behind me and rub from the base of his neck to his forehead and back again. I turn to face him. 'Look,

204

even your facial hair is longer.' I cup his chin, my thumb stroking his cheek.

'It's easier to look after,' he says. 'Two minutes in the shower, and boom, I'm done.'

'Well, that's a lie. What about your eyebrows?' I smooth them, although they're perfect. 'It must take longer than two minutes for you to get these so immaculate.'

'Very funny.' He kisses my crown.

The fire snaps and crackles, its smoke twisting to meet the sea mist. I lean back against his chest and stare into the fire. He takes a strand of my hair, wrapping the curl around his finger.

'I swear I'm a closet pyromaniac,' I say. 'I love fire. When we were little, Mum would rug us up, pack a basket of potatoes wrapped in foil and meet Dad on the back beach where he'd have been fishing for the last few hours. The boys and I would trudge up and down the dunes, dragging driftwood for a fire, Mum commandeering the pieces she liked the shape of to take home, before stacking the timber into a teepee and lighting the bottom pieces. Matty and Tommy, always helpful, would move around the tiny flames, panting and puffing enthusiastically to help them along, blowing them out in their excitement.' I laugh at the memory.

'Not you?' asks Paul.

'I had braces for years. Half of what I'd have blown would have been saliva.'

'Sexy.'

'I know, right?'

'You have no idea.' His breath warms my neck.

'Weird.' I say. 'We haven't had one yet.'

'One what?'

'A fire.'

'This isn't a fire?'

'No, I mean my family. Although I'm not complaining. They almost always end in a fight or a vomit. Sometimes both.'

'What?'

'Mum would remember to wrap potatoes in foil, get butter, even salt and freakin' pepper, but she'd always forget a knife, so Dad'd have to use his manky old fishing knife.'

'Fish guts and baked potato. Nice.'

The ocean continues its endless thump against the shore, the wood shifts and protests in vivid sparks, my vision dotted, Paul's breathing soft. He runs his fingers up and down my arms.

'Look up, Cat.' The sea mist has moved behind us into shore and the stars look so close I could touch them. They're almost unrealistic, like they're painted on, obscene in their multitude.

'Perfection,' I say.

'Again, you have no idea.'

Later, we kick sand over the fire, extinguishing every hint of it.

'You're okay with the dark?' Paul's arm is around my shoulder, pulling me into his warmth.

'Aren't you here to protect me from any scary boogiemen on the beach?'

'Why, yes, I am.'

'Anyway, this is my secret superpower, so it's more like I'll protect you. You know how I said Mum always forgets to bring a knife? She also forgets a torch. I have the best night vision, so it's always my job to lead the way through the dunes. Still, I love it so much. I know it's silly.'

'Why silly?'

'Well, by rights, at my age I should resent spending time with my family.'

'Your family is pretty cool.'

'Yeah, they are, really. We'll have to do it again this summer, just one last time.'

'Why one last time?'

'This time next year, I'll be in the city, starting uni, and all that.'

'It's not a once you're out, you're out, Cat. It's ninety minutes away.'

'Once I'm out, I'm definitely out.'

Paul stops and his arm drops from my shoulder.

'That's a bit full on, isn't it? I know you have big plans, and that's awesome, but it's not all or nothing. You don't have to turn your back on your whole life here, yeah? What about your family? What about me? You're never going to come home again?'

'Let's just go.' I walk ahead, the sand shifting beneath my feet.

'Seriously? You're just going to walk away?'

'Why are we even arguing about this? None of this is new to you.'

He walks to catch up. 'Cat, we're not arguing. I'm just wondering where I fit into this future vision of your life.'

'Well, I don't know, really, do you? I mean, do you want to? Like when the summer's over and I go back to school?'

'Are you kidding me, Cat? For a smart girl you're pretty freakin' oblivious sometimes. You know how I feel about you.' He shakes his head, then grabs both of my hands and pulls me so we're chest to chest. 'I'm not playing around here. I don't want to say it but being with you is like having my skin stripped from my body. It's like you can see all the way through me, and it scares the crap out of me, but man, all I want is to be with you. Not just now, not just this summer. We've been over this. This isn't just summer holiday shit here between us, Cat. You know what I'm saying? I told you I love you and I freakin' mean it.'

'I didn't plan for this, you and me. I'd planned nothing other than setting up my future, that and avoiding Nonna. You know what this year means to me, getting the marks I need, getting out of this place, it's everything.'

'I know that, Cat, and you're going to smash it. You're gonna get whatever you want. But you don't even know what that is yet, which is how it should be. No one knows what the fuck they want half the time, especially at your age.'

'I know exactly what I want,' I say, shaking him off. I walk down the beach, feet sinking in the sand.

'Do you even want to be a doctor? Or a lawyer?'

'What are you talking about?' I say over my shoulder.

'Stop, Cat.' He tugs my wrist. 'We're talking here, don't walk away.'

'Fine.' I sit on the sand.

'What's with that don't waste the marks stuff? You said that to your aunty.' He sits beside me; his mass is nothing but gentle patience.

'What do you mean?'

'You'll do well, that's obvious, but how can you waste marks you don't even have yet? Don't you think you should do something you like, not something just because your score says you can?'

'That's missing the point,' I shrug. 'I have to get good grades to get good options. Just because you were happy to settle for being a tradie doesn't mean I'd be okay with whatever happens, happens.'

'I didn't have a freakin' choice, Cat. My brother died. You think I could fuck off to the city and leave my parents?'

My mouth goes dry as what he's said sinks into my thick head.

'I didn't mean settle. You're an amazing builder, Dad loves working with you.' I wince at my condescension. 'I'm sorry, Paul.'

'Of course I wanted to go. I wanted to leave long before my brother and all that shit, so I get it. I know this place is too small for you, Cat. I fucking get it. I'll back you with whatever you go for. Whatever you need, I've got you.'

'That's easy now; it's summer. What about when school goes back? I'll be studying for five hours every night. Five hours, Paul.' It's the first time I've even thought about the logistics of what Year Twelve will look like. I don't even get home from school until after four. If I start homework at five, stop for whatever Mum or Dad burns for dinner, I'll be still going at ten o'clock at night. And I'll be studying all weekend, too. 'When do you think we'll ever see each other?'

'Babe, I do have a job. You know that, don't you?' Paul says. 'Once I finish up with Mick and work goes back, I know we won't see as much of each other as we have been, but I'll take whatever I can get.' He lifts my chin and leans down to kiss me. It's light and soft, nothing like how we kissed by the fire but with no less intensity. 'I'm not an idiot, Cat. I know this can't last forever. Once you hit uni, you'll have a new life and friends and all that. But can we worry about that when we get there? Until then, let's just go for it. I've never felt like this about anyone. Let's take it as far as we can for as long as we can. What do you think? You in?'

I rise to my feet, shaking more than a little, my throat thick. It's going to hurt like hell walking away from this, from him.

'I'm in.'

39

I'M on the balcony in my bikini top and shorts, legs crossed, science text spread open over my thighs, highlighter in hand. Earphones drown out the incessant noise from under the house when suddenly there's hands over my eyes. I yank out my earphones.

'Guess who?'

'No way!' I jump out of my seat. 'JB! What are you doing here?' I throw my arms around his neck, and he lifts me off my feet, spinning me around while we scream, holler and whoop.

'Miss me, did you, Trines?'

'Put me down before I vomit, you shithead.' I push against his chest. 'I don't believe this!'

'Believe it, gorgeous!' He hugs me again and bends to hug Mum who has come outside at all the high-pitched screaming, mostly JB's. 'Angela! Merry Christmas, Happy New Year, what's for dinner?'

'Enough!' I say. 'How are you even here?'

'Took the thumbs-up bus.'

'You hitchhiked? That's so dangerous, even for a weapon like you!'

'Who's going to mess with this specimen?' He flexes his muscles.

'Yeah, yeah, put it away.' I punch his arm, then tousle his blonde hair, grown long and floppy since the end of the school year.

'JB!' Tommy races across the balcony, Matty behind him. Tommy throws his arms around JB and he mock-stumbles.

'Woah, little mate, look at you! You been working out, dude? Hey Matty, how are you? You've shot up too!'

'We got new games for Christmas,' says Tommy. 'Come play, wait

210

until you see how good I am.'

'You're shit, Tommy,' says Matty, 'I kick your arse.'

'You're shit. I kicked your arse two minutes ago.'

'Language,' says Mum.

'Matty, Tommy, can you back off a bit?' I put a hand on Tommy to restrain him.

'What, you think I can't take on these two?' JB flips Tommy upside down with one arm and brandishes his legs at Matty like a sword. Tommy's squeals of excitement and laughter bounce off the walls. Matty dives for JB's waist and drops to his knees, trying to use his inconsiderable weight to drag him to the ground.

'Seriously?' I turn to Mum. 'Can you do something, please?'

JB sprawls on the balcony, feigning defeat, his legs draped over Matty as Tommy scrambles to his feet.

'Guess what?' Tommy says.

'I can't even begin to guess, mate. Hit me.'

'Cat's in love with her lover.'

'Oh my God. Mum!'

'Good to see you, mate,' Dad materialises from nowhere and JB leaps to his feet. Dad hugs him, slapping his back. 'You good? Work going well?'

'Work's work,' says JB, shrugging.

'Cat...' Mum tilts her head, almost imperceptibly.

'Oh shit, of course!' I put my hand on Paul's shoulder. 'JB, this is Paul. Paul, meet JB.'

'G'day, mate.' Paul holds out his hand. They're almost the same height and I'm standing between them looking up like a little kid, my head swivelling, a ridiculous smile stretching my face.

'How's it going?' JB takes his hand.

'Yeah, good,' says Paul, his arm coming around my shoulder.

'So I see,' he winks. 'How'd you get Trines' head out of a textbook?'

'Trines?' Paul's eyebrow raises.

'Trines, Caterina, latrines,' JB grins. 'She loves it.'

'No, she does not love it,' I say. 'It's an annoying AF nickname I've been telling him to stop calling me for years. Anyway, you can talk, JB. I bet you're miles ahead of me, of everyone. I also heard you're fit as too.' I slap his abs. 'Freakin' overachiever.'

'How's Mum, JB?' says Mum.

'Yeah, she's good, Angela, you know Mum.'

'Tell her we're overdue a long lunch. Bring on the return to school so us mums can get back to our real lives.'

'That's so nice, Mum, glad to see we mean so much to you,' says Matty.

'She said to say the same thing to you,' says JB, 'only she wants a liquid lunch.'

'Speaking of, it's pretty much beer o'clock.' Dad checks his watch. 'Paul? JB?'

'Not for me, Mick, training tonight. I'm grabbing a ride with Scampo.'

Dad walks inside, dusting his hands on his dirty shirt.

'What? You're not staying?' My shoulders drop. 'I haven't seen you for ages, *literally months*, and you're blowing me off for football?'

'Trines, you know the old man.' He shrugs. 'He'll blow a gasket if I'm not there tomorrow. All I've done since school is work, train, read and sleep. If it wasn't for preseason, it would have just been work, read and sleep. As it is I'm lucky he pissed off to the races, so here I am.'

'Here you are!' I lightly punch his chest. 'Man, you have buffed up, haven't you?'

'Careful, gorgeous, you break it, you buy it.'

Dad returns, two beers in hand and offers one to Paul.

'Sorry, not for me, either, thanks Mick,' says Paul. 'I've got to go help the old man. I'll see you later, Cat?' He kisses me on the cheek then shakes JB's hand. 'Good to meet you.'

'Yeah, you too,' says JB. Paul disappears down the stairs as Tommy grabs JB's arm.

'Come on, JB, let's play.'

'That's a no, Tommy,' I say. 'I promise you next time JB comes we'll play with you for as long as you want.'

'Are you guys going to the beach? Can I come?' Matty says.

'What do you think?' I almost feel bad as his face lights up. I grab my t-shirt off the chair. 'That's a no, too. Let's go, JB.'

40

'MAN, how hot is it?' says JB as we walk to the beach.

'It's oppressive. Intolerable, even. Like your hat.' I reach up to knock it off, but he stands at his full height. I have no chance.

'Ooh, look who's collecting big English words,' he says. 'Intolerable is standing on the side of the highway when it's four hundred degrees begging for a ride. Still, I couldn't pass up the chance to see you, even though I knew I'd cop nothing but abuse.'

'Ah, you love it.'

'Seriously, though, how are you? You good?'

'I'm so good, you have no idea how good I am.'

'And the surfer, seems intense. He a good guy?'

'He's the best.' I find myself blushing. The sweat trickling down behind my ear tells me that the heat of the day will mask a blush as exertion.

'Is he though?' JB's voice lacks his jovial tone.

'What do you mean?'

'Nothing,' he says. 'Just something Scampo said.'

'What did Ant say to you?'

'Usual shit, that the surfer's a bit of a player, stories about him and his mates and what they're into. Is he treating you well?'

'What, so you're my dad now?'

He gives me a light shove. 'We'll be gone soon anyway, won't we, metal mouth?'

'You're going to have to find another insult for me,' I say, baring my teeth.

'You'll always be metal mouth to me, baby girl,' he says. 'How's this dickhead?'

There's a banged up four-wheel drive parked directly in front of the access gate stopping anyone from driving down the path to the clubhouse and to the lookout, and of course stopping any of the lifeys from being able to get out. It's rust-speckled and there's a set of fishing rods attached to the roof racks. The silver glare from surfboard covers reflects through the back windows. Cavey. He's clearly taken umbrage to the lifeys closing the gate, restricting car access to the lookout to the chosen few.

'Ugh, this is the ongoing war over the keepers of this beach,' I say, 'the lifeguards or the surfers. Check it out.' A skinny young kid in a wetsuit framed by two middle-aged lifeys make a big show of taking down the car's license plate number. I cannot wait to have all this territorial bullshit behind me.

JB puts his arm around my waist to lift me up over the carpark barrier before he jumps it.

'You are such a showoff.' I swing my towel at him.

'I'm the king of the box jumps,' he says, 'Google it.'

We run down into the ocean and dive under the waves. I'm so light and happy with my best friend beside me after such a long time that I'm as buoyant as an inflatable toy. The water slicks over my skin, cold and enlivening.

We bob to the sway of the waves. 'So, your dad, you doing okay?'

'I have a mantra, Cat, you want to hear it?'

'Not if it's a meditation mantra. They're so crap.'

'What, the queen of overthinking finds it hard to meditate? There's a surprise. Finally, something you're not perfect at.' I splash water in his face. 'No, it's not a meditation mantra, it's a JB mantra. It's "just one more year, just one more year."'

'That bad?'

'It is what it is. Just bring on the end of the year and our ticket out. So don't get too attached to your surfer. But first...' He dives under the water, grabbing my legs to drag me under.

'Fuckwit!' I laugh as I emerge from the water. As he swims away from me, the muscles in his shoulders reflect the sea and the sun. I have no hope catching him, so I float on my back, letting my hair swan behind me, then follow him up the beach to where we dumped our stuff.

'Hot chips?' I ask.

'Yeah, that'd be good, I'm meeting Scampo at the shop.'

There's a group of city kids kicking a soccer ball in the wet sand. As we pass by the lifeys, one of them says, 'Check it out: they're playing wogball.'

'What did you say?' I spin around. At least they have the decency to wipe their smirks and look sheepish. Not one of them in the whole group looks me in the eye. 'Yeah, that's what I thought. Heroes, aren't you?'

'Calm down, all right?' A beast of a man crosses his arms over his red and yellow oversized polo and widens his stance, pale flabby legs like two concrete pillars planted into the sand. I see myself reflected in his mirrored sunglasses, my face red, my teeth set, and man, if he had any sense, he'd back away rapidly. 'If it weren't for us "heroes" you wouldn't feel safe on this beach so you might want to show some respect.'

I can't help but laugh. 'Are you kidding me? Show *you* respect? You know when I feel safest on this beach? It's at the end of the summer when you racist, redneck wannabes go back to where you came from.'

'That's enough, miss,' he says, 'we're volunteers, here keeping you safe out of our sense of community. We don't have to take your abuse; I suggest you leave the beach before we use our authority to demand it.'

'Well, there's two jokes on you, bud,' says JB. 'We're leaving anyway, and guess what? You have no authority. None. Although you do have a code of conduct, don't you? And I'd bet my left teste that your code of conduct doesn't include racism, am I right?'

'For your information we operate under the council bylaws and your very presence on this beach constitutes a—'

'Do you really think we're going to debate with a racist ignoramus like you?' I say. 'Why would we do that when it will take me less than five minutes to write an official complaint to whoever sits on top of you, and to their boss, and their boss? I'm going to write to their boss, too. Let's go, JB.' I yank JB's hand.

'Boom!' JB high fives me as he finishes telling Ant about the lifey encounter. The three of us are sitting at a table out the front of Sadie's, a massive parcel of hot chips steaming between us. 'Bringing out the big guns, an official complaint! Spoken like a true private school girl.'

'And you took it to the high ground by bringing your testicles into it, didn't you?'

A car horn toots and I turn to see Paul parking in front of our table.

'What's so funny?' He drops down to sit beside me on the bench.

'This sweet, innocent-looking chick just made a grown man cry,' says JB. 'She scares the crap out of me every time she opens her mouth, don't you gorgeous?'

'You call me a chick again and you will be scared.'

'Who's the lucky guy?' says Paul.

'Cat tore the lifeys a new one.' Ant tosses a chip high into the air, catching it with his mouth. 'Got all lawyer on them. Man, I wish I could have seen it,' he says, chomping through the chip.

'He's exaggerating, just for a change.' I lick the salt off my fingertips. 'Meanwhile, I'm in desperate need of water. Anyone want anything?'

'I've got you,' Paul and JB say in unison.

'Sorry.' JB facepalms. 'Force of habit. Yeah, of course.'

'All good.' Paul goes into Sadie's. I reach across and whack Ant's arm.

'Ow, what was that for?' he says, mock scowling.

'Oh, don't be a baby. I barely touched you. It's a thank you for helping me catch up with my best friend.' I knock JB's hat off to tussle his hair with both hands. 'Even if he has an unhealthy obsession with hair product.'

'Hands off, Trines!' JB bats me away. 'The ladies love it.'

'Yeah, I can tell, look at you fighting them off.'

'Don't look but there's one giving me "come hither" eyes right now,' he says, smirking.

I turn, and there's Isabel sitting across the road at the pub, true to form, eyeballing my best friend.

'Trust me, you do not want to touch that.' I clench my teeth. 'Honestly, not even with hospital grade disinfectant and a hazmat suit. I forbid it. You hear me?'

'Forbid what?' Paul places a glass bottle of water in front of me.

'Baby girl's under the misguided impression that I have to run everything past her,' says JB. 'It's bizarre how you think you have a say in my love life.'

'Love life?' I scoff. 'That's a laugh. I don't think you could call a five-minute hook up in the toilets "love". You know the rules. My best friend *does not* hook up with my mortal nemesis under *any* circumstances. Do I make myself clear?'

'You are so easy to wind up,' he says, bopping me on the nose. 'I'm not here to hook up; I'm here to see you. Calm down, chickaboo.'

'Why is everyone telling me to calm down all the time?' I take a swig of water. 'If everyone didn't push my buttons I wouldn't need to calm down.'

'I hear meditation helps.' JB winks. 'Anyway, we'd better head now, hey Scampo?' He rises off the bench. 'Man, it's been so good seeing you. Come here, gorgeous.' He hugs me, shaking me from side to side. 'See you in a couple of weeks.' He shakes Paul's hand. 'Take care of her, man.'

'On it,' Paul says.

<h1 style="text-align:center">41</h1>

'CAT, I'm trying really hard here. I don't want to be a dick about this, I know you say you're just friends and all that, but the way he looks at you? Calling you gorgeous all the time? Baby girl? His hands all over you? That doesn't look like friends.'

'For someone trying not to be a dick that's pretty much all that's coming across,' I say. 'JB and I are friends. *Just* friends. I don't know why it's such a difficult concept for you to understand. Maybe because you constantly have girls throwing themselves at you that you have no idea what it's like to connect with someone on a different level.' My fingers tap against the window of Paul's car as he drives along the coast road. My legs crossed, my chest tight, the air between us feels like a snarly rabid dog. 'Anyway, I don't care what it looks like to you or to anyone else. JB's been there from the start, he's like a brother to me. He'll always be there for me.'

'So, you're telling me you've never gone there.'

'Are you kidding me? Even if I had, would it matter? Could you be any more hypocritical?'

'What's that supposed to mean?'

'Oh, I don't know, maybe the fact that you said yourself that you've been with more girls than you can count. Everywhere we go you have Isabel Dillon all over you. And you think it's okay to question me and JB?' *Ugh, here we go.* My throat scratches as I feel the telltale prickle of tears behind my eyes. I jam my fists into my sockets and take a deep breath. 'I'm not in the mood for the night market anymore. Let's just forget it.' My voice breaks.

He pulls onto the shoulder of the road and I clutch the grab handle to stop from sliding off the car seat, feet now firmly planted on the floor.

Paul pulls the handbrake up and turns to me. 'I'm so sorry, Cat. I feel like such a dick, please don't cry.' His Adam's apple shifts slowly up and down his throat.

'I'm not crying.' A tear snakes its way down my cheek.

'What's this then?' He holds it aloft on his thumb. It glistens in the late afternoon sun streaming through the window, a tiny rainbow prism within. He sighs. 'I'm sorry, this is my shit, not yours.'

'What does that even mean?'

'It means I shouldn't have put all that on you like that. I felt like I was third wheeling there and JB? He's from your world, babe. His mother is friends with yours. He's the private school, golden boy, rich kid, he's your future in the city, he's more you than…' He chokes on the last word.

'Stop,' I interrupt. 'The private school, golden boy, rich kid? This jealous thing you've got going on is one thing, and let me tell you, it's doing absolutely nothing for me, but having a crack at JB? He has shit going on that you couldn't even imagine.'

'I'm just saying, I wouldn't blame you.' He looks down at his interlocked fingers, then opens his palms, shrugging. 'He's a good one.'

'You're my good one, don't you get it?' I unclick my seatbelt to hurl myself across the seat. My hands over his ears, I lift his head to look me in the eye. 'You hear me?'

'I hear you,' Paul says, 'they can hear you in the city.' He kisses me. 'I really am sorry. Seriously, there's no words for how sorry I am. You want me to take you home?'

'No way.' I wriggle my way onto his lap, my legs stretched across the seat, the window hot against my back, my body twisted against his. 'I'm sorry I yelled. But if you want to go do your own thing it's all good.'

'My own thing?' His finger traces its way across my face and my neck. 'I just want to be wherever you are.'

A car horn honks in passing and my body jerks, the steering wheel jamming me right in the sweet spot between my ribs. I wince. 'Then let's not be here, hey? Night market?'

'Sounds like a plan.' He turns his indicator on. Ten minutes later we're parking in town.

'How good is summer?' I say. The jetty is packed, the parkland adjacent crammed with market stalls selling everything from scented candles through to wind catchers, preserves and chutneys, and framed prints. As we wander past the stalls, I pause in front of a glass cabinet filled with jewellery. A kaleidoscope of green, amber and aquamarine glints in the late afternoon sun, luminous. 'Do you make these?' I smile at the woman behind the table. 'They're beautiful.'

'I do,' she says. 'I live a couple of hours up the coast, and every morning I walk on the beach collecting sea glass, then every afternoon I turn them into these pieces. Are you visiting from the city?'

'No, I live in the next town. I collect sea glass too. I've never seen aquas like yours.'

'This is going to sound super woo-woo, but I feel like I made this piece just for you,' the woman says. She unlocks the cabinet and holds a necklace towards me. 'The aquamarine would look stunning against your beautiful tan.' It's an off-center long oval, wider at the top than the bottom, like a lopsided heart. It's half the length of my thumb, connected to a silver chain with a casing that's so delicate it almost disappears against the vibrance of the glass. She places a mirror on the cabinet, and I hold it against my chest. 'It even goes with your shell,' she nods at my fishing line and shell necklace.

'It's beautiful.' I hold it up to the light, furtively looking at the price tag. 'Whoa, and it's a little bit out of my price range.' I hand it back.

'We'll take it.' Paul pulls out his wallet.

'No, it's all good,' I say. 'I'm just looking.'

'And I'm just buying. You want to wear it now, Cat?'

'Are you sure?' I run a tentative finger over its glossy finish.

'Done and dusted,' he says. 'Can you please take the tag off?'

'You don't have to do this.'

'I want to,' he says. 'Turn around and let's put it on.'

'Are you absolutely positive?' I'm already piling my hair on my head. 'Thank you so much.' I kiss him and turn back to the mirror, grinning. 'I love it.'

Seagulls squawk and squabble in packs up and down the beach, fighting for chips. We lean against the jetty railing watching kids jump between fishing lines into the sea, ignoring the 'no jumping' signs plastered everywhere. I have an ice-cream cone in one hand, my other is resting against the waistband of Paul's board shorts, my fingers curled against his skin.

There's a cheer as a fisher triumphantly lands a calamari. He mock bows right as black ink squirts all over the jetty's timber, sending a pair of tween boys squealing out of the line of fire. He's removing the hook, a posse of little kids with their heads peering into his catch bucket when a passerby trips over his rod and the hook sinks into the fleshy base of a small thumb. A little girl's scream pierces the air and blood spurts, mixing with the squid ink and fish scales.

'Livvy!' A woman tears across the jetty. She so closely resembles the child that she has to be her mother. She sinks to her knees next to the little girl. A curious onlooker pauses to see what's happening and the colour drains from her face. Her eyes roll back, and she faints, stopped from hitting the decks by the fisher who's also holding the child's arm upright, blood flowing over the fisher's fingers. Paul's ice-cream goes into the water as he moves next to the fisher and gently lowers the woman to the deck.

People crowd around, stickybeaking. The blonde girl, who wouldn't be more than five, is red faced and snot nosed. She wails and reaches for her mum whose mouth is gaping like the fish that are being reeled in up and down the jetty. Ice-cream dribbles down the cone onto my fingers, sticky. I quickly do a cleanup job around the rim of the cone with my tongue while Paul crouches down on his haunches before the little girl.

'Liv? Is that your name?' says Paul. 'What is that short for?

Olivia?' She nods her head, her wails softening into small sniffles. 'I love that name! It's weird though, I didn't know fish could be called Olivia.'

'I'm not a fish. I'm a kid!' Paul takes a closer look at her finger and her sobs pierce my eardrums. 'It hurts. It hurts.'

'What? You're not a fish? Then let's get you unhooked. Mate, cut us some line?' The fisher slashes through the line on the rod and winds out metres of it. He hands a loop to Paul.

'Shouldn't someone call an ambulance?' asks the fisher.

'Maybe for her.' Paul gestures towards the woman passed out on the deck. A man kneels over her, using a cap to fan her down. 'Help me out, mate?' Paul loops the fishing line around the hook. 'Just press down here for me. Better with your thumb, hold it down flat, not too hard, yeah? Okay, Liv, how old are you?'

'I'm four!' she wails.

'Four? Okay, you're a big kid then, aren't you? I want you to count to three with me. Can you do that? One, two…' Paul yanks the line, and the hook comes clean out of her skin.

'Three,' says Liv.

'It's out, little mate,' Paul says. 'Look!' He brandishes the hook. 'You're such a brave kid.'

'No three?' she asks, incredulously.

'No three! You're all good. Here, just hold this tight.' He pulls a napkin from his ice-cream cone from his pocket and pads it against her thumb to stem the blood.

'You are just a bundle of never-ending surprises, aren't you,' I say to Paul as he comes to stand beside me, hands awkwardly by his sides. 'You saved that kid's life. How'd you know how to do that?'

'I don't know how many people die each year from a fishing hook in a thumb, but yeah, I'm basically just a hero,' he says, 'they'll make movies about today. Meanwhile, thanks for saving me some ice-cream.'

'Yeah, sorry about that, I was just too caught up in watching my superhero boyfriend save the day.'

'You crack me up,' he says. 'There's blood everywhere, people are fainting and there's you, calmly watching it all unfold, eating ice-cream. You'd be an amazing doctor.'

'It's weird; I'm okay with blood but no good with vomit. Besides, I knew you had it all under control. Maybe you're the one that should do medicine?'

'Yeah, right, as if.' He scoffs.

'Don't you dare go limiting my boyfriend's potential.' I poke him in the chest. 'But I've been thinking about that, actually. Something you said to me, about if I want to be a doctor, do you remember?'

'When we had that bonfire, just you and me?'

'Yep. The thing is, I don't think I do. I don't even like hospitals; even the smell of them gets to me.' I screw up my nose, thinking of that weird laundry smell, the acrid handwash, the food, oh God, the corn smell of the food. 'And you know my issues assignment? I keep looking at the articles about climate change and asylum seekers and I'm not saying they're not important, they are, but I keep gravitating towards articles about misogyny. If I'm interested in that, then wouldn't that tell me that law is where I should go? What do you think?'

'I think you should breathe.' he says, and he's right. I'm almost panting after getting that soliloquy out. 'But Cat, that makes perfect sense. If anyone's going to tear shit up, it's you, and a law degree is only going to help you do that. Go for it.'

'So, I'm going to be a lawyer then,' I say.

'Looks like it.'

'Meanwhile, I wouldn't mind washing my hands, they feel so gross.'

'Yours feel gross?' Paul holds his aloft, smeared with blood and squid ink. We walk across the car park to the fish cleaning platform where some kind soul has left liquid handwash.

42

'HEY, babe,' Paul drops to the sand beside me. He nods at the book I'm holding. 'Looks like another one bites the dust?'

I flick to the back page.

'Yep, just another twenty-two pages and I am D-O-N-E.'

'How's it going?'

'Better than I expected, look.' I turn the pages and he takes in my highlights and scribbles. 'You surfing?'

'It's average, but yeah, going to give it a crack. You want to come in for a quick swim?'

'Let me get this done, and I'll see. Where's your board?'

'Top of the dune.' I look behind me, and there are the Neanderthals high above me, surveying the surf. 'Hey, I've been thinking.'

'That sounds dangerous,' I say. 'You okay? You need a massage?'

'Very funny.' He nudges my shoulder with his. 'And yes, I do, actually. Right now would be great. Maybe with your lips.' He pulls me to him and kisses me.

'Hey!' I say against his lips, but I take my time in moving back from his kiss. 'Can't you see I'm working?'

'Well, something's working.' He sits up. 'But you're right, stop kissing me. You're very distracting. Go back to your book.'

'You started it, but what were you going to say? What have you been thinking?'

'I was thinking it's time we go out properly, you know, have a proper date. Dinner in town. Movies. What do you think?'

'I'd love that. When?'

'Tonight?'

'Sounds good. I'll get Mum or Dad to drop me off at your house?'

'Oh hell, no,' he laughs. 'It's a date; I'll pick you up. Around seven? Give you a chance to get some work done. I don't want to get yelled at again for taking you away from the most important year of your life.'

'Point taken. Off you go. Go play with your friends.'

'Yeah, yeah, I'm going,' he says. 'See you out in the water?'

'Yeah, maybe.'

I watch him lope up the beach, his shoulders impossibly wide, the muscles in his back tapering down. A dog trots towards him, its owners lagging, and Paul crouches down to pet it. *Ugh. Could he be any more perfect?* I return to my textbook and try to convince myself that the amoebic structure is infinitely more interesting and appealing than my boyfriend. Sweat trickles down my spine, and my brain is starting to feel foggy. I read the same paragraph three times. I take a slug of water and it's warm. There's shouting coming from the dune; the Neanderthals run down, boards under their arms. Paul waves, I close my book and rise.

'You all done?' His arm comes around me when I reach him. 'That was quick.'

'Nope. I've had enough for now.' I wrap my arms around his waist. 'I can't seem to concentrate; I keep thinking about that massage I owe you. You know, the one with my lips?'

'I know the one,' he says, 'and now I can't concentrate.'

'Hey, Paulie,' Tom yells. 'That a gun in your wetsuit, or are you just happy to see Cat?' The Neanderthals laugh and Paul blushes and shifts his surfboard.

'Can still see it, mate,' Tom says.

'They can see that one from space,' Cavey says.

'The Great Wall of Batter's Cove,' Tom hoots.

'Yeah, yeah.' Paul turns his back on them. 'Okay, that's embarrassing. See what you do to me?'

'Apparently the International Space Station can see what I do to you,' I say. 'I don't know if I'm flattered or just mortified.'

'I'm mortified,' he says. 'Come on, let's get in the water. That cures everything.'

'I didn't realise you needed a cure for me, but whatever,' I say. 'I'm not going past the shallows, though.'

'Yes, you are,' he says. 'It's safer out the back and you'll be with me.'

'You sure?'

'Positive. Let's go.'

We move through the swell, Paul duck diving under the waves on his board, resurfacing each time to find me beside him. 'Do you want to hold on to my leg rope? You okay, babe?'

'I'm all good.' And I am. It's the furthest I've been out all summer. I dive through the waves, the sun pulsing through the green, the whitewash luminescent. I swim out the back, Paul paddling beside me, far beyond the Neanderthals at the line up. Paul straddles his board.

'Take a seat.' He slaps the deck.

'Is there room?'

'There's plenty.' He holds his hands out and wrenches me out of the water and across his board. 'Now just swing your leg over.'

'This isn't very dignified or lady-like.' I cross my hands across my lap. 'Nonna would spontaneously stroke if she saw this. No wonder the girls wear board shorts.'

'I won't look,' Paul says. 'I'm a gentleman, remember?'

'So you keep telling me. You know you're looking right now, don't you?'

'I'm only human,' he says. 'But you're right. I've barely recovered from the beach incident. If it bothers you, scoot a bit closer.'

'I was born to scoot closer to you,' I say, 'watch me scoot. Don't I scoot well?'

'You scoot like a boss.' His arms enclose me, my head tucked under his chin. My bathers have shifted and the wax from his board is sticking into my, well, where surf wax doesn't need to stick.

'Isn't this going to make it hard for you to surf?' His wetsuit is cool and soft against my body. His hands move across my back.

'I've never been so happy to miss the lineup. You, the sun, the water, your skin. If I die now, I'll die a happy man.'

'Me too,' I say. 'Happy girl, not man. But your wetsuit sucks. Why am I almost naked and you're like a nun here? How is that fair?'

'Not fair at all,' he says, 'but man, it's the only thing keeping me together right now. Hold on, babe.' He tips himself off the surfboard. I grip the decks as it wobbles precariously. He pops up beside me, bobbing in the water.

'Why'd you do that?'

'Just need to cool off a bit,' he says. 'You okay?'

'Actually, my hips feel like they're going to pop from their sockets.' He holds the board steady while I swing my legs around to lie face down. I cross my arms and rest my chin on my wrists. Paul moves to the front of the board to face me. Salt flakes crust his eyelashes and eyebrows.

'That better?'

'This is awesome,' I say, 'I reckon I could sleep here. Maybe surfing isn't so bad after all.'

'Technically, this isn't actually surfing,' he says, 'but I'm glad you like hanging out with me in my natural habitat.'

'I love it.' I lift myself up on my elbows. 'And I love you, Paul Lightwood.

'I love you, Caterina Kelty.'

43

I SNEAK a look at the time. Less than half an hour until the movie ends, but the way my waistband is squeezing the life out of my bladder I know that waiting isn't an option. The movie has no chance of commanding my attention; between the protests of my bladder and my tongue working at a random piece of popcorn stuck right between my front teeth I can't concentrate on anything other than relief from both.

'Be back in a minute,' I whisper to Paul.

Stooped, I edge my way past countless knees in the darkened cinema. In the ladies, I grab my Christmas tree, the tiny pick that's been my smile's best friend for years now. It's been forever since my braces came off but after years of being denied my favourite movie snack, popcorn remains a terrifying, paranoia-inducing novelty. Did I really have to eat three quarters of a tub the size of a toddler? As I floss, a girl comes out of a stall and washes her hands. She smiles at me in the mirror.

'Popcorn stuck in your teeth?' she says. 'It's the worst, isn't it?'

'So annoying.' I pull my fist out of my mouth. I give the pick a rinse under the water and wash my hands.

'Wait, you're here with Paul Lightwood, aren't you? I thought it was him.'

'Um, yes,' I say, 'sorry, do I know you? I mean, have we met?' I feel the heat of my flush move up my neck and I turn my back on my reflection. She's at least a head taller than me even without considering her perfectly formed bun that balances on the top of her head. She's heavily made up with immaculate cat eyes I've only ever seen in what

229

I've always assumed were photoshopped images. She leans into her reflection to apply lipstick in a deep shade of red.

'No, we don't know each other,' she says, smacking her lips together. 'I live up north, but I went to school with Paul and Cavey and the guys.' She settles back into her heels and smoothes her hair. 'Paulie's still drop dead gorgeous like he was at school. Age suits him; from what I saw, he's even hotter. I heard Paulie was seeing someone, but I didn't know it was "movies-seeing", that's full on. I'm Bec.'

'Um, yeah,' I say. 'I'm Cat.'

'You look like a nice girl.' She leaves her reflection to face me, twisting her lipstick between her hands, her angular arms jutting. 'This feels like my civic duty to the next generation, but maybe you should stick to boys your own age. They'll be less likely to give you a sexually transmitted disease. Okay? Enjoy the movie. Tell Paulie Bec Farmer says "hey".'

My pulse rushes in my ears as the door closes behind her. What the actual? I put my hands under the cold water, then lay my palms flat against my flaming cheeks. I take in my quickly slapped on mascara, my hair a tangled, dishevelled mess. I was going for effortlessly cool in my band t-shirt and denim skirt ensemble, but I look like a scrappy little country teenager. I take a deep breath, pull my shoulders back and return to the cinema. This time I don't even bother to pretend to stoop as I bash into the knees of the people in our row.

'All good?' Paul's hand is heavy and hot on my knee. I nod, crossing my legs, nudging his hand, my eyes fixed on the screen. I can't make sense of what's playing out in front of me, the actors could be speaking another language. The audience laughs, and I flinch, startled. I turn my head to look behind me and all I can see through the dark is buns; it feels like every person in the entire cinema is watching me. I dig my fingers into the armrests and will myself to calm down. The movie can't end soon enough — the lights are barely up and I'm on my feet, shifting and fidgeting, waiting for all the people beside me in the aisle to leave the cinema.

'What did you think?' Paul says, his hand low on the back of my hip.

'I think if these people don't stop taking their sweet time and get their act together, I might actually lose my shit.'

'I meant the movie. You like it?'

'Yeah, it was good. Funny. Look, I just really want to get out of here,' I say and finally people begin shuffling their way out into the aisle.

'You okay, babe?' Paul takes my hand as we step out into the night, the smell of a thunderstorm hovering in the heat.

'I was,' I say, 'right up until a glamazon in the ladies told me to stick to someone my own age. Bec, she said her name was. Another one of your hundreds, I'm guessing?'

'What?'

'Well, she said she went to school with you and Cavey. Said to say "hey". "Hey from Bec Farmer." She also said you'll give me a disease. Charming, hey? I've always loved being bailed up in the ladies by someone's ex-girlfriend.'

'Bec Farmer? I haven't seen her in years. I didn't even know she was still around. Last I heard she lived up north. I think Cavey keeps in touch, but I haven't seen her since school.'

'I can't tell you how much fun it was being patronised by one of your ex-girlfriends.'

'Oh man,' Paul rubs his hand across the back of his head and sighs. 'She's not an ex-girlfriend. Not even close. She was just a pain in the arse freakin' drama queen at school. Looks like nothing's changed there.'

'Okay, so how do you grownups put it? You're saying you never went there?'

'Oh no, I went there; I'm not going to stand here and lie to your face, Cat. But we were never a thing. God no. We just hooked up a couple of times. In fact, if I had a disease, which I don't, she would have been the one handing it out.'

'That's like poetry. They should put that on t-shirts.'

'Very funny,' he laughs and tugs my hand behind his back. 'It's crap you had to deal with that. I'm so sorry.'

'It's not your fault.' I drop my head to my chest. 'It was just a bit weird, you know? Like at school being told off by one of the teachers. I'm standing there feeling like an immature, grungy hobbit next to this glamazon with perfect makeup.'

He holds my chin between his thumb and finger and lifts it so I have nowhere to look but his eyes. 'Number one, stop saying glamazon. She was never a glamazon. Her name at school was cake-face because she used to cake it on. Number two, don't ever call my beautiful girlfriend a hobbit. You want to talk perfect? Look in the mirror, Cat. You could be a model.'

'You are so sweet, Lightwood.' I rise onto my toes, my arms around his neck. 'You're also a massive liar. I don't even wear makeup.'

'I'll let you in on a secret, Kelty. I hate makeup.' His thumb sweeps the side of my face from my chin to the scar in my hairline and circles back down again. 'The fact that you don't wear makeup is right up there in the top ten of my *I Love Cat* list.'

'There's a Cat list?'

'There is. All about why I love you. It's massive.'

'Interesting. What else is on this list?'

'That's for me to know and you to find out, babe.'

'Come on, what's number three?'

'Well, I'd have to look.'

'What? You don't know?'

'It's a pretty big list, Cat. Too big to keep track of. I'm adding to it every day. Seriously, I've had to start a spreadsheet. It's taking up so much space, I might have to upgrade my data. Anyway, you hungry? Want to grab something?'

'After dinner and then that giant tub of popcorn? And the ice-cream? I'm about to explode. Although, I could go some chocolate… Are you still hungry?'

'No, I'm all good.' He opens my car door. 'I'm just not in a hurry to take you home.'

'I'm in no hurry to go home.'

'Where do you want to go?'

'What about your house?'

'And watch the late-night news with my oldies? Yeah, nah.'

'Come on, I'd love to see your bedroom. You've seen mine.'

'Nothing to see, babe, and it's the last place I want to hang with you. We can do better than that.'

<h1 style="text-align:center">44</h1>

WE pull into the car park at Rip Bay. We're the only car here and as Paul kills the ignition we sink into darkness. The ocean is black before us, and the lights of Batter's Cove seem impossibly far away. The horizon is the faintest sliver of light and the stars fan over us.

'I've been thinking,' I say. 'You know when you look straight out to sea and the horizon looks flat? You can kind of understand why people thought the world was flat. But when you look up at the stars, see them curving up and around, it's like, of course, the planet's a globe, yeah? And yet there's those people out there who still believe the world's flat and that billionaires want to insert a freakin' computer chip into humans for better phone reception. People really freak me out.'

'People are the worst.' Paul unclicks his seatbelt and turns to face me, leaning against his door. 'That's what you've been thinking? That the world isn't flat?'

'I'm also thinking it's cold tonight,' I hold out an arm. 'Look, goosebumps. Do you have one of your giant hoodies?'

'For some strange reason they keep disappearing. Now, there's a conspiracy for you. Come here, I've got you.' I nestle against him like a baby koala. He's like the world's best hot water bottle.

'Question,' I say against his chest, his heartbeat thrumming in my ear.

'Here we go.' His lips graze the top of my head.

'Do you not want your family to know about me?'

'What are you talking about? You met them when we went to get your books.'

'Yeah, but that was in the context of working for my dad.'

'You know that driving Miss Caterina isn't part of my job description, don't you? I did that because I had a massive crush on the boss' daughter and wanted to get you alone in my car for four hours.' He gently tickles my ribs and I squirm closer into him.

'Why didn't you want to take me to your house tonight? Are you embarrassed about me?'

'Cat, no, why would you even think that? In what universe would I be embarrassed?'

'Maybe I'm overthinking it, but it feels like whenever I mention your family you just shut it down.' I'm so glad it's dark because I can feel my cheeks heat. 'Did your mum not like me? Is it the whole jailbait thing?'

'Fuck, I'd hoped you'd forgotten about that,' he chuckles softly and rubs his head. 'Of course she liked you, who wouldn't? She was just a bit shocked. I walked in the house with a beautiful girl and threw her for a bit of a six.'

'What do you mean?'

'You know the other day, when you were saying you never have time for yourself, that there's always people at your house?'

I grimace, picturing myself in full tantrum-mode.

'Your house is a place where people like hanging out,' he continues. 'Your brothers' mates are in and out. The way JB turned up was like he lived there. I know this summer's a bit weird with your friends away, but Mick's told me that most weekends you have friends staying over.'

'That's true,' I say. 'Especially Em.' I tell Paul about Em's father, always travelling for work for a company that's a mix between the government, a bank and the church. 'Her parents aren't together,' I say. 'Her mum lives on a farm on the other side of the city but Em wanted to stay down here with her dad, even though he's never home. They have this amazing beach house. Bliss, yeah?'

'Sounds awesome.'

'According to Em, it's lonely and boring. She hates it, but the rest of us love it. She used to have a live-in nanny but her dad got rid of her once Em turned 16. She has no one to answer to, she can come and go as she likes. The only place she wants to come and go to is our house.'

'I get it,' he says. 'That's my place. I'd rather be anywhere than my house.'

'So where do you go with your friends?'

'Surfing. The pub. Sadie's.'

'But, why?' I'm truly flummoxed.

'You were there, Cat. The creepy fucking dolls, my old man in the recliner talking non-stop about nothing, Mum cleaning all the time. Don't get me wrong, they love me, I know that. It's just different since… well, since we lost Pete.'

'What was he like?'

'He was much older than me. There was him and then Michael, he's the smartarse prick that lives in Melbourne, and then six years later there's me. Surprise! So, there were eight years between us. Michael treated me like shit, but Pete wasn't like that. He was funny, everyone loved him. He'd walk into the room, and we'd all be laughing over nothing. It was just good being around him, you know?'

'When did you say that he died?' I can barely get the words out.

'It's nearly been five years.'

'So, you were younger than me now?' I do the maths in my head. 'That's so awful, Paul.'

'Yeah, it was pretty shit.' His fingers drum against the steering wheel. 'I was going into Year Eleven. He wasn't living at home then or anything, so nothing really changed, but everything changed.' His chest rises and falls against me. He sighs heavily. 'I never knew what I'd be coming home to with Mum crying or the old man just sitting there, so I stopped letting my mates come home after school. Mum was famous for her after-school snacks, but after Pete, that all stopped. Except for Cavey, he kept coming, I couldn't stop him, and he was cool. But you're the first girl I've ever brought home.'

'Seriously?'

'Yep, and I only did it because your mum pushed you into my car. But you were so cool with everything, you just sat there talking, so natural.'

'I'd love to see them again, Paul,' I say. 'My parents know you so well, I'd love yours to know me too.'

'Dad's been busting my balls about you coming for dinner. But don't feel obligated.'

'Are you kidding? I'd love to.' His arms tighten around me.

'Cat?'

'Paul?'

'I've never told anyone any of that shit.'

'Really?'

'Yep,' he says. 'I don't even know the last time I said my brother's name.'

'I'm glad you told me.' I kiss his hand, clutching my shoulder. I put my hand under his t-shirt to feel his skin. 'Man, you are so warm. How aren't you cold?'

'I read about this weird way to get warm once, but it's kind of hard to get your head around.'

'I'm a smart girl, so try explaining it to me and I'll see if I can understand. Maybe talk slowly.'

'Well, it involves taking your clothes off first.' His fingers move up and down my bare arms.

'Hmmm, that does seem counter-productive,' I say.

'I saw it on a movie once. It was one that you have to be 18 to watch, so I don't think it's something you would have seen. It had this really weird soundtrack, like *"boom chicka wow wow."* From what I saw, it works in raising body heat.'

'That a fact?'

'If I saw it, it must be true.'

'Who am I to argue with that?' I yank my t-shirt off over my head.

'No, Cat, I'm only kidding,' he says. 'Honestly, babe.'

'Your turn,' I tug at his t-shirt, and he moves away from my hand. 'What? Come on, Mr Never-Wear-A-Shirt. We have a hypothesis to test. Do not make me rip this off you; I'm stronger than I look.'

'No doubt about that.' He pulls off his t-shirt. His elbow collides with my temple as he lifts the fabric over his head. 'Oh shit, babe, I'm so sorry, are you okay?'

'I'll be better when you kiss me,' I say and then my pulse races, my heart stops, my skin burns and angels descend from the heavens singing. Well, actually, they don't, which is a complete travesty because the way he kisses? The way his hands move up and down my spine? The feel of his skin against mine? They should. 'Don't you dare stop.' He shifts in his seat.

'You know you've got me trapped here.' He pushes my hair back out of my face. 'I'm jammed between the most beautiful, amazing girl in the world and the door. This is why I need a new car, something with a bit more room to move. This freakin' door handle is sticking right into my back. Can you sit up a bit?'

'You just whacked me in the head with your enormous manly elbow. I think you can tolerate a door handle in the back.'

'I was hoping you'd forgotten about that.'

'I nearly had, but then you stopped kissing me. You'd better kiss me again.'

'You're so bossy.' He smiles and slides a finger along my jawline.

'You love it.'

'I do. And I love you.'

I lose all track of the conversation and time and gravity and all the fundamentals of life on earth until he pulls away.

'Let me swap sides.' He lifts himself across to the passenger seat in one motion. Even with me on top of him, it's like I'm no heavier than a napkin placed across his lap. 'That's better.' His arms wrap around my body, enclosing me against his skin and for a moment I wonder if you can die from feeling this incredible flush of craving, so acute, so delicious in the pit of my stomach.

Passing headlights illuminate the whole car. I cover my bra with my hands. 'Hope they enjoyed the show.'

'I know I am,' Paul says, head back against the seat, his hand on my hip, fingers tracing the arch of my hip bone.

'It's got an amazing soundtrack.' Music fills the car, low, the singer almost growling and purring through the speakers, doing nothing to assuage my, well, lust is the only word for what I'm feeling right now. 'What is this, your sexy time playlist?'

'It is now,' he says. 'Cat, what are you doing?'

'Getting comfortable,' I say, unbuttoning my denim skirt.

'Yeah, no you're not.' He stays my hand. 'We probably should get going now, get you home.'

'Are you freakin' serious?' I say. 'You want to go?'

'Leaving is the last thing in the world I want to do.'

'Well why would you say let's go?' I grab his face between my hands, my fingers spread wide. 'Here's the thing: I love you. Do you love me?'

'You know I do, that's not even a question.'

'Why do you keep pushing me away? Are you just not that into me? Because it feels like you are. Seriously. I can *feel* you're into me, right now. You know what I'm saying?' I look down between us.

'Cat, I'm so into you I could explode. I really, *really* want to be with you, not just now, not just tonight, but for the long haul.'

'So, we're in agreement, because I really, *really* want to be with you too. Like *really*, really. I thought me sitting on top of you barely dressed is evidence enough. And you went to all the trouble of making a sexy time playlist.' I lean in to kiss him but he holds my face between his hands.

'I just don't want you to feel like I'm pushing you into anything you don't want to do or that you're not ready for.'

'Here we go again. Yes, yes, I get it, you're so much older and wiser than me. How could I forget? You're worse than my parents, worse even than Nonna, and she's the actual worst of the worst. Can you please stop treating me like a child?'

'So, making sure you're okay with being together is treating you like a child? It's called consent, Cat.'

'Well, I'm giving you my full consent to take off this annoying skirt that's cutting off my circulation. We're staying here, and we're fogging up these windows.'

'You're the boss,' he says. 'They're pretty fogged up already, though. Look.' He reaches across me, index finger extended. He draws a heart in the condensation, then touches the middle of my chest, the tip of his finger cold against my skin. I shiver. 'I didn't make a sexy time playlist. But I know for a fact that I won't be able to hear any of this music ever again without thinking about you and how beautiful you look tonight. I never knew that it was even possible to feel so in love like this. I swear, touching you feels freakin' sacred.'

My heart rate is spiking, my chest lifting in anticipation. 'Then, touch me.'

45

IT'S been hot since I woke up. I can see the peaks of the ocean from the balcony, choppy and rough. I'm buzzy and tingly all over, the feeling that only comes from being taken way past the point of delirium by a beautiful walking surfer god. I feel so happy I could sing as I walk to the beach, and to prove it, I belt out a tune, our song, while no one is around.

As I reach the surf beach car park I decide to stop and use the bathroom before I hit the beach. I must still be delirious; normally I'd prefer to pee myself in public than expose myself to a plague from that toilet block. It's an ugly, roofless brick box, divided in two by a sad, solitary brick wall. Inside, the floor is covered with sand and what I hope is sea water. I'm barefoot as usual, so go right up on my toes to avoid stepping in the tea-coloured puddles. There's a row of three toilets with that special ambiance only found in public toilets. The bowls are rust-stained, the toilets sans seats – not that in a million years I'd ever sit down on one – and opposite the toilets are three showers, all missing doors. Water cascades from the middle shower and there's Isabel, standing inside in only her undies.

'Kitty Cat.' She turns off the water. Her feet are bare, the red of her toenails shocking against the pale of her pruned feet. 'Can I help you?'

'Why would you ever shower *here*?'

'Where else? Are you inviting me to your place? Are we friends now?' She wraps a towel around herself.

'You're the one who stopped talking to me, Isabel. I'm the boring Stuck-Up Bitch, remember?'

'Funny that's the way you remember it.' She drops the towel onto the bench and pulls on a dress.

'Whatever.'

'Whatever,' she mimics me in a high voice.

'Is that supposed to burn?' I slow clap. 'Good on you. Look at yourself, showering in this cesspit. What are you trying to wash off?'

'You're such a hypocrite. The Gap is Skanksville, but doing the deed in a car on the side of the road is, what was the word? Special? No, wait, that's not it. Sacred! Yes, I hear *your* hookup was sacred. I'm surprised you can even walk from what Cavey told me.'

'What?' My mouth goes dry.

'I heard you had quite the night.'

'What exactly did you hear?'

'Nothing that I haven't already had, me and half of the population.'

'What are you even talking about? You two were never a thing.'

'You're so deluded, Cat. Look at you, thinking you have your hot boyfriend wrapped around your little finger. You think he'd choose you? Really?'

'He did choose me, Isabel. All summer he's chosen me. He chose me last night.'

'Yeah, I know last night he was with you. Everyone knows. He did what no one thought was possible and hooked up with the stuck-up rich girl. How long do you think until he gets bored of you and goes back to being with someone who has a personality?'

'Like you? Yeah, right.'

'Wouldn't be the first time. Or even the third or the fourth.' She rubs at her wet hair with her towel. 'That's if I wanted to, but I like Cavey. He's not so up himself.'

'Good one. You think Paul would touch someone like you with a ten-foot pole? And yet I'm delusional.'

'God, how gullible can you be? You might have him locked down this summer, but what about the summer before this and the summer before that? Ooh, that reminds me. Remember the last time we bumped into each other here?'

'I do. You pulled an all-nighter, and you were angry I wasn't okay with that.' The memory floods. Isabel sitting on the bench, a long red scratch down her leg, teeth chattering, telling me that after I'd left a Gap party she'd stayed with the Neanderthals. There was a fire, stars, vodka from the bottle, waking on the beach right before sunrise. 'We were 15. You called me a stuck-up virgin and told me to fuck off.'

'If you hadn't dumped me, you could have had him long before now. You might've worked out he's different once he's had his fun and grown bored. But you couldn't get away from me quick enough, could you, Cat?'

'Don't put that on me. You didn't want to know me after that summer.'

'Keep telling yourself that story,' she says. She bats her hand in the air. 'It's ancient history. You think he loves you? Ha! You really think everything he's said to you he hasn't already said to every other girl he's hooked up with? He knows what he's missing while he's hanging with you and now that he's had his *sacred* night it's just a matter of time before he dumps you.'

'That is the fucking funniest thing I've ever heard. We're done here. Enjoy your sexually transmitted disease.' I turn to leave.

'Again, you have the sacred and I have the disease. Nice one. You just think you're so much better than everyone else on the planet, don't you, Cat?'

'Maybe not the planet, but I'm sure as shit better than you.' I walk out the toilet block shaking as she hurls insults at my back.

46

THE ocean is cold to the point of painful. I float on my back, staring up and through the blue of the sky. There's too much depth of colour; it hurts my eyes. I deep dive to the bottom, kicking hard to grasp a handful of sand. As I resurface, I let it trickle through my fingers until all that's left is a layer of grit in the webs of my fingers.

How am I so naive? It's no secret that Paul has the sexual history of a freakin' rockstar, but even so, would he have actually been with Isabel freakin' Dillon? That morning that I saw her, shivering in the toilets, she said she'd had the best night of her life. I didn't believe her. I didn't know what to make of what she was saying. I didn't want to know. She'd entered a territory that felt dangerous, that we were too young for, that there was too much we didn't know. I'd heard rumours of what happens at Gap parties when there's only the Neanderthals left. But Isabel had scratches all over her legs, she was shaking, hugging herself. When I asked her if she was really okay, like really okay, she just yelled at me. Did Paul know about Isabel on the beach that night with his friends? Oh my God, was he there?

I can't even think about that. But what about Isabel knowing all about us at Rip Bay? How could Paul be with me, kiss me goodnight at my house, tell me he loves me and then tell his mates the second after he took me home? Paul my boyfriend, Paul who played with my hair, Paul who sat at our family dining table, who freakin' drove my Nonna home. *My* Paul. The hottest of the hot. The beautiful, walking surfer god. King of the Neanderthals. I *know* these guys. He's just as much a misogynistic, lying, dipshit Neanderthal as the rest of them.

I let the waves push me towards the shore. I lie down on my

stomach where the water barely ripples as it meets the sand. My body feels cold, but the sun is aggressive, its rays pulsing against my skin as if testing for pressure points. I rest my head on my folded arms. Up and down the beach, families are settling their belongings, erecting sun protection tents, shaking out beach towels, issuing instructions to their children. Above them at the lookout, the Neanderthals are gathered, looking out to the bombora where the surf is building. Right in the middle is *my* Neanderthal. I roll over and stand. I run to where the ocean is deep enough to dive and I throw myself through a wave, washing all the sand from my body.

As I leave the water, I pull the elastic off my wrist. A deep, red imprint remains where it sank into my skin. I twist my hair into a top knot and secure it with two loops of the elastic. I pull my dress over my head. The fabric clings to my body as I gather up my stuff and head for the stairs. As I climb, Paul spots me, his face lighting up and showcasing his perfect, straight teeth. I lift my hand, my middle finger extended. His smile drops.

I move past the lookout at the top of the stairs, my legs pumping with every intention of walking past them, avoiding eye contact, going straight home. Paul's coming towards me through the lookout. I push past him, but he grabs my arm and halts my escape.

'What's wrong?' he says. I shake my arm free.

'So much for sacred.' I push my finger into his breastbone, my voice low and quivering, my teeth clenched. 'You repulse me.'

'Trouble in paradise, Paulie?' smirks Tom.

'Oh, fuck off, Tom,' I say.

He backs away, his hands up in mock surrender. 'What have I done?'

'Not just you. All of you. You're all scum. And you?' I turn to Paul. 'You're the worst. You're just as vile as the rest of them. More so, because you pretend that you're not. Or was that just so you could hook up with the Stuck-Up Bitch?'

'What are you on about?' Paul's face is red, brows furrowed. He tries to take my arm and I back away.

'Don't touch me.'

'Cat, I have no idea what you are talking about.'

'Ask your fuckwit friends. They know everything, apparently.' I turn and run through the lookout, down the track, taking the shortcut to the road. Tears threaten to overflow. There are footsteps behind me, Paul's calling my name, but I don't stop running. He catches me at the roadside, encasing me in his arms.

'Babe, what's wrong? What's happened?'

I wriggle out of his hold and shove him away from me. 'Last night? Being with me is sacred? So sacred that you tell your friends?'

'Are you kidding? It was the best night of my life. It *was* sacred.'

'I don't think you actually know what sacred means, because if you did, every one of your Neanderthal friends and half of Batter's Cove wouldn't know about it.'

'What?'

'Cavey told Isabel about our "sacred" night, and she was so thrilled to tell me she knew all about it. How'd she know that exact word to use, Paul?'

'Of course I told my best mate about us. You're the best thing that's ever happened to me. Are you telling me you haven't told your friends?'

'No, I haven't. It hasn't even been twenty-four hours. And even if I did, they wouldn't have spread it around and shared all the dirty details. Your mates are pigs. And me? I'm the most ignorant fuckwit in the world for not realising sooner that you are too.' I push the tears away from my eyes, my hands in fists. I'm yelling now and a family ushers their kids to the other side of the road. 'It's not even bad enough that everyone knows because you couldn't wait to tell them about hooking up with the Stuck-Up Bitch. What about the way you think it's okay to treat women like meat, Isabel Dillon and God knows who else?'

'Cat, I've had nothing to do with Isabel since I don't even know when. I think I kissed her at a party one time, years ago, but that's it. Nothing happened. It meant absolutely nothing. I know she's hooked up with Cavey and maybe Tom but what they do has nothing to do with me.' His jaw is working, his teeth clenched. 'The idea of it makes me want to vomit. I told you this, babe. There's crap that I'd never want you to know about, not in a million years. Because it's from a lifetime ago, and because it's not me.'

'A lifetime ago? Not last summer? Not even last year? Who even are you when I'm not around? It doesn't matter because now I know. Every disgusting, misogynistic detail. Let me guess, Isabel asked for it, am I right?'

'Cat, this is bullshit. I'm in love with you. You, Cat.'

'You think I can even look at you, knowing what you're a part of?'

'I'm not part of anything.'

'You really don't get it, do you Paul?' My heart is racing, and it feels like it's going to snap my ribs with its force. 'Okay, so what you're saying is that you don't treat people like human garbage, good for you. But what about your mates? I see the way Cavey talks about girls. He makes my skin crawl. You're so obviously okay with that.'

'I'm not okay with it Cat, but what do you want me to do? He's my best mate. He was the only one who was there after Pete.' He tugs my wrist and I pull it behind my back like a child holding out. 'Cat, please, none of that has anything to do with us.'

'You think there's an us? There is no us. There's just me and there's you, and a dirty hookup that all your friends know about.'

'Cat, stop. Don't say that. I'm sorry I told Cavey, I never in a million years thought it'd go past him, and I'm going to fucking kill him, but we can sort this out.'

'I don't even want to look at you. Go hang with your a-hole friends and leave me alone.'

I run and don't look back. I run all the way home. My lungs are heaving out of my chest, my toes are bleeding, but I keep going until I get to the familiar balcony stairs, then I go into the shower, and I cry.

47

I WAKE in semi-darkness. Shafts of light force their way through the gaps between the blinds and the windows. I move through the house, each space has its own halo. It's silent and a note on the bench from Mum tells me Dad's out fishing, she and the boys have gone into town. There's a smiley face, a love heart and line after line of kisses, followed by *P.S. Paul came to see you.*

They knew something was up when I came barrelling through the door. I can only imagine what I looked like, barefoot, stubbed and bleeding toes, puffing and panting, face bright red and sweat-stained, crying uncontrollably. When I left the bathroom, a good half hour later, my parents had taken turns to knock on my door to ask what had happened. I just told them the truth; I'd broken up with Paul for being a giant misogynistic creep, and to leave me alone. I ripped the doona off my bed and buried myself under the sheet, willing sleep to take pity on me and knock me out for the day. My exhaustion from sprinting home and from crying resulted in a horrible restless sleep that was more dozing and confused dreaming than blissful slumber.

I gulp about a litre of water from the tap. It's almost five and I'm starving. I haven't eaten anything since this morning's mango, so I go to pull apart the roast chicken in the fridge. It sits in a layer of orange jelly and my stomach flips. I snap off some chocolate from the block in the fridge and the cliché doesn't escape me. If I didn't feel so shit I'd probably laugh at the irony of sad girl finding solace in chocolate.

Back in my room, I survey my feet. My toes are a mess of scabs from stubbing them on every rock from the beach to home. I go through my drawers until I find the thickest, softest, spongiest sports socks I own. I put them on with my runners, lying abandoned at the foot of my wardrobe since the first day of this new year, the day I walked into Paul at Sadie's, the day he handed me a glass water bottle and I fell completely in love with him then and there, on the spot. My feet cushioned, it's the most pampered they've felt for weeks after a summer of taking a pounding with salt water, rocks, asphalt and gravel. I splash my face and brush my teeth. I think about putting a brush through my hair, but that's torture I'm just not in the mood for. I pull the back door locked behind me.

It takes me half an hour or so to get to the back beach, ducking in and out of streets, cutting through vacant blocks and then across a paddock to the coastal scrub. As I scale the sand dunes, I see a rocky outcrop, a Dad-shaped being on the point. My runners sink into the soft sand.

'The first of the Dirty Three!' he says as I sit on the rock beside him. 'How you doing, Bella?'

'Shattered. So tired I could sleep for a week.' That's not half of it; I'm weathered. Battered. Bruised. I feel older than Nonna and that the world has just tripped me over, kicked me in the head and then sat on me.

'I wish I could tell you this is the last time you'll feel like this,' says Dad. 'I can't. But I can tell you that feeling like this is temporary, and it's these arse kickings that turn you into the person you're meant to be.'

'You mean stronger?'

'Yes, but that's not just it. You're already strong. You came out strong. Probably too strong.' He chuckles ruefully and shakes his head before his smile drops. 'I saw Paul.'

'And did he tell you he's an a-hole and a creep?'

'He told me that he trusted the wrong person with some information that didn't need sharing.'

'There's an understatement,' I say.

'He's devastated, Cat,' says Dad. 'He thinks he's really messed up. It's your call, but he obviously cares about you and you care about him, so why write him off based on something someone else did to him? If you're feeling betrayed, so is he.'

'Totally not interested, Dad.' I shrug and cross my arms around my knees. 'He's wasted enough of my time and energy as it is. I have far too much I should be thinking about. Anyway, my friends would hate him if they knew what he's done. *I* hate him for what he's done.'

'That's the thing about strength,' says Dad. 'Sometimes you can be too strong, too hard, too inflexible. You've heard that old proverb about an oak tree breaking in the storm? None of us are perfect, Cat.' He walks towards the ocean's edge, reeling in his line. There's a giant tangle of seaweed caught on his hook. 'We all have our flaws; we all do and say things we regret. The difference between good people, smart people, the people with real strength, is that they admit when they're wrong, they work hard to better themselves. That's Paul. It shouldn't matter to you what your friends think, it should matter what you think. And if you can't see someone trying for better, seeing you as a way to help them become better, well then, Cat, I don't think you should see that as a strength. It's a weakness. And it's sad.'

'So, you think I should just forget that he's a total deadshit with no respect for women, is that what you're saying?'

'Don't be so dramatic all the time, Cat. You know that's not what I'm saying. And you know that's not him. What I'm saying is to take him at face value and how he treats you. I don't know the ins and outs of what happened, and believe me, I don't want to, but from what I do know? You're ending something based on the small-town gossip machine, and that's on you, kid. You're not a slave to that.'

'Is it gossip when it's my so-called-boyfriend talking about me? About our relationship?'

'Paul's not a shit-talker. I know that. You know that. He just made a bad call.'

'And that's my responsibility?'

'Of course not. But do you really want to call it quits? Is it really worth that? That's all I'm saying.'

'It's all so confusing,' I say. 'Last night, I had it all sorted out in my head, and today I feel like I'm the biggest dipshit on the planet.'

'I know,' says Dad. 'But, Bella, you're 17. Expecting perfection from yourself and from other people is unrealistic. More than that, it's unfair. Of course, Paul's made mistakes in his life. You're going to make mistakes in yours too, Cat. You have to so you grow and learn. You're our baby girl, we'll always love you. You're going to make bad decisions, but you'll make more good than bad. Pass me the pliers, Cat.' He crouches down on his haunches to free the hook out of the seaweed. 'Don't be so hard on yourself and don't be so hard on everyone else. Paul's family's gone through shit that's the stuff of nightmares. I'm not making excuses for anything but don't crucify the bloke because of what he may or may not have done long before he was seeing you, or for him opening his gob to the wrong bloke. Paul's a good one. And he loves you. I wouldn't say that if I didn't believe it.'

'Dad, how am I going to survive without you next year when I go to the city?' I duck under his fishing rod to hug him.

'I don't even want to think about that.' He kisses my forehead.

A whistle pierces the beach. It's Tommy. Mum's beside him; they're carrying a picnic basket between them.

'Bonfire?' says Dad.

'Absolutely.' I step across the rocks to meet them.

48

'ARE you feeling better, darling?' Mum says as she approaches. 'You slept for hours.'

'Where's Matty?'

'Paul took him into town to get some potatoes,' says Tommy. I glance at Mum and she shrugs her shoulders.

'Poor guy looked miserable. I thought a baked potato was in order.'

'Baked potatoes and hanging out with Matteo Kelty will cheer him up? You didn't think to ask me how I feel about inviting my ex-boyfriend to our family bonfire?'

'I don't think it's as bad as that,' she says, and I burst into tears. 'Oh, Cat, come here.' She wraps her arms around me and strokes my back. 'Everything's going to be okay, darling.'

'It's really not, Mum,' I say between sobs. 'I was so angry, I yelled and cried, and I told him I hate him, but I love him. I told him I never want to see him again. It's all so shit. And I'm so, so angry. He betrayed me. He betrayed what we have. It's so freakin' humiliating.'

'Cat, think about it logically. Did anything really happen other than Paul telling his best friend that he's in love? I know you feel betrayed, but do you think that's betrayal?'

'It's more than that, Mum.' I rub my fists into my eyes. 'I might just go home before they get here. I need to think, get my head clear.'

'I think you owe it to yourself and to Paul to stay and sort this out,' says Mum.

'What do I even say to him?'

She holds me out at arms-length to look me in the eyes. 'Here's a tip, Cat, for once in your life, don't say anything. Let him speak.'

'What's the point? It's all over, I just know it.' Tears spring afresh and I push my arms up into the sleeves of my hoodie, which, as I look down, I realise is Paul's, just one of the collection that is all over my bedroom. 'How symbolic is this?' I hold up the sleeves. 'He gave me this to wear that first night at the Gap party so I wouldn't be cold, and now I'm wearing it when he's coming to break up with me.'

'Oh, my heart, you silly, silly girl,' says Mum. 'He's not coming to break up with you. He's in love with you, Cat.'

'I've messed up everything and this is all your fault, Mum,' I cry, snot and tears flowing freely. 'I told you I didn't want to see anyone, I just wanted to get my shit together for school, but you were the one who kept going on about freakin' work life balance and then he was always there and you and Dad were okay with me seeing him and even freakin' Nonna liked him and so did I but his friends are like something out of my issues assessment and he doesn't give a shit and even random mums on the beach look at me like what's he doing with you when he could be with anyone, and I ignored all that, because I listened to you, Mum, and now I love him and I called his friends scum and I should just be thinking about one thing and that's my education but all I can think about is Paul freakin' Lightwood.' My breaths come in ragged gasps and my face is so wet I may as well have dunked it in the ocean.

'For the love of God, stop crying. Cat, you're being hysterical,' says Mum as she wipes the mess of my face with her jacket sleeve.

'I can't.' I fill the clean slate with more tears.

'You'd better, because look, here he comes with Matty. Pull yourself together. Here.' She pulls a tissue from her pocket and it's older than Nonna, older even than the fossils dotting these rocks, but I take it anyway. 'You talk to Paul; I'll keep the boys with me.'

'How do I look?' I sniff. I don't need her to tell me; I can feel my eyes are red, swollen slits, my mouth quivering.

'Terrible, but so does he.' She hugs me and kisses the top of my head.

I walk down to the water's edge, breathing deeply, trying to compose myself while my chest heaves and shudders. I glance over my shoulder, and Matty's dropped to the sand beside Mum and Tommy. Paul's walking towards me.

'Hey, Cat.' Paul stands beside me. 'Your Mum invited me; I hope that's okay.'

I shrug, not game to speak, not physically able to. I watch the tide flow dangerously close to my runners.

'I came to see you earlier, but your parents said to give you a bit of space,' he says. His eyes are bloodshot and his hood is pulled up over his head. His hands are jammed hard into his pockets and the fabric strains against his fists. 'Cat, I know you're thinking I've been with Isabel Dillon this summer, but I swear on my life that I haven't. Last summer, at a few parties, off my face, we might have kissed, but it never meant anything. You have to believe me.'

'And you have to believe that what we did – you and me? It meant something. It wasn't a hook up, not to me, and that's because you made me feel like it wasn't. So, hearing that you saw it as something that could be public knowledge spread around your mates just hurt me in a way I can't even explain.'

'I'm sorry, Cat. I'm so, so sorry. I stuffed up. I saw Cavey after I dropped you home, and stopped and had a quick beer, just me and him. I don't even know why I told him. I was just so happy, Cat.'

I nod, crying, because I do know that happiness. I was that happy too.

'I was so happy, and I told who I thought was my best mate. Never in a million years did I think he'd be anything but happy for me, but I was wrong. I've known who he is for too long and I've let myself ignore it. No more… I'm done with him.' He gently touches my sea glass necklace and it clinks against my shell. 'Cat, I've done some stupid, stupid things in my life. I was wasted through high school, and my parents were too caught up in their own grief over my brother to give a shit about me. All I've ever had is my mates and surfing and my job, the same shit, different day. Then your old man offers me a summer job working on something I could actually give a shit about and you crashed your way into my world.' He looks at me with that smile, his elbows jutting as his hands sink into the back of his waistband. 'My head's been spinning ever since and for the first time in my life, I feel… not worthless. You see me. I can be worthy. I swear I'll never do anything to hurt you again, I promise. Being yours? You being mine? Cat, that is everything. It's like that song, *your heart my core.* I am so in love with you, that's bottom line, low key all there is to say.' He shrugs. 'That's all I've got, beautiful. That's my big speech.'

'It's a very good speech.' I wipe the tears from my face.

'You think?'

'I do. Don't forget I was debating team captain, so I know a good speech. That was right up there.'

'Now it's your turn.' He glances at me and crosses his arms.

'Paul, I love you. That's all I've got. That's my big speech.' My voice shakes and I lay my palm against his cheek, his stubble scratchy.

He closes his eyes and tilts his head, leaning into my hand, his jaw flexing.

'It's a very good speech. I'll take it.' He wraps his arms around me, hugging me, squeezing me. I sneak my hands under his hoodie to feel his skin and we kiss and it's like time comes to a halt, the waves stop breaking, the world stops turning.

'You're shaking,' I whisper.

'I thought for sure I'd blown it with you, Cat, and we're only getting started.'

'I should never have gone off at you like that. I just had all these stories, all these rumours, all these questions banging around in my head. Why would someone like you want someone like me if it wasn't a joke?'

'Cat…'

'No, let me finish. I was so wrong to doubt you, Paul, and I was so, so wrong to doubt you and me. I can't tell you how sorry I am. And the way I yelled at you? I thought *I'd* blown it with *you*, and I wouldn't blame you if you decided that I was just far too much for you.'

'Too much? Never enough.'

'Stop, Matty, you dickhead.' The wind carries my brothers' yells. We turn to see Matty chasing Tommy down the beach, waving a stick impaled with a fish head. Dad's crouched over his tackle box and Mum's got the fire cranking. Embers spit into the sky as she sits by the fire, wrapping potatoes in foil, the stem of a glass of red wine buried in the sand beside her at an alarming angle.

'Ugh, way to kill a moment,' I say. 'Can I tempt you with a toasted marshmallow?'

'Why, yes, I do believe you can.' He takes my hand and we walk across to join Mum by the fire.

'There's actually something you should know.' I pass Paul a flaming marshmallow. 'You might want to brace yourself.'

'I'm a big boy, I can take it.' He blows out the flames, his cheeks puffing. 'Do your worst, Kelty.'

'Okay, this might come as a surprise to you, but I have a bit of a temper.'

Mum and Dad hoot with laughter.

'Really?' says Paul. 'I hadn't noticed.'

EPILOGUE

'DRIVE safe, Cat, and call us when you arrive.' Mum moves beside Dad, his arm coming around her shoulder as her lip trembles.

'Can I have your bedroom?' says Tommy, throwing his arms around me, his head down. He hugs me, hard.

'This is a joke,' says Matty. 'She'll be back in a couple of weeks for the long weekend. We already had the Festival of Cat celebration when she got her marks, and again when she got into law and freakin' again when she got that scholarship. Do we really need to drag out a big dramatic farewell?'

'Come here and kiss your sister goodbye.' I hold my arms out. I'm still genuinely in shock about the scholarship. Who could have ever guessed that the issues assignment I started last summer ended up in federal parliament after a local politician heard about it on a school visit? If it wasn't for that, I know for a fact that my scholarship application would have gone nowhere. Another fact? My assignment about misogyny and sexism wouldn't have been half as good if I hadn't have gone to see Isabel Dillon at the end of last summer, just her and me, talking, away from all the rumours and bitchiness. I don't know that we'll ever be real friends, but I think now at least we get each other. 'I'm going to miss you, turdburger.'

'Me too,' he says, tears in his eyes. 'Shut up.' He brushes them away when I give him a teasing smirk.

'Caterina, remember where you come from,' Nonna says to me in Italian. 'You're a good girl, you've worked so hard, you make me very proud to be your Nonna.'

'Don't let the petrol gauge go under half.' Dad wraps me in a hug.

'I love you, baby girl. We're so proud of you. Go grab the world; it's yours.'

'I love you too.' I don't even bother to stop the tears.

'Ugh, enough,' drawls Matty. 'I'm going upstairs.'

'Don't you even think of it.' Nonna grabs him by the ear and even though he towers above her he lets her. 'You stand there and show your sister some respect. The way you behave? You'll be needing her as your lawyer.'

'Man, it's like she's going off to war,' he mutters.

'Let's give them some space,' says Mum. 'Come on, guys. Mama, don't you have some biscotti for the boys? Cat, we'll talk to you later.' She shepherds Dad and Matty up the stairs like she's herding cats. Matty swings on his arms up the stair railings, Nonna admonishes him as she leads Tommy into what she calls her house under the stairs. Pots spilling over with red geraniums flank her doorway. She blows me a kiss and I blow her one in return.

'You all set?' says Paul.

'I think so,' I say. 'Thank your mum for the cupcakes. That was really sweet of her. And it's just my clothes, my books, a few bits and pieces. And this, of course.' I pull my sea glass necklace out from under my top.

'Me too,' says Paul, and tugs his t-shirt down to reveal his shell necklace.

'We really need to sort out that situation with something a little more robust,' I say.

'Are you kidding? I love it. And I love you, Cat.'

'I love you.' My voice wobbles.

'Oh, babe, please don't cry. This is what you always wanted. Uni, the city, an amazing place with Sal and JB. You smashed it! It's all good. I'll see you in a couple of weeks, yeah?'

'It just feels hard, all of a sudden. I don't want to leave you.'

'You're not. You're ninety minutes down the road. No biggie. I am so proud of you, my beautiful girlfriend, the soon to be lawyer, already tearing shit up. You got the playlist I made you? Crank it up, babe, and let's do this shit.'

'Kiss me,' I say, and he takes my head in his hands, and kisses my forehead, my nose, my chin. 'Kiss me properly.'

'Still so bossy,' he says. 'I'm getting there.' He kisses me until my head swims. 'Drive safe, babe, and we'll talk later. I love you.'

'I love you.' I click the seatbelt and check my mirror. As I drive down my street, I see my family on the balcony, waving, and Paul at the foot of the driveway, his hands in the back of his waistband. I hit a button and music floods the car.

'Never dare dreamed, ever me, ever you, ever more, your heart my core, my dream come true, my dream come true.'

ACKNOWLEDGEMENTS

This book was written on the lands of the Woiwurrung Wurundjeri and Boon Wurrung People. I pay my respects to their elders past and present and acknowledge their continuing connection to land, waters and culture. Australia was and always will be Aboriginal land.

Thank you to Carolyn Martinez and the team at Hawkeye Publishing: firstly, for awarding this novel the Hawkeye Publishing Manuscript Development Prize, and secondly, for falling in love with my story and giving it a home among an incredible stable of authors. A massive thank you to my editors for elevating my novel with such generosity, passion and care. Your comments had me squealing in delight.

In 2020, when you-know-what happened, I crossed paths professionally with someone who mentioned they liked to play around with words. That conversation led to a recurring appointment in my calendar: Writing with Ali. Ali is now my writing bestie and how truly serendipitous to be on a writing date with Ali when I received *that* email offering me a contract. We cleared the cafe with our screams of joy.

There are so many people that helped bring this book baby to life. I wrote it in sprints with my fabulous Band of Batchers and during epic cheese-filled writing retreats with Ali, Jaqui, Caroline, Melitta, Julie and Riss. Nicole and Hanna Vine provided appropriate sibling insult suggestions and wardrobe advice. Najiye Polat gave unequivocal horticultural feedback that still makes me wince and laugh in equal measure. My circle of friends and family have offered so much support and excitement for my writing and it's a pretty special feeling knowing

I have such formidable humans in my corner. Sorry about the state of my floors.

I've been a member of Writers Victoria since dinosaurs roamed the earth, and they are a phenomenal organisation supporting writers in myriad ways. A full-day workshop with Eliza Henry-Jones about grief and loss in YA fiction helped me flesh out the complexity of emotions in this story, and Eliza's writing inspires me to the point of needing a lie down.

This book is an ode to summer and to the beach. I was blessed to grow up on a farm on the coast where I always had a book in my hand. Thanks to my beautiful parents for always encouraging my love of reading and writing and for giving me an idyllic childhood and adolescence. Together, with my favourite brother Saher, you gave me enough family dynamics fodder to fuel countless novels. The matriarchs in our family certainly helped fill the well.

Thanks to my husband Raph for being my unwavering cheerleader, for the sticky notes and the workplace bragging. You're my rock and I couldn't do any of the things without you.

I dedicate this book to my daughters, Gabriella and Alessia. They're the loves of my life, and this is a story about the beauty and complexity of teenage girlhood and of laying claim to one's own life. You inspire me every day with your insights and your spirits.

ABOUT THE AUTHOR

HOLLY CARDAMONE is a Melbourne-based communications specialist and author. Her writing has appeared in publications as diverse as bridal tomes and in fashion magazines, in trade publications, and in the large dailies. Her debut novel, *Summer, in Between* was the 2024 winner of the Hawkeye Publishing Manuscript Development Prize. Holly was a finalist in the Romance Writers of Australia Sweet Treats 2024 Anthology and has been long and short listed in a number of national writing awards.

She's a mother of two, wife to a devilishly handsome Carlton Football Club tragic, and slave to the most beautiful boy in the world, Buddy the Australian Shepherd. She's also a voracious reader who has been known to mumble 'just one more page' on more than a handful of occasions.

BOOK CLUB QUESTIONS

1. How, if at all, did this book relate to your own coming of age? Did it evoke any memories or create any connections for you?
2. What were some of your favourite scenes from the book? Why did they stand out to you?
3. Who was your favourite character and why? Which character did you find the most complex or intriguing and why?
4. Which character did you relate to or empathise with the most and why? Which character did you dislike or disagree with the most and why?
5. What do you think happens to the characters after the novel ends?
6. How did the novel explore themes such as love, trust, family, identity, misogyny, or feminism?
7. What's the significance of the title?
8. Despite having many comedic moments, the novel contains some very serious and hard issues, including misogyny and casual racism. Do you think the comedy makes this more palatable or does it minimise the heaviness?
9. The book is set in a very specific small town backdrop. Does this make it hard to relate to, or are Cat's concerns universal regardless of setting?
10. Why do you think that many coming of age novels are popular and universally enjoyed by adults as well as YA? Do you think that people of varying ages read and experience the book differently?
11. Some of the tropes in *Summer, in Between* are small town, grumpy/sunshine, coming of age, first love, he falls first. What's your favourite trope?

If you liked what you read today, please tell your friends or post a review
about what you enjoyed.

Summer, in Between is available at hawkeyebooks.com.au
and all good bookstores and libraries.

....

If you loved *Summer, in Between* you'll also enjoy:
Salt Runs Through by Mark Rafidi
New Year's Eve by Sarah Todman
Road to Freedom by Gabrielle Davis
Welcome to Blackwood by Khaiah Thomson
Moontide by Mary Greenwood
LightWorkers by Anna Sarelas